Trial of Tears

Chris Semal

ISBN: 0-9837-1900-4
ISBN-13: 9780983719007

I'd like to dedicate this book to anyone deciding whether to keep going on in a creative project, whether it be music, writing or any other art. If you throw up your hands in disgust at the crappiness of the business end, or the people who don't believe in you, that's when the….. No, the terrorists don't win, but neither do you. Do you really want to be in a tie with a terrorist?

Thanks to Mike Shohl for doing a great editing job, reminding me of what was working and kicking my butt on the rest. Thanks to Julie Schoerke, Marissa DeCuir & Samantha Lien of JKS Communications for making sure this novel gets into all the right hands, as well as the left hands. Thanks to Lucinda Blumenfeld for patiently answering so many of my newbie questions. Thanks to Jeff West, owner of Ultrasound Studios, who has given me some great stories (Sadie is not one of them) and put up with my decibels for some 30 years.

Thanks to my friend Julien Brinas, who was very instrumental in putting my website, www.chrissemal.com, together and helped significantly with the cover (especially the tears, which were a real pain to get right), designed by Robin Ludwig Design Inc. All in all, I owe Julien a lot more drinks.

Thanks to all the readers of early drafts of this story and the good, bad & ugly feedback they gave me in return, all valuable. A first time novelist can't possibly see the forest for the trees.

Thanks to Neil Peart of Rush for allowing me to use one of the many, many brilliant lines of lyrics that he includes regularly in all his songs. He is equally a master of words as well as percussion. The quote in this book comes from 'Hemispheres' and is reprinted by permission.

Thanks to Cannon Publications LLC for making life easy for me. There's a line about having a fool for a client, but that's probably just sour grapes from some disgruntled individual.

Thanks to my wife, Isabelle, for keeping her doubts about my sanity to herself, except in moments of stress, and for being wonderful in general.

I'd also like to thank my late cat Axel, who so kindly and graciously shared the chair that most of this was written in.

1

"You have to admit that dumpsters are an underrated form of lodging," he said to himself, nestled snugly among the stained newspapers, food wrappers, and assorted detritus surrounding him. He reached into a pocket of the tattered brown jacket he had found in another dumpster, a few blocks north of his present location and extracted the rewards of three-and-a-half hard hours of panhandling: a fifth of one hundred proof vodka just purchased at a discount liquor store. Vodka was an acquired taste, one of the last acquisitions Jerry Hince could count as his. One of the others was a memory that faded, gratefully enough, after only half a bottle. The cracks in the sidewalk of society don't seem that wide, but it's possible to slip through them with enough lubrication.

"Donald Trump doesn't have room for me at the Plaza? Well, I can show that bushy-eyebrowed asswipe a thing or two about fine accommodations," he chortled and cracked the plastic cap off the bottle. Something near his feet was emitting a rank smell, so he shifted around and foraged, the dim light from the lamppost at the far side of the alley slicing through a gap in the dumpster lid. His hands touched wax paper. He pulled it close to his squinting eyes, and when he realized he had found half of a past-its-prime roast beef and provolone cheese hero, his mouth cracked into a piano smile.

"I'm sorry, sir, the Oak Room seems to be closed at the moment. Please dial 0 for twenty-four hour dumpster service. Would you like me to put the 'Do not disturb unless you're a hooker looking to give a freebie' sign on the lid?" He laughed and took a healthy pull from the bottle. "If only I could get cable in here, I'd be set. And if I could lick my balls, I'd never leave. Now where's the bathroom? Ah, here it is." He turned forty-five degrees to his right, unzipped his pants, and urinated into some broken-up cardboard boxes. Some drops splashed back on him, but he didn't care. He was settling in for the night, and, with any luck, the police wouldn't come around to roust him. This neighborhood was residential and reasonably quiet at night. Aside from a few late night party crawlers coming home from Greenwich Village clubs and bars, there wasn't much chance that anyone would give him any trouble, certainly with the dumpster being so far down in the dark side of the narrow alley. He'd made the mistake of crashing in one in Alphabet City the year before, unaware it was gang territory. It had cost him five teeth, forty-three stitches, and the medics had never found the top half of his right ear. A better bargain than the arm and the leg it would have cost him to stay at the Plaza, but costly nonetheless.

About an hour of quiet contentment had passed for Jerry, though he measured time in bottle levels and not with a watch, when he heard a car slow down at the street end of the alley.

"Chrisht, the goddamn cops here," he slurred, and wiped some moldy crumbs of provolone from his beard with his sleeve. He peered through the four-inch crack in the dumpster lid and saw the headlights of a long black sedan go dark. The front doors opened, two large men emerged, went back to the trunk and opened it.

"Hey Cinderella, better get out before this carriage turns into a pumpkin," said one of the men. His voice rumbled like a truck rolling through a tunnel. They leaned into the trunk, pulling out a very thin, very terrified young Hispanic man by his belt and the scruff of his collar and flung him to the ground at the entry of the alley.

"Your fairy godfather's not very happy with you. You're supposed to be sprinkling the magic dust, not snorting it, asshole!" The other voice was smooth and mellifluous, like a radio announcer's, but with a rising inflection towards the end of his sentences. He wheeled and kicked the prone man in the side twice. Unable to defend himself due to the handcuffs that pinioned his arms behind his back, he squirmed to avoid direct hits, but the steel-toed, pointed boots unerringly found their mark. A rib snapped.

"Bunny, this ain't right!" he shouted, "You know me. I didn't rip him off. I'm not that stupid. Don't cap me, man. Please, man."

"Come on, Liquid. How's it gonna look if every dipshit dips into the bags they're supposed to be selling? This is a business, not a party. We gotta make you look a little bad, set an example, you know?" said the first man. They dragged him further back into the alley, away from the street.

Jerry was fascinated. Cable TV at the Plaza Hotel wasn't jack compared to this drama unfolding before him. He couldn't make out the features of the young Hispanic because his dark, lank hair was hanging over his face, but the other two faces were coming into focus. The one with the pointed boots had the standard early 90's look: goatee, ponytail, two earrings in each ear, black bomber jacket, and black jeans. The only thing missing was the baseball cap turned around with the bill facing back. There seemed to be something strangely wrong with his face, however. Maybe it was the light playing tricks, but one eye looked like it had been dragged down his cheek a half-inch or so. It gave him the kind of expression one associates with paintings in haunted houses, the ones where the eyes follow you around the room. The other man, referred to as Bunny by the unfortunate Liquid, resembled a sadistic Mr. Clean on steroids, with an enormous black walrus mustache. Close to six foot eight and coupled with his gleaming bald head, he would have made a great battering ram, if anyone had the strength to lift him. He was dressed in khakis and a sports coat, as if there was a country club social at the back of the alley. The thought occurred to Jerry that even if he had to pick these two individuals out of a police lineup, no one would ever believe him.

They pulled up twelve yards short of the dumpster and slammed Liquid hard against the rough brick wall. Bunny hit him with a short left jab to the solar plexus and he dropped to his knees, gasping for air.

"Hey Ronno, did ya ever see that shitty movie with Demi Moore?" Bunny said, turning to his partner.

"The one where she's a stripper? Loved it. What a rack! I never returned it to the rental store." Ronno replied.

"No, the really, really bad one where they redid some old book. If you got caught messing around when you're married they painted a big red 'A' on your forehead."

"What, 'A' for asshole?"

"No, 'A' for aardvark, moron. It stands for adulterer. Anyway, this gives me an idea for our friend here," he said, a cruel expression flickering across his face. From his back pocket he removed a vicious looking six inch spring-loaded serrated knife. He grabbed Liquid by the hair, jerking him up from his kneeling position and drew the blade across his forehead, a half inch below the hairline. Blood poured from the wound and the young man screamed. Bunny growled, "Shut up!" and slammed his head back against the wall. He then turned the knife and sliced Liquid from the bridge of the nose up to the other incision.

"Every time you look in the mirror now, you'll have a subtle reminder of what a bad decision you made when you decided to rip off Frank Bender. Nobody likes a thief, especially a stupid one."

Liquid moaned, his face a mask of blood. "Please, man, let me go. I swear on my mom, my kids, anything. I never took much. Just a little here and there." He looked up imploringly at his captors. "Hey, I've got some money stashed. You can have it. Just let me go."

"You must have kissed a lot of frogs to get to be the prince you are now. You want to kiss a weasel? Tell you what, Cindy, you do that and maybe we'll let you go. C'mon, sweetheart, pucker up," said Ronno, straddling Liquid's head.

"What the fuck, Ronno. You always have to get perverse when we're trying to get something done," Bunny said, his mouth tightening. "Don't be mixing business and pleasure," Ronno unzipped his pants and dangled his penis in front of Liquid's face. Even with the blood stinging, his eyes bulged with terror.

"Hey man, this is fucked up. Bunny, I'm a man, man. Don't let this shit go down. We know each other a long time. I don't deserve this."

"You're right," answered Bunny. He pulled out a silenced automatic pistol from a holster inside his jacket and shot Liquid twice in the head. He slid to the ground, the bricks behind him revealing a darker red color.

"You almost shot my dick off!" exclaimed Ronno.

Bunny laughed. "My aim's not that good. I could never hit a target that small. Gimme a hand getting this useless mess into the dumpster."

It took a second, maybe two, but it suddenly dawned on Jerry there was a very real problem here. As entertainment, this was excellent, but he had no intention of becoming part of the act, and it looked like the fourth wall of this particular piece of theater was falling down in chunks. The two thugs dragged the body toward the dumpster while he hastily burrowed as quietly as he could further into the depths of the garbage. He pulled the urine drenched cardboard over him, praying that all parts of him were covered.

They lifted the lid off the dumpster, picked up the body, and hefted it into the bin. Jerry was compressed further down and fought the panic overtaking him when he grasped that blood and brain fluid were dripping onto the left side of his face. He desperately tried to keep his breathing regular, but was fighting a losing battle against hyperventilation.

"Man, it smells like piss in there," said Ronno, grimacing.

"It's going to smell a lot worse in a couple of days, with this Indian summer heat. What's this?" Bunny picked up

Jerry's half full bottle of vodka and said, "Looks like someone was throwing themselves a party in here."

Jerry snapped. He screamed and thrashed, trying to get away from the bleeding body lying on top of him, and finally poked his head through the uppermost layer of the garbage in the bin only to see the killers looking back down at him

"Why, hello there!" said Bunny, with a benign smile, as if welcoming a guest who'd been unaccountably delayed. "Nice place you've got here. Who does your decorating? Looks like you've gotten some tips from Martha Stewart. Is she in there, too?" He playfully looked around the upper strata of garbage.

"Don't shoot me! I'm not going to say anything. I didn't see anything. I didn't hear anything," Jerry implored.

"Don't worry, I'm not going to shoot you. This kinda reminds me of 'Tommy' by the Who," said Bunny. He sang, in a passable baritone voice, "Wino, can you hear me? Can you feel me near you?"

"Or maybe Sergeant Schultz from Hogan's Heroes," added Ronno with a smirk. "I see nuttink. I hear nuttink."

"Do you remember that out of the way Italian restaurant on Arthur Avenue we were at last week?" Bunny said, unscrewing the cap of the vodka bottle. "They served this great penne a la vodka, best I ever had, and I loved the cherries jubilee they had for dessert," Bunny said, the smile still brilliant under the mustache, and poured the rest of the bottle over Jerry's head and splashed it around the dumpster. "They bring it out, put the sauce on it and light it up."

Jerry desperately scrambled to find some purchase to pull himself up, but nothing was solid enough to hold his weight. Bunny pulled out a book of matches and lit one, set the rest of the book on fire, and tossed it into the dumpster. Jerry screamed as the dumpster quickly burst into flame. He'd managed to free one arm from underneath Liquid's corpse and windmilled it around frantically in an effort to beat out the flames, but to no avail. The cardboard beneath him ignited and the contents of the dumpster collapsed downwards. With an anguished howl, he slumped and fell back into the blaze. After a few seconds, just before Ronno reached over and flipped the lid back on to the dumpster with the motion of a slam dunk, he could see the features beginning to char and melt on the drunk's face. One last keening scream was cut off suddenly and a sickly smelling smoke billowed out from the side of the lid.

"I highly recommend the marinated swill pot flambé here, though, frankly, the service leaves something to be desired," Ronno chuckled, looking around in vain for something to clean his bloody hands with. "For crissakes, where's a napkin when you need one?"

They returned to the waiting car and, as Bunny opened the door, he scowled.

"One thing bothers me, though, Ronno."

"Yeah?" asked Ronno. He turned and looked at Bunny from across the roof of the car.

"I think you're getting your fairy tales mixed up. It wasn't Cinderella going around kissing frogs."

Ronno shrugged.

"Yeah. It's possible."

2

It was the second loudest noise Pete Watts had ever heard in his life. He raced out of the office/reception area down the hallway to Rehearsal Studio C, flung open the door and was greeted by the sight of wisps of smoke wafting gently upwards from the speaker cones of the P.A. system. A gathering of slightly, and some not so slightly, stoned musicians looked dully back at him.

"What the hell was that?" demanded Pete.

"Sorry, dude," replied one of the musicians. "We couldn't get the thing to work, so Luther turned up the volume all the way on the P.A. and I finally found the switch that turned it on. Awesome sound, huh, dude? Could we do it again so I could get it on my sampler?" The musician adjusted the strap on a pearl white Ibanez Flying V guitar slung over his shoulder and ran a hand through a truly impressive number of colors dyed into his shoulder length hair.

Pete went over to the P.A. console, turned it off, counted to ten and took a deep breath before he turned back to the band.

"O.K., that's it. I have had it! You guys are barred from here. It was bad enough when you did the Keith Moon tribute and I had to replace half the drum set, or when you did the Jimi does Berkeley thing and set off the fire alarms and sprinkler system. You know, I even have to admit the Ozzy Osbourne bat thing was funny, though I had to clean it up afterwards, but this is just way too much. You guys have just cooked a seven thousand dollar P.A.!"

One of the girls hanging out by the drum riser strode over to Pete. She looked to be about fifteen, though one can never really tell with girls sporting crew cuts. She was wearing about as much black as a person can wear and her liberally applied eyeliner would have made a silent screen movie star proud. She handed him a platinum MasterCard and said in a voice that sounded as if Barbie dolls were produced on the Jersey shore, "Daddy will take care of it. Just give it back to me next week when we come back. And why don't you get black wallpaper and some candles for this room, too? It looks so fuckin' wholesome."

Pete looked around the room. He saw the names of bands scrawled and spray painted on the cracked gray plaster of the walls, a ratty, tattered carpet of indiscernible color that made up for its lack of threads with a large and varied collection of cigarette butts, beer bottle caps and stains of unknown origin,

"I like it just the way it is, thanks. But I will get the P.A. fixed. You sure this'll be O.K. with your old man, Ariel?"

"I think he'll be back from L.A. with his new girlfriend next month. He just signs anything I put in front of him and asks how school has been, as if I went." The corners of her mouth twisted.

Pete walked back to the office wondering why he had to constantly claw and scratch to make ends meet while other people lived the good life. Then again, he did have a chance, once. Nah, he thought, it would have been dirty. He heard the phone ring, picked it up and said,

"Half Moon Bay Studios. Can I help you?"

"Hello. I'm looking for Dick Hertz. Is he there?"

"Very funny, Styx."

"You sound about as cheerful as a rash. What's up?"

Johnny "Styx" Kostykian was one of those people you had to meet to believe he truly existed. As infuriating as he was lovable, there were times when Pete wished that Mr. and Mrs. Kostykian had reconsidered bringing a child into this world, but when the chips were down, there was no one better in a bad situation. His mind moved in a seemingly parallel universe to the one most folks inhabit, and Pete had to admit that when he was out with Johnny, he found himself involved in conversations which, in their own particular New Yorkish kind of way, couldn't possibly happen anywhere else. Johnny's improbable, though highly successful, methods in procuring female companionship were legendary.

"You know those clowns who call themselves 'The Jokers'? Well, these dingle berries just fried my best P.A. It's going to be in the shop for at least a week, if I'm lucky. One of the bimbi hanging with their drummer offered to pay for it, but I'm going to be rescheduling bands out of that room until it's fixed and that's going to be a royal pain," said Pete.

"I always said P.A. stood for pain in the ass, instead of public address. But I have a feeling, my man, that if you play your cards right tonight, it could stand for pelvis adjuster. I met a pair of lovelies today, and I'm in a sharing mood. Why don't you come down to the Pyramid Club on Avenue A and Sixth street tonight? We're gonna to head down around 11:00," suggested Johnny.

"Sixth and A? Haven't been down in that nabe in a while. I read somewhere that the lettered avenues of the lower east side stand for A – Adventurous, B – Bold, C – Crazy and D – Dead."

"That's a good line. I might use it someday. So, how about it?"

"I don't know. Angeline's been giving me a hard time about staying out late, and that's just for working here. She'd have a foal if she knew I was out with the likes of you."

"Tell her you've got to give me a hand with my latest jingle," Styx replied. He was constantly involved in one new project or another. His current career path consisted of writing commercial jingles for an advertising company. Pete and Johnny had been in numerous bands throughout their teenage years, Pete on the drums and Johnny on bass guitar. You'd think with a nickname like "Styx", they would have reversed their instruments, but life is funny that way.

"What are you working on right now?" asked Pete

"I think I've got a good account this time. It's for the Elsie Milk Company. You know, the one with the dancing cow wearing a hula dress on the carton. I wrote this jaunty little tune and the lyrics go something like this:

Milk, milk, the answer is milk.

Cold as ice and smooth as silk.

Cuts through me like a knife through butter,

All that joy from one cow's udder.

So, what do you think?"

"You should change the last line to 'These lyrics make me shudder.' Christ, that's awful. The Elsie Milk Company should have pictures of missing advertising lyricists on their cartons after they hear that one," replied Pete.

"Oh come on, it's not so bad. Maybe it ain't Springsteen, but that's not what's required here. Now at least you have a legitimate reason to meet me at the club. Save me from my own weird talents!"

"All right, all right. I'll go if I don't catch too much flack at home. But you're buying the first round," he said.

He hung up the phone and looked at the three calendars hanging on the wall in front of him, next to one of his prize possessions, an autographed photo of Anne and Nancy Wilson of Heart, each calendar displaying the schedules of the different rehearsal studios rooms. Monday nights usually weren't very busy, the last band due to finish at 10:00. At least he'd have time to go home and shower, not that anyone at the Pyramid Club would notice or care. The cuckoo clock on the far wall, the cuckoo dangling from a noose, read 7:30 and he ordered sesame chicken and boiled dumplings from the Chinese take out place around the corner. The deliveryman showed up about eight minutes later. Pete wondered if they didn't cook the stuff in the elevator on the way up, it got there so fast.

After he ushered the last band out and helped Greg, his assistant, make sure all the musical equipment in the different rooms was present and accounted for, he locked up and took the subway down to the Spring Street stop. Pete walked the three blocks to his building and then the four flights up to his apartment.

The expression "it ain't much, but I call it home" was aptly applied here. An L-shaped one bedroom flat, it seemed a strange war had broken out between the furniture and diverse pieces of sound equipment, with both sides taking heavy casualties, more of a Japanese standoff than a Mexican one. A guitar amplifier head stood with its top off, thus rendering it headless, an assortment of diodes lay next to it, perched on a three-legged chair, the fourth leg a prosthesis consisting of four stacked Manhattan telephone directories. The couch had escaped the battle fairly unscathed, but the desk in the corner of the living room was surrounded and had surrendered long ago to a tangled mass of wire and speaker cones, a flag of colonization consisting of a Zildjian drum cymbal perched triumphantly on top of a fractured electric guitar neck.

Looking at it as if he were seeing it for the first time, he realized he'd seen worse in some of the local Soho art galleries and thought if he'd had a catchy title for it, maybe "The Mound of Music", he'd be able to sell it to some wealthy art collector. He could undoubtedly use the money, not to mention the space on the desk. The light on the answering machine was blinking. He depressed the answer button and a soft, almost feline voice replaced the silence,

"Hi, it's me. It looks like recording is going to be running late again tonight and I'll be meeting up with Paul and some guy from the record company afterwards for a couple of pops, so don't wait up. See you later, sugar. Bye."

"So much for needing an excuse to hit the Pyramid Club tonight," Pete said to himself. He slipped out of his jeans and shirt and jumped into the shower. The shower was kind enough to remain at the same temperature for the entire time he was under it. This was rare and Pete took it as a good omen for the evening ahead of him.

He studied his reflection in the full-length oval bedroom mirror and thought of the line from the Indiana Jones movie: "It ain't the years, it's the mileage". He had just passed his thirty-third birthday, but there was a quality in the eyes that spoke of someone who had lived longer, though not necessarily happier. His dark brown hair was longish, not quite curling down to his shoulders, but getting close. His nose had never fully recovered from the breaking it had received five years back. It gave some character to a face that otherwise would have been sort of blandly good looking, the kind of face that went largely unnoticed, a useful trait when working as an undercover narcotics cop, his former occupation.

He didn't miss it all that much. Still, there were times he longed for the adrenaline surges that came with the work. Sometimes adrenaline is your friend, sometimes it's not, he thought, and buttoned a navy blue shirt. He put on a pair of black boots and wrapped a white lizard skin belt around his leather pants. After deciding the autumn evening was still warm enough to wear a light jacket, he flicked off the lights, locked the door and stepped out into the night.

He flagged down a passing taxi and pulled up in front of the East Village club ten minutes later. Pete knew it made a better impression on the bouncer if you stepped out of a cab rather than strolling up to the door if you arrived at the club solo. A stretch limo with a bevy of beauties is the surest way to get in with a smile, but since the stretch was in the shop and he'd misplaced his bevy, the taxi would have to do. As he stepped through the door he could hear a band in the back room chewing their way through a cover of Iggy Pop's "I Wanna Be Your Dog".

Though it was only 11:15, there was already a healthy crowd for a Monday night and it took him a couple of minutes to find Johnny. He was at the end of the long, scarred oak bar in the front room, talking animatedly with two young women who looked like they could be from the Swedish bikini team. Johnny looked up and saw Pete squeezing past a two hundred plus pound woman dressed in pink spandex and rabbit ears and waved him over. Pete finally made it down to the end of the bar and ordered a beer. "Looks like the Energizer Bunny has been doing pretty well this year and is eating up most of its residuals," he said.

"Hey guy, good to see you. I'd like to introduce you to Kyra and Astrid. Ladies, this is the gentleman I was just telling you about: Peter Watts, third in line to the Tasmanian throne," said Johnny. The two women flashed perfect teeth at Pete.

"Does this mean you'll get to rule over that cute little cartoon character?" asked Astrid, the shorter of the two, "I always used to watch Bugs Bunny cartoons when I was growing up in Stockholm."

"Astrid and Kyra are here doing a commercial for Speedo swimwear," said Johnny with a proud smile, "and I've just been given the account. For some reason, they pulled me off the Elsie milk account and want me to come up with a jingle for this one. It's undoubtedly going to be a passionate love song." He took Kyra's hand and kissed it while looking deep into her eyes.

Kyra blushed, looked away and giggled, "Oh, Johnny, I never know when you're being serious."

"I think I know how it's going to go already," he said. "When inspiration hits me, it hits me hard. Something like this:

One thing that's guaranteed—o
She's the one I really need—o
My beautiful lady Swede—o
Wrapped in a shining Speedo."

The two women laughed and clapped their hands. Pete shook his head. "Your inspiration hit me pretty hard too, pal.

My beer just went flat with that last one. You sure there's no inbreed—o going on in your family?"

"You're just jealous because your muse left you a long time ago and took out a restraining order against you."

"Most amusing. Hey, one of the tables in the back room is freeing up. Do you all want to sit down? I've been on my feet all day," said Pete. He ushered them through a low doorway and they took a table near the wall. The band had commenced a vivisection of Garbage's "I'm Only Happy When it Rains". Pete winced as he watched the guitarist, dressed in a harlequin's costume with wraparound sunglasses and combat boots, strangle the chords. At the end of the song, the audience looked on in disbelief as the bassist answered the cell phone ringing in his pocket. He spoke hurriedly to the caller and hung up, an embarrassed grin on his face.

"These guys are atrocious. What made you pick this place tonight? Are they covering some of your jingles?" he asked Johnny.

"These guys are called End Over End. You see the guy playing keyboards all dressed in red over on the left? That's Dale Patterson. He got signed a few months ago by Magma Records to a huge contract with a big advance. Apparently, his manager has a lot of pull with the label and he's quite talented. He's got it all: he sings, plays and produces good industrial dance tunes. His record just came out last week, and it's being hyped all over the place."

"Then what's he doing with these guys? It sounds like they were walking in front of a Salvation Army store and found some instruments on the sidewalk."

"Ah, they're just some of his old friends from high school. He thought it would be a hoot to do this gig. I know the drummer from a show I did with him a while back. He said to come down and he'd introduce us."

"Do you think they would play some Ace of Base if we asked them nicely?" asked Kyra.

"Yeah, I'd like to hear Ace of Base debased by these guys," said Pete with a laugh. The guitar player announced they would play "Come Out and Play" by the Offspring as the last song in the set, but not to worry as they'd be back in twenty minutes for more. This time the song held together reasonably well until the end, when all four musicians tried to end the song on the four different beats of the measure. They all stopped and looked at each other. The drummer counted out, "1,2,3,4" and they were able to bring it to a crashing conclusion. The drummer waved when he saw the foursome sitting at the table, and signaled for Johnny to order him a beer. He wiped his face off with a towel, jumped off the tiny stage and came over to them. A waitress took their order.

Johnny introduced the drummer, a friendly-looking British fellow named Griff. "Kyra here was wondering if you guys would play something by Ace of Base in the next set."

"Who?" queried the drummer, "Oh, those Europop blokes with the two birds singing. Bloody Abba of the nineties. Sorry, luv, don't know any by them. I hate that stuff with the drum machines."

"Pete's a drummer too," Johnny said to Griff. "You guys are just worried that those machines'll take your jobs. Hey, at least they always show up to rehearsals on time and never get too drunk to play." He looked around the table conspiratorially. "What do you call a person who likes to hang around musicians?"

"I don't know. What?" asked Kyra.

"A drummer," replied Johnny with a loud guffaw. The two women looked at each other perplexedly.

"It's a stupid musician's joke," explained Pete "Like: how many bass players does it take to screw in a light bulb?"

Kyra smiled and shook her head.

"None. A keyboard player can do it with his left hand."

Sensing they were losing the interest of the women, Johnny tried another tack. "I guess you had to be there. Hey Griff, how about it, you gonna introduce us to Dale?"

"Sure. He's another wanker with the bloody drum machines. I tell you, he's been dodgy of late. We'd scheduled four or five rehearsals for this little gig and he only made it to one. I know he's likely to be hitting it big soon, but it can't sound very tight when that happens."

"Only one rehearsal? We couldn't tell," said Pete, thinking of the fine line between diplomacy and hypocrisy.

"Yer being generous, mate. I know it sounds like a bloody Chinese fire drill up there," replied Griff. He motioned to the keyboard player, who was staring down intently at his synthesizer. He finally looked up, squinted at them and ambled over to the table. "Dale, I'd like you to meet some friends of mine."

"Yeah, yeah. Hi. How's everyone doing? Hey, I gotta do something. I'll be back in a few," he mumbled. He waved vaguely and shuffled off in the direction of the bar.

"Wow, that was without a doubt something I'll be able to tell my grandchildren about," said Johnny. He turned to Griff. "What's with him?"

"Sod all if I know. I ain't seen 'im in years, and Noddy over there," he pointed to the harlequined guitarist, "he rings me up and says we're going to do a one-off as a lark. Dale used to be a genuinely open, friendly bloke. I mean, I know fame is supposed to change people, but the clock's barely started on his fifteen minutes yet."

"I know what you mean. I'm often amazed I've managed to stay as humble as I have," said Johnny with a solemn look. "I've even managed to carry some of my less fortunate friends with me on my inexorable climb to the top." He nodded his head toward Pete.

"Can you see over the rim of the toilet yet?" retorted Pete.

"Not yet. Maybe if I get on the shoulders of the Tidy Bowl man, I'll catch a glimpse of what lies beyond these blue waters."

The table rocked with laughter. Pete thought it might be a better idea to concentrate on Astrid, judging from the way Kyra was looking at Johnny, kind of like a hungry jaguar eyeing an antelope, though an antelope was not the animal Pete would have compared Johnny to, if truth be told. A sheep dog would have been a better match. With his shaggy blond, grown-out bowl haircut and engaging lopsided grin, he looked somewhat like Johnny Ramone gone California. In any case, Astrid was definitely nothing to sneeze at, though he did wonder about what that said about his current lady love and their relationship.

His girlfriend Angeline was fascinating, exotic, sensual and ruthless. She would have been perfectly cast as a villainess in a James Bond movie. Her name would be Heather Hither, or something along those lines, and she would keep a throwing knife in her garter belt. Then again, Astrid would be the professor's daughter that Bond would save from peril. Pete tried to think of a name for her, maybe Golden Delicious. That would be about right. She must have been reading his mind because at that moment she turned and gave him a wink. "I think drums are the most primal, sexy instruments in the world. Have you been playing for a long time?" she asked.

"Ever since I was a kid. I used to drive my parents crazy. I'd play on everything in the house with a pair of sawed-off broomstick handles until my dad finally broke down and bought me a second-hand set. I guess he figured that if I had the set down in the basement, the rest of the furniture upstairs would be safer," Pete said, taking a pull from his beer bottle.

"Yeah, he used to beat on a lot of things when he was a kid," Johnny said. Pete issued him a warning look. Johnny grinned mischievously. "We had a lot of fun jamming in that tiny basement, though. Some of those parties, oh baby!"

"I remember when you tried to turn the washing machine into a bong. Christ, I got in trouble for that. My mom never could figure out why all her sheets came out smelling the way they did. And remember when we tried to do the indoor fireworks display?"

"I hate to interrupt your holiday down memory lane, but I've got another set to play. You fancy Rush? We're going to do a couple of numbers by them next," said Griff as he finished his beer and got up.

Pete cringed inwardly at the thought of his favorite band being manhandled by this ensemble, but smiled anyway. "Kick some ass," he said.

"Sure, mate. Nice to meet you all. Noddy, you ready to go?" he shouted over to the guitarist, still on the stage, attempting to tune his instrument. He was using an electronic tuner with a dying battery, which would only respond to being smacked against a hard object, in this case, the stage itself.

"Yeah, Slasher's at the bar, hitting on the barmaid. You seen Dale?" was his reply.

The bassist returned with a round of free beers, compliments of the barmaid. "We're going on again?" he asked.

"Yeah. Where the fuck is Dale? Bloody hell."

"I don't know. I thought he was back here with you guys," replied the bass player. He was dressed like a cross between a Hare Krishna and a Hell's Angel, with a dab of Tallulah Bankhead thrown in for good measure.

"If these guys are going to be a while, I'll excuse myself for a minute," said Pete. He found his way to the men's room. He stepped up to the dingy urinal and read the witticisms scrawled on the tiles in front of him. One particular limerick written to the left of the urinal handle in black magic marker caught his attention. It read:

There once was a girl named Alice

Who used a dynamite stick for a phallus.

They found her vagina

In North Carolina

And part of her anus in Dallas.

Now if only Johnny could come up with something that good was the thought crossing Pete's mind when he noticed the red lizard skin boot sticking out from underneath the far stall toward the back of the bathroom. He thought he recognized it and called over,

"Hey, guy, I think the rest of your band is looking for you. They want to get the next set going."

No answer. He started toward the stall.

"Hey, Dale. You in there?"

Still no answer. The bathroom door swung open and a clearly annoyed Griff stomped in, muttering to himself. He stopped when he saw the boot.

"Fucking hell, there he is. C'mon Dale, be quick about it. We're ready to go back on."

"I think you might have a problem here," said Pete. He knocked on the stall door. "You O.K. in there?"

The boot didn't move. Exasperated, Griff came up next to Pete and shook the door. No activity from the boot.

"C'mon, mate, wake up in there. Time to go." Pete stepped into the next stall on the right, stood on the toilet seat, and looked over the partition.

"Oh shit!"

He scrambled down rapidly, came around and, with one well-placed blow, kicked in the stall door.

"Sweet Jesus," whispered Griff. Dale Patterson was slumped on the toilet seat, eyes open and glazed, his belt wrapped tightly around his biceps and a syringe sticking out of his left forearm. His gaze had fixed on a broken tile just below the air vent near the ceiling. A thin trickle of blood had rolled down toward his wrist and was pooling into his palm. There was still some blood left in the syringe. He bolted from the bathroom and raced over to the barmaid in the front room, who was leaning over the bar and whispering something into the bass player's ear.

"Hey! Call 911, get the paramedics, now! You've got an O.D. in the bathroom. Quick!" he shouted at her. Startled for an instant, she then reached for the telephone behind the bar. He ran back into the bathroom and pushed past a pale and wide-eyed Griff into the stall. He felt for a pulse on Patterson's neck. Couldn't feel anything.

"Help me get him out of there. Stretch him out on the floor."

Griff took Patterson by the legs while Pete reached around and grabbed under the arms. They maneuvered him out of the stall, onto the grimy tile floor.

"Shit! What do we do? What do we do?" asked Griff. A couple of club regulars poked their heads through the door to see what the commotion was. Pete ripped Dale's shirt open and put his ear to his chest, trying in vain to hear a heartbeat. A small glassine envelope containing brown powder fell out of the breast pocket of Dale's shirt. Pete then pressed both hands hard on the sternum rhythmically in an effort to revive the heart. As focused as he was on trying to resuscitate Dale, Pete couldn't help but notice the crude drawing of a laughing clown's face with a bright red nose stamped on the envelope. Four minutes later, the paramedics arrived, ushered him out of the bathroom and attempted revival themselves. Ashen, Pete returned to the concerned looks of the others. He related the events of the last minutes as the paramedics removed the body on a stretcher and into the ambulance. The shocked band members followed behind in their rented van. A policeman was questioning the barmaid and she sent him over in Pete's direction.

"You the guy who found him?" The cop asked.

When Pete looked up, the officer did a double take and exclaimed, "Pete, hey what's up? You're the one that found the guy? Shit, I haven't seen you in a dog's age. How ya doing?"

"Hi, Manny," Pete replied. "We used to work together," he explained to the rest of the table. He turned back to the policeman. "I found him in the last stall. I had to kick the door in and drag him out, but he didn't respond to CPR. I tried not to touch anything else."

"Yeah, he's gone, all right. All my years on the force and I never get used to these scenes," said the officer, shaking his head. "I hate to ask you, Pete, but you gotta come down to the station and give a statement. You know the routine." He looked around the table and noticed the ladies' presence. "Oh, hell, I guess it can wait til tomorrow. This stiff ain't going nowhere. The guys'll be glad to see you, at least most of them. I'll tell the Reaper you're coming."

Charles "The Grim Reaper" Grimson was a sergeant in the division Pete used to work in. He was also Pete's ex-father-in-law. They had always gotten along well, though they didn't see much of each other anymore.

"Yeah, say 'hi' to Charlie for me and tell him I'll be by sometime tomorrow morning. Take it easy, Manny. Let's get together for a beer sometime," Pete said as the officer left.

"Christ. What a nightmare. Are you O.K., buddy?" said Johnny, a worried look on his face. Astrid came around the table and put her arm around him. Pete lowered his head and stared at his bottle of beer.

"That was thoroughly strange, seeing that guy dead on the floor. I felt like I was caught in some weird time warp. Everything just came flying back at me, all the things I've tried to forget. Christ, all the bodies, the guns, and that explosion. I'll tell you," he said, looking up at them, "that was the loudest noise I've ever heard."

3

"C'mon, let's get out of here," said Johnny, after spending a couple of minutes watching Pete stare down into his empty beer bottle, absently peeling the label with his thumbnail. "There's this new place uptown that just opened up a couple of weeks ago, Electric Willie's, and I've been meaning to go check it out. It's supposed to be kinda outrageous. Designers, supermodels, rock stars, plumbers, serial killers, nuns, they've got it all."

It was drizzling lightly outside. They were able to flag down a passing taxi a few minutes later and wend their way to the Upper East Side of Manhattan. Johnny sensed Pete was lost on an unlit strip of his psyche and filled the silence with ramblings, diverting the ladies while Pete gradually got his bearings. He had never seen his friend so shaken in all the years they had known each other. Astrid was looking at him with concern and put a hand on his arm reassuringly. He turned to her with a fragile smile and said,

"Sorry about this. I guess I'm not the best company in the world right now."

"Don't let him fool you. This is a considerable improvement from what he's usually like at this time," said Johnny, looking at the two blondes. "Mostly after midnight he's usually up on the bar doing the can-can with the transvestites that hang out in there. The impressive part is that, even at his age, he gets his ankles up around his ears, better even than some of them."

Had there not been female company in the taxi, Pete would have offered to do the can-can on a certain part of Johnny's anatomy. He opted instead for a glare that brought a chuckle.

"There. That's more like the guy I've come to know and love."

A few moments later, they pulled up in front of a canopied nightclub complete with a doorman with huge biceps and a dour expression. A bristling handlebar mustache added to his threatening demeanor. A trio of drunks in expensive suits and Wall Street haircuts were doing their best to dissuade him from throwing them out.

"Do you know who I am?" shouted one of the florid faced suits, "I'll have you fired. I'm good friends with the owner."

"Get out of here before I decide to go Cro-Mag on your sorry ass," replied the doorman.

"Hey, the bitch was asking for it. Who was she not to want to have a drink with me?" said another, who, though still technically standing on two feet, was having trouble keeping his equilibrium and addressed the air next to the bouncer.

"Weebles wobble, but they don't fall down," said Johnny to Pete in a low voice. "There's nothing more boring than a drunk yuppie, except maybe a straight yuppie."

"You gentlemen will soon enter an area I like to call 'The Pain Zone'. Get the fuck out of here before something bad happens to your shiny little suits and you have to explain this to your wives, who are doubtless gonna treat you worse than I ever will," growled the doorman.

"You'll be sorry," said the first and pulled his friends away. "This neighborhood's turned to shit since they closed the Surf Club." They stopped and looked unfocusedly at Pete, Johnny and their dates before piling into a black car service sedan waiting in front of the club.

"Hey, Jimmy, what's happening?" said Johnny, knocking fists with the doorman. "If I read about a drive-by shooting up here tomorrow in the *Post*, I'll know who did it."

"Mr. Styx, how you doing tonight?" replied the doorman with a polite nod, "I'm supposed to work the door, but sometimes I think the job title should be 'garbage man' because I always wind up throwing the trash out."

"I can see what you mean. How long you been working up here?"

"Ever since they closed down the Limelight again," replied Jimmy. "Do you ever walk into a place without at least one beautiful woman on your arm?" He smiled at the two ladies and held the door open. "Bobo, comp these four for me." he called over to the cashier standing inside the doorway.

Once inside, they beheld a bizarre neon, fur and chrome jungle. Behind the bar on the left was an impressive collection of vibrators and other electrical stimulants hanging from a rack over the glasses. The top shelf liquor bottles were all capped by non-electric stimulators. Apparently, the safety of the bartenders was a strong consideration in this establishment, as it would be potentially embarrassing for the bar to have one of them electrocute themselves while pouring a drink for a patron. Ambient acid jazz music pulsed behind the din of voices. There was a row of brown leather backed booths with faux zebra skin trim on the right and Johnny guided them to a vacant one. They made small talk, waiting for one of the overworked waitresses to notice them.

Astrid drew laughs with her observation of how many people wore sunglasses after dark in New York when her country was known as the land of the midnight sun. Pete commented on how flawless the ladies' English was and Kyra replied, not too unkindly, that, unlike in American schools, European children are taught foreign languages from infancy. Finally, a waitress arrived and took their order. The booth was a bit cramped for four people, but Pete didn't mind being squeezed in close to Astrid. The mixture of his beer and her perfume was getting to him in a big way, not to mention that he was still way off balance from the evening's activities.

He'd been in similar situations before and hadn't hesitated to make a complete idiot of himself by moving too fast, too soon. A gallery of foolish, wasted opportunities and clumsy passes flashed through his brain like a video on fast forward and a voice in his head said, "Take it easy, be natural." He'd successfully ignored this voice many times in the past and was poised to do it again. But, just as his hand was reaching under the table for her inner thigh, Johnny whispered to him,

"Hey, guy, check it out; nine o'clock at the back bar. Isn't that Angeline?"

Pete's view was partially blocked by a large black man with a beehive hairdo, but he craned his neck and was able to see the profile of a beautiful Eurasian woman with swept-back shoulder length hair. There was no mistaking that profile, or the moon-shaped jade earrings he'd given her for her last birthday. She was standing at the bar with a man wearing a green silk jumpsuit, his long graying hair in a ponytail wrapped by a leather thong. She laughed as he whispered in her ear and slowly caressed her neck. She whispered something back to him, ran her tongue around the rim of his earlobe, and finished her drink.

They got up, the man helping her on with her bolero jacket, and walked toward the exit, oblivious to the intense scrutiny. Pete was sorely tempted to confront the pair. The beer muscles and desire to spill some blood were tempered by the knowledge that it wouldn't get him anywhere, and he had what could be a promising situation developing right next to him. If this had been a cartoon, angel and devil characters would have appeared on his shoulders to debate his options.

"Easy, Trigger. Down, boy. Take it easy, guy," said Johnny quietly, gripping Pete's shoulder "I know you're having a shitty night. Don't go making it worse."

"Is something wrong?" asked Astrid, "You look like you've seen a ghost."

"No, it's nothing," Pete answered. He clenched his teeth and stretched his lips in an unconvincing attempt at a smile. "I was thinking about how that poor guy looked when we had him stretched out on the floor. I'll be fine. Anyone feel like doing a shot of something other than heroin tonight? Maybe a kamikaze or eight? Or would you ladies prefer tequila?"

Much to Pete and Johnny's surprise, the Swedes had never sampled tequila before. He signaled the waitress, who was luckily in the area this time. She returned with a tray full of glasses, depositing them in threesomes before each. After dedicating the first two shots to the memories of Stevie Ray Vaughan and Captain Kangaroo, the mood turned decidedly lighter. Pete understood that if he had any hopes at all of salvaging a dreadful evening, he should concentrate on the present, which seemed at the moment to be looking up. The two women excused themselves and got up, a bit unsteadily, to go to the bathroom, leaving Pete and Johnny alone for a couple of minutes.

"Jesus, what a night!" said Pete "I sure hope hell's won't be this bad when I get there. It can't be."

"Well, hell's a little warmer. But it's not the heat; it's the humility."

"C'mon, man, be serious. What is going on here? Who was that dried-up, lime colored shithead poseur with Angeline? She left me a message she'd be out with Paul, the guy who's producing her demo, after they'd finished recording the background vocals, and that's not him. Poppa Stevens is a short, chunky guy. I've seen pictures of him. Christ, how many times has she lied to me? This makes me wonder."

"As useless as it is to tell you, I think I know how you feel. It sucks when someone abuses your trust. I never like to throw my two cents worth when it's someone else's relationship, but this doesn't exactly surprise me. Whenever I see her, with you or without you, there are always sixteen guys around her like flies on shit, and she doesn't exactly discourage their attention, if you know what I mean. Not that she's going to do all of them, but……," Johnny hesitated, noting from his friend's expression that he was doing more harm than good. "Hey, at the same point, it says a lot about you that she sticks around with you most of the time. She sees something in you, I can tell. I know this sounds a little on the lame side, but you know what I'm saying, don't you?"

"That I'm some pathetic shmuck? Yeah, I think I get your drift, douche boy, loud and clear. What's she doing with me, anyway? She's looking to climb her way up the ladder of the music business and I'm running a crummy rehearsal studio, barely getting by on a shoestring."

"Good analogy you're using there, bud. She's climbing up the ladder and you're a rung, albeit a low one. Think of how Madonna's first boyfriends in New York felt when she kept ditching them for the next one. It's kind of like a food chain."

Pete couldn't help but laugh at that bit of imagery.

"I guess that makes me plankton then, doesn't it?"

"I've always thought of you as a crustacean, judging from your underwear, but if the shoe fits…"

"I know, I know. It's just I feel stupid now." He pressed his forearm dramatically against his forehead. "I feel so used, so tawdry."

"You know what would be stupid? To waste more time on a lost cause right now. Don't cry over spilled beer. Those two lovely Swedish meatballs will back in a minute and I'd put up money that you'll be astride Astrid within the hour."

"It would be nice to have something go right tonight, for a change. This hasn't exactly been a picnic so far." He spied the two women making their way back to the booth. They chatted a while longer and then, after downing his last shot, Pete checked his watch and said, "I'm sorry, but I now have to be up early to go to the police precinct, so I can't stay out super late." He turned toward Astrid. "I'm cabbing it downtown. Can I drop you off on the way home?"

"I'd like that," she answered with a warm look.

They went outside to hail a cab. The rain had dissipated into a light, cool mist and they had no trouble finding transportation. Astrid was staying at a midtown hotel on Lexington Avenue and, as the taxi slowed down and pulled to the curb in front of the hotel, suggested they sample the wet bar in her room. He choked back an unfortunate pun and paid the cabby. The hotel doorman opened the taxi door for them and steered them into the lobby. The elevator took them to the thirty-eighth floor.

Once in the elegantly furnished room, she mentioned the beautiful view of the city skyline and pushed open the French doors leading out to a narrow balcony. Astrid returned with a split of champagne from the wet bar and a couple of water glasses from the bathroom. Even from the relatively close proximity, the view of the top of the Empire State Building was lost in the mist, though a halo of light was still discernible in the night.

"It makes me feel like this whole city is mine from up here," she said, taking a sip from her glass. "When I was in grade school, my parents took me on a holiday to Holland and we went to a place where a whole miniature town had been set up, called Madurodam. That's what this makes me think of. Of course, there is a touch more attitude here."

"I kind of like your attitude," said Pete. He leaned over and kissed her, lightly at first, and then more urgently. Her lips melted against his and their tongues entwined. "You want to go inside? I'm getting wet out here."

"So am I," she said with a look of pure heat.

Astrid took his hand and led him back toward the bed, though they didn't get there until close to an hour later. He slowly undressed her, kissing her wherever skin was being exposed. They sank to the plush carpeting, her arms and legs wrapped around him. She gasped as his questing fingers slid under her panties and gently stroked her, all the while kissing her nipples through her bra, which he soon removed.

She fumbled with the buttons of his shirt before simply grabbing the collar and ripping it wide open to feel his skin against hers. The shirt had been a present from Angeline, but at this juncture Pete didn't mind too much. His mouth continued its inexorable path down her body, stopping at diverse scenic points of interest until arriving at its intended destination. Her lace panties proved to be no match for his teeth.

She wrapped her thighs tightly around his neck and groaned from deep within, pushing her pelvis hard into his face. Having his oxygen supply cut off had never been as exciting and he knew if he didn't get his pants off soon they would simply pop open from the pressure within. He presently realized his hands were free, as her legs had such a tight grip around him that he was able to unbuckle his belt and slide his pants and underwear down to his knees.

She released his neck from her thighs, rolled over on to her knees, and looked back over her shoulder at Pete, beckoning with her eyes. Pete didn't especially need to be beckoned at that point, but it's always good to be sure. He mounted her from behind and she said something in Swedish. It didn't sound like "stop" in any language he knew and he started rocking, picking up speed as she bucked frantically. Her guttural scream of passion, when she came, set him off and he released deep inside her. Spent, they remained in that position for a few more seconds until they both rolled over and collapsed on the floor.

"Oh, that was wonderful, but I think I burned my knees on the carpet," said Astrid. She slung an arm over Pete's chest.

"You and me both, babe," he answered. They both raised their legs towards the ceiling to survey the damage, matching red marks on their knees. "Could you give me a hand getting out of these boots? They're tight as hell and I've had too much too drink."

"Me too, at least I've had too much to drink. After that, I don't think I'll ever be tight as hell again. God, you were in me to the hilt," she said. She turned and yanked hard on his left boot, almost falling over backward when it finally came off. The right one came off somewhat more easily and she slid off his pants, which were bunched up around his calves.

"Free at last," he said. "Oh, Astrid, that was terrific."

They dozed the sleep of spent lovers for a few minutes before she nudged Pete.

"Come on. The swimsuit company has paid for the bed for a couple of nights. We might as well use it."

Once in the bed, they began caressing each other. After a few minutes, she straddled him, raised herself up, and slid his now resuscitated member inside her. This time was less frantic and she unhurriedly rode him to climax. Her chest heaved and she tossed her mane of blond hair about in passion. She squeezed her pelvic muscles rhythmically around him until he felt a great swell come over him. He sighed mightily and held her close against his chest, their perspiration mingling, then slowly drying in the soft autumn breeze blowing through the open balcony doors.

"Oh Christ, you are too much," Pete whispered. She made a low noise in her throat and curled up next to him.

Pete awoke sometime before dawn, his body glistening from sweat and his heart beating fast from an awful nightmare that, for the life of him, he could not remember, except a feeling of dread hanging on like a bad aftertaste. He slid from between the sheets and sauntered out, naked, on to the balcony.

The rain had stopped sometime during the night, though the streets, empty but for a few passing cars, still shone. The dream faded quickly as the breeze dried his skin. He appreciated that rarely does one get the gift to see the city from this view and in this frame of mind simultaneously. It was a very peaceful, private and spiritual moment. He cherished it, knowing how fleeting it was, and that tomorrow he would be dragged back into a past he sought to leave behind. After a few minutes, he returned to the room, closing the doors behind him, and saw Astrid's blond hair fanned on the pillow. He smiled, yawned, climbed back into bed and slept untroubled until the next morning.

4

A ray of sunlight slanting through the window woke Pete up. He shifted a few inches and barely caught himself from falling over the side of the bed. Throughout the night Astrid had gradually gained strategic control of the bed through assorted rollover maneuvers and had left Pete with only the width of his body to sleep in. She was a petite woman and he had no idea what she would want with all the space in a king sized bed, but she had made the most of it, whatever the reason, her lithe limbs sprawled out deliciously over the red satin expanse.

He sighed, memories of the previous evening's festivities flooding back to him, and leaned over to kiss her neck gently. She murmured softly and threw an arm over his chest, burying her head in his shoulder. He craned his neck to look at the digital clock and could only see the first digit, a nine. Knowing what was facing him today, he stretched out the placid moment as long as he could, but knew it was only a temporary respite from the inevitable. He gradually disengaged himself, one limb at a time, careful not to wake her, and entered the sumptuous black marble bathroom.

He marveled at the quantity of skin care and makeup products arrayed around the rim of the sink and thought a small fortune could be made by mixing mayonnaise, peanut butter and water in a bottle, calling it virgin yak milk extract or something equally exotic, and claiming it to be an exceptional exfoliant, or whatever it was that removed the dead leaves from the skin of women around the world. Pete turned on the shower and in a few moments the steam misted the large mirrors. He stepped into what, for him, was a little slice of heaven.

The shower in his apartment was a truly squalid affair, a weak sluice of water dribbling down at a snail's pace in an unpredictable vast range of temperatures, one extreme following another without hesitation, without warning, without mercy, into a payphone booth sized space. There was even a telephone in the hotel bathroom, next to the toilet, though he couldn't think of whom he'd want to call from this particular perch.

This shower was the size of a walk-in closet, with a white marble bench on one wall, and he let the hot water pound his back and neck from six spigots jutting from the wall. His muscles loosened and he whistled quietly to himself, an old song by Cheap Trick that he couldn't quite remember the title to. Soon the bathroom, sizable as it was, was completely fogged in. As he cleared scented soap from his eyes, he saw a shape gradually emerging from the mist. The door to the shower opened and a soft voice said,

"There you are. Am I too late or are there any areas left on you that still need cleaning?"

"It so happens I reserved a couple of spots for exactly this contingency. Choose your weapon: washcloth, hand or tongue."

"I have something else in mind that should prove equally effective, if you don't mind. Pass me the soap, please."

Pete complied and Astrid briefly rinsed herself under the flowing water and then began working up lather between her palms. She then massaged her breasts with her soapy hands until they looked like Mr. Bubble's happiest fantasy and turned her eyes up at Pete, his interest piqued.

"You missed a spot on your back."

"You know, I never seem to be able to get that one spot clean, try as I might. Can you help me, or is there no hope?"

He'd never felt so safe turning his back on someone in his life and his confidence was amply rewarded. She rubbed herself against him, giving him a combination massage and back scratch he wouldn't soon forget.

"Did you know I was a medical student at the University of Malmo before I chose to model? I could have become a proctologist." She slid a finger between his ass cheeks and stopped before the point of no return. Pete let out a yelp and spun around. "Oh, here's another spot you didn't get to. You know, you are a very, very dirty man."

"You don't know the half of it."

"I think I'd like to know all of it."

After massaging him to fullness, she sat him down on the shower bench and wrapped her arms around his neck. Astrid kneeled on the bench and lowered herself on him, feeling him slide deep inside. She rocked back and forth faster and faster. Their lips locked frantically. Finally she pulled her head back away from him, her wet hair clinging to her fine cheekbones, arched her back and let out a long, sensuous sigh. Feeling the contractions within her, his resistance gave way and a thunderous orgasm coursed through his entire body.

She kissed him lightly and asked, "Are you feeling cleaner now?"

"In body and in mind," he replied with a smile, "you are something else."

"I ordered some breakfast before I came to the shower. I had a feeling we might work up an appetite."

They had just finished toweling each other dry when they heard a knock and a muffled call of "room service" sounded from the other side of the front door. Astrid hurriedly threw on a long white terrycloth bathrobe hanging from a hook on the door and let in a tuxedoed waiter who wheeled in a serving tray laden with food and beverages. The waiter lifted up the long, lace tablecloth and, from a range of drawers and slots in the tray, produced silverware, china, fruit juices, two long stemmed champagne glasses and a chilled bottle of Dom Perignon. He then lifted the covers of platters with a flourish, steam rising from the eggs Florentine nestled in the middle of an arrangement of smoked salmon

"Will there be anything else?" he asked, before presenting her with the bill.

"No. That will be fine. Please put the 'Do not disturb' sign back on the door on your way out. Thank you," replied Astrid. The waiter bowed his head and exited.

"I was going to grab a bagel with a schmeer on the way to the station, but I hate to waste good food," said Pete, eyeing the expansive, and expensive, spread while he towel dried his hair.

"It's only fair. You've filled me up and I should do the same for you," she replied with a smile. The smile turned wistful, and she added, "I like you a lot. I wish I didn't have to leave tomorrow morning. There's something about your eyes I could get used to looking at."

"You're leaving so soon? Damn!" Pete said, surprised. "I know what you're saying. It's so easy being with you, too, at least when I don't feel like I'm going to turn into a geyser. If time's not on our side, at least let's make the most of it. You doing anything for dinner tonight?"

"Are you offering me that delicious body of yours or are you talking about a restaurant?"

"I'd be happy to be your plat du jour, or prix fixe, or prick fix, or whatever you want, but I was thinking of this little place I know in Soho. It's kind of intimate and the food's great. Do you like French food?"

"I'd love to go. I've got a photo shoot this afternoon at the Bronx Zoo, but why don't you pick me up around 7:30 or so," she answered while they helped themselves to the salmon, eggs, sausages and bacon.

"After all this, I won't be able to eat anything before dinner," he said, surveying the contents of his plate.

"Coffee?" she asked and poured two cups full in response to his affirmation. She motioned to the bottle of champagne and said, "Can you pop the cork for me? Not that you haven't already, a couple of times."

"Sure. I don't know if I should indulge, though. I want to keep a clear head this morning. I've got to make my statement at the precinct today and have to do it with the man who used to be my father-in-law. He's a great guy, and all, but I'm not at all looking forward to this. This brings back memories I'd just as soon leave behind."

"I must admit I'm glad to hear he's not your current father-in-law. You don't have a current father-in-law, do you?" She gave him an appraising look. Pete shook his head no and sipped his coffee. "Perhaps you'd like to switch jobs with me today? You might have a good time wearing leopard patterned bathing suits in front of caged leopards and I find men in uniforms kind of sexy. Do you have any pictures of yourself in your police outfit?"

"Not with me, no. Besides, I only wore a uniform for a couple of years. I was undercover most of the time after that. Call it underdressed for success. You look as ratty or indistinct as possible and try to blend in. I had the grunge look down long before it became a fashion statement." He looked at the champagne bottle and said, "You know, on second thought, it would be kind of silly to let this good stuff pass me by. Maybe one little glass won't hurt."

"Would you like some juice in it? There's some orange, but I like it with peach nectar. It's called a Bellini."

"Sounds good to me. Is that caviar?" he said, motioning to one of the dishes, "My God, I've heard of breakfasts of champions, but this…"

"A breakfast fit for a thoroughbred. But I think it's time you were farmed out to stud," She leaned over and slid her hand up his thigh.

"No, no, please. I've got to get my day started. Let me save something for tonight," He removed her hand and kissed it.

"If you're not willing, maybe I'll find some beast at the zoo this afternoon that can keep up with me," she pouted.

"If you're going to be wearing leopard skin bathing suits, it'll only be a matter of minutes before you find one."

He opened the bottle of champagne and filled the glasses halfway. Astrid topped them off with the peach nectar. They dug into their breakfasts, sampling each dish. After one last cup of coffee, Pete stretched and threw on his clothes. They laughed when Pete went to button his shirt and did a double take before remembering the way she had ripped it open the previous night. A couple of the buttons remained attached, so it didn't look too obvious. Pete kissed Astrid goodbye and promised he would pick her up in the hotel lobby around 7:30 that evening.

He strolled over to a bus stop, one block north of the hotel, took the bus downtown and made his way a few blocks west to his apartment, where he changed his clothes.

The precinct station wasn't very far away and he soon climbed the still-familiar six steps to the heavy wooden door. It had been scarred over the years by punks carving initials and various slogans, some legible, some obscene, others unfinished, as they had been caught in the act. All were covered in heavy layers of stain and varnish, the oldest ones barely visible, having receded to fossil status. The door handle, however, was a highly polished bronze, a stark contrast to the wood, which had seen better days. Pete hadn't been through this door in four years. He climbed the steps and arrived at the front desk, where a sullen looking uniform was filling out forms, his cap pushed back from his forehead.

"Hi. I'm here to make a statement on an O.D. at the Pyramid Club last night. Guy named Dale Patterson."

"Why didn't they bring you in last night?" asked the cop.

"Yo, Petey, where you been?" shouted another policeman from the other end of the room. He poked his head into an adjacent office and said, "Hey, guys. So's here." Two more officers hurried from the room and came over to him.

"Hey little drummer boy, what's the word?" called out one of them, a tall black man with the nametag "Weaver".

"Man, we never see you around here no more," said the shorter, dark haired officer on his left, his tag emblazoned "Impeliterri". "You been hiding, boy?"

"Yeah, you don't call, you don't write. You look like you haven't been eating right either. Either that or you been taking it in the can too much and the food comes right out your asshole 'cause there's nothing left to block it," said the third man, nameplate of "Tippins", with a loud guffaw.

"Mikey, if anyone could do that to me, it wouldn't be you. You could fuck a squirrel while it was asleep and it wouldn't wake up, you needle dick," retorted Pete.

The four men met and threw their arms around each other, the three cops trying to squeeze the breath out of Pete. "That's a hell of a choke hold. You guys couldn't choke your chickens with that," Pete said.

"Hey, Heller," said Impeliterri. He motioned to the cop at the desk, who was observing the reunion with a disapproving glare, "You know Pete 'So' Watts? He did a lot of good things with us a few years back, before he went civilian. This guy was the shit."

"Yeah, I've heard about you," said Heller, lifting a finger in Pete's direction. "Not a happy ending."

"What, you was waiting for the fat lady to sing?" said Tippins to Heller, "It didn't happen, 'cause I was banging your wife that night and she was screamin', not singin'."

"I'm surprised you can remember back that far, you drunken sack of shit," retorted Heller.

"Gentlemen, I find this kind of discourse intolerable," a burly, white-haired police sergeant, looking like a football linebacker gone a bit to seed, paused as he ascended the final step to the room and said, "Peter, you big turd, where the fuck have you been? Christ, I know we're not family anymore, but you could come down sometimes. I finally see you again, and it's only because you're fucking here on fucking business."

"Charlie, I don't know what to say...Shit, it's not you," Pete said.

"Don't say nothing. Let me look at you," said Charlie Grimson. He strode across the room, gripped Pete by the shoulders and looked him in the eyes. "You doing alright? Everything O.K.?"

"Yeah, everything's fine. How about you? You're looking good for an old fart," said Pete, clapping Charlie on the back. "How's Rosie doing? Is she still working at Bloomingdale's?"

"Yeah, she's still there. She's still as pretty as a picture, too. Looks just like her mother, God bless her memory."

"Good thing she didn't take after you, Reaper. Good work is hard to find in the circus," said Weaver. The rest of the policemen unsuccessfully smothered their laughs.

"I'm going to bust you down so far you'll be looking forward to cleaning up after the horses at the Saint Patty's parade."

"I'll take it," retorted Weaver with a laugh, "the horses are cleaner than the Irishmen. Smarter, too. And I won't even go into the difference in the way they're hung."

"Damn, I miss this crap," said Pete with a rueful expression. "You wouldn't believe the people I have to deal with these days. It's like day care for overgrown kids."

"You mean you miss the charming folk we deal with on a daily basis? That's kinda hard to believe," said Impelliteri, the Brooklyn accent dripping from every word.

"Only a complete wacko would miss the scum. It's you guys, shooting the shit, taking your money while playing cards. Oops," he glanced over at Charlie.

"What's this? You rat turds were playing cards, gambling on duty?" said Charlie, hands mockingly on his hips, "I can't believe it, you doing this behind my back. What, you were afraid I'd take all your money?"

"We wanted you to have something left for your retirement. Isn't it in about twenty minutes?" replied Weaver.

"Weaver, you know, you've always been like a son to me. It's why I always wondered your father didn't suspect why you're so much lighter skinned than he is." The other officers hooted. Charlie turned, put a brawny hand on Pete's back and escorted him to the office the other policemen had recently emerged from. "Let's get this shit over with quick and maybe we can go to Clan Den and throw a few back, maybe something to eat, too." He gave Pete a wink.

"Hey, Petey, I'm having a barbeque next Saturday," called Tippins. "Why don't you come? You can check out the new deck. These guys'll all be there and Eileen would love to see you. Maybe we could put some meat on your scrawny bones."

"I'd love to, Mikey; sounds great. But didn't Eileen tell you she only likes to see me when you're not around? Unless you're the one hiding in the closet taking notes. Nah, probably not. Must be one of her other boyfriends," replied Pete, with an evil grin. "Sounds great. I'll be there. You still at the same place, five blocks away from the Jamaica station?"

Tippins nodded. "Same place as always. Do me a favor, would ya, and wear men's clothing, for a change, on Saturday."

Pete and Charlie went into the office and sat down at a decrepit desk covered with so many coffee mug stains that it looked like the Olympic planning committee had gotten drunk there when they'd planned their logo years ago. Charlie hit a key on a computer planted in a garden of paper, and said proudly, "See, I've made it to the nineties. A few years ago, I'd have used this thing for a goddamned paperweight and now I've finally figured out how to turn it on. I've been thinking about buying one for the house. Maybe I'll even go and make myself a web page or something."

Pete smiled, thinking of his gruff ex-father-in-law going on line and getting into some bizarre chat room, discussing the pros and cons of being a vampire with some aspiring teenage bloodsuckers.

"Sounds like a great idea, Charlie."

"So, you want to tell me what happened last night?"

Pete recounted the previous night's events that had occurred at the Pyramid Club with minimal prompting from Charlie, only occasionally asking a question regarding details, such as the position of Patterson's body on the toilet seat, but not interrupting much. Pete's training kicked back in rapidly and he provided a clear and concise statement.

Charlie input all the details into the computer, typing with his two index fingers and pushed the save button. "I guess that's that," He cocked his head. "On one hand, I'm happy you were there 'cause I can count on your observation and police perspective. At the same time, I've got a good guess as to what that did to you inside, like you can't escape this bullshit."

"Were there any prints on that bag of heroin he was carrying?" asked Pete.

"The only clean ones we got were the vic's. A couple of others were too smudged to get anything. We checked that weird clown logo in our database, but no matches, and no one in narco has seen it before. We sent the heroin to the lab for testing. This is gonna be a real publicity clusterfuck. You ever heard of this guy, Patterson?"

"Not before last night, Charlie, but the way the music business runs nowadays, everything is viral and careers can be made in a week."

"I'm way too old for all this bullshit," he replied with a wave of his hand. "Give me Elvis, Fats Domino or Jerry Lee Lewis any day of the week."

Charlie hesitated, looked down and fiddled with a pencil before looking back up. "You know, it's not exactly like I feel responsible for what went down five years ago; it's more like a helplessness. I know you. I also saw what Rosie went through, like you had died. She treated me like a leper for a while, like it was my goddamned fault you got hooked. It's taken a while for us to get back to a semi-normal father-daughter relationship again. Or at least as normal as a couple of nut cases like us can have." He chuckled before turning serious again. "What I'm trying to say is…Shit, I'm not good at this crap. I should have looked out for you better than I did, should've seen it coming. Maybe I could've done something. You're the closest thing to a son I ever had."

"Hell, Charlie, c'mon, don't beat yourself up. I just got caught up. It was like being in a tornado. I'm lucky I got my feet back on the ground again."

Charlie's eyes crinkled. "Whaddaya say we wrap this up and get the hell outta here?"

Pete was about to agree when Impelliteri stuck his head through the door. "Hey, Reaper, the O.D.'s manager, Richie Roeper, just showed to make his statement. You want me to take it or you want to talk to him?"

"You take care of it, Vinnie, we're going out to grab something, be back in a couple of hours."

"Sure, chief. No problem." He closed the door.

"Hey Petey, by the way, you still living in the same place?" Charlie asked.

"Yeah. It ain't much, but you know......"

"The reason I ask is: you didn't happen to hear or see anything funky going on last night? Not a block away from where you live we found two burnt bodies in a dumpster. We I.D.'d one guy, some shit-heel drug runner. The other guy we have no clue on yet. Boy, it stunk like hell in that alley!"

"No, Charlie, not a thing." Pete shrugged. "My neighborhood's quiet most of the time."

They put their jackets on and headed out of the office. As they passed the front desk, Pete noticed the man Impelliteri was leading to another office on the far side of the station. He was wearing a crisp looking gray suit matching his long hair, held in a ponytail by a strip of leather. He turned while entering the office and Pete recognized him as the man who had left Electric Willie's the night before with Angeline. Pete's eyes widened and he said in an incredulous tone,

"That motherfucker is Patterson's manager?"

"Why, you know the guy?" asked Charlie.

"Well, no, not really. Ah, sort of," he stammered. "What I mean is I've never met the guy, never been introduced."

Pete knew he was floundering and debated whether to tell Charlie about the rest of his evening. He knew Charlie most likely wouldn't be shocked to hear the details of Pete's love life, but still felt somewhat uncomfortable discussing it with him, and preferred to avoid it, if possible. Nevertheless, he tried to decide if this was at all pertinent to the investigation, his instincts warning him. After a moment's hesitation, Pete realized that through this coincidence, he had at least learned the man's name, and said, "I've just heard it said this guy's a real scumbag. You know, these people in the music business." Pete figured it was a close enough assessment and besides, he didn't feel like lying to Charlie.

"I'll bet that business is crawling with guys like that. Rat bastards," said Charlie. He put a beefy arm around Pete's shoulder. "Fuck 'em all. Hey, like a pistol, the first six rounds are on me." They went down the stairs, through the door and out on the street.

5

"Hold on to something, this is gonna hurt a little," Ronno said. He stubbed his cigarette into a Murano crystal ashtray, brushed back a lock of greasy hair from his forehead, and lifted the forceps with a steady hand from an ornate Louis XIV desk.

"Hang on a sec, let me take another hit before you start."

A hand bearing a scorpion tattoo fished into the ashtray and extracted half of a very large spliff, still smoldering. As he gripped it between his thumb and first finger, the scorpion's stinger, running up his thumb, seemed to undulate, as if sensing an unseen enemy. Lying face down on the burgundy Chesterfield leather couch, he raised it to his lips, drew in a prodigious amount of smoke and savored the taste. He held it in for fifteen seconds, before slowly exhaling with a sigh.

"Nothing like a little Hawaiian. Mmm. Alright, Ronno, go ahead. Let's get this over with."

"At least it looks like the bullet's still in one piece. I don't want to be fishing around for fragments. Still, you're gonna want to get some soft pillows to sit on for a week or so. Not for nothing, though, I'd rather be in your shoes than that scumbag in the other room."

"Don't wash the bullet off when you pull it out. I want to personally feed it to him."

"Sure, boss. Alright, here goes." Ronno positioned himself, held the man's left buttock firmly in his hand, and deftly pulled out the bullet in one rapid motion after plunging the forceps into the wound. "Got it."

"Nice. I'll never regret sending you to med school," he said through tightly gritted teeth.

"Don't move, I've got to sew this up and put a bandage on it. All I could find was green thread, Hope that's O.K."

"Only if the Band-Aid has tiny flowers on it. Why would I give a damn? I can't see it anyway." He relit the now-extinct joint and inhaled slowly, the last tendrils of smoke going up his nose. "You clean it out good. That's one place I sure as hell don't want to get an infection. Ooh," he winced as Ronno applied the disinfectant. "That shit's worse than taking a bullet in the first place."

"Good thing your butt's not too hairy, it'll make taking this bandage off and cleaning the wound a little easier on you. We're going to have to do that a couple of times a day for a while," said Ronno. He carefully made the stitches and applied gauze bandages.

"I'll get a nurse to do that. You've seen enough of my ass for today. Get me someone who'll know what to do afterwards while my pants are still down."

"I've got just the woman for you. Remember me telling you about Alice? She's a very interesting lady, many hidden talents."

"Is this another one of your enema stories? I don't want to hear about that crap now. Jesus, you are one kinky bastard. C'mon, help me roll over and get my pants back up. Christ, what a pain in the ass this is." He looked over at Ronno, realizing his unwitting pun, and roared with laughter. "And I'm definitely going to take this out on someone. What's the line from the movie with the guy with all the needles sticking out of his face?"

"Hellraiser?"

"Yeah, that one. That's one funny movie. He tells this poor bastard: *Even in hell, your suffering will be legendary.* The scumbag who tried to take me out, his suffering's gonna be legendary in Bensonhurst. Let's go check him out, see if Bunny's left anything to work with."

He rolled over gingerly and, with Ronno steadying his arm, gradually straightened from a crouched position until he rose to his full height, about five-foot-three-inches.

"This ain't too comfortable," he said and loosely buckled his belt. "I think I might have to go to sweatpants or bathrobes for a while, maybe get the Hugh Hefner look going. Well, aside from Billy's funeral. I gotta get dressed up for that. You're going to take care of everything for me on that, right? I want this to be top shelf, Ronno. Get three hundred grand in cash ready for his family, too. His wife's got a kid on the way. He went down protecting me and I never let loyalty go unrepaid. Disloyalty, too."

Frank Bender gave Ronno a sidelong glance.

"I'll take care of anything or anyone needs taking care of. You know that," replied Ronno, who swallowed dryly and noticed the temperature in the room always seemed to get a few degrees warmer when under Frank Bender's scrutiny.

Bunny had commented to him once, when they were on a job, that their boss had something inside him very few men possess, a commanding presence comparable to Alexander the Great or Napoleon. It was the very lack of physical stature that made him so much more imposing. With his sharp features, piercing gaze and slick jet black hair, Bender always had the immediate attention of any room from the moment he entered it, and men whose ferocity would never be questioned on the street always eagerly sought his approval.

Every so often though, through the years, some upstart would try to make a name for himself by trying to muscle in on Bender's rigidly defined, although vast, territory. The quality of their deaths would be such that no further attempts would occur as long as recollection held. This, however, was not an industry known for either for longevity or long memories. By the same token, unlike Napoleon and Alexander, Bender had never tried to expand his territory past manageable means, never courted unnecessary danger, and was respected by the other crime lords of the city. In New York there's always enough to go around for everyone, if no one gets too greedy, he thought. Bender, an ardent student of history, was aware of what happened when a conqueror's reach exceeded his grasp.

"Shall we check in on our honored guest?" he said, a forbidding expression on his face. He hobbled toward the door and swung it open, emerging into a stately foyer. Oak paneling covered the walls lit by an enormous Venetian crystal chandelier. An oriental rug stretched across most of the floor. More antique furniture gave the room the feeling of a sumptuous nineteenth century European sitting room. Ronno opened another door at the end of the foyer and they stepped into a well-stocked game room. A drop cloth had been spread out in one corner and a dreadlocked bloody mess lay face down unconscious on it, his hands tied tightly behind his back with nylon restraints.

"I appreciate you taking care not to mess up the floor, Bunny," said Bender to the very large man wearing a black tank top standing next to the drop cloth, liberally stained with red, brown and other discolored patches. "You get anything out of him?"

"Not much. I got a couple of things in him, though. You're gonna have to replace one of the pool cues. Don't worry, I didn't use the Balabushka, just the one that was a little warped. Good for trick shots and those hard-to-reach places."

"God, you two guys," Bender sighed. "Can't you just cut off fingers and toes like everyone else? You have a strange way of expressing yourselves artistically."

"I got that covered too, boss. You might have to speak up a bit louder to him, he's become a little hard of hearing," remarked Bunny. He held up a pair of ears previously covered by the aforementioned dreadlocks. "Heads or tails?" He flipped one of them with his thumb like a coin. They watched the ear's trajectory as it landed lobe down. "Also, I may not know what he knows yet, but he won't be using the expression 'the nose knows' in the near future," He grinned and pointed to one patch on the drop cloth where a large flap of flesh lay next to some broken shards of tooth.

"Shit, is he still alive? Bunny, I want some answers from this piece of garbage. If he's not, you've got a very big problem on your hands."

"Not to worry," said Bunny confidently, though his grin disappeared. "Ronno's favorite nurse, Alice, was here a couple of minutes ago, checking him out, and gave him as clean a bill of health as he's gonna have for a while. He should cherish these moments. You know, you've got nothing without your health."

"Wake him up, Ronno."

"Sure, boss," Ronno went behind the bar, filling up an ice bucket with cold water from the sink. "This is gonna make for some wake up call." He took a container of iodized salt and emptied it into the bucket. "Bunny, roll him over for me, willya?"

"If you want to really do a number on him, you should throw in some of that disinfectant you used on me," said Bender with a steely laugh, still smarting from Ronno's ministrations. Bunny grabbed the prone man's arms and flipped him over effortlessly, exposing a gruesomely ravaged face.

Ronno recoiled and said, "Wow! This one's not winning any beauty contests in the near future. Jesus, even I look cute next to him. Ooh, man. Bunny, you did a real piece of work here." He leaned over, twisted a few dreadlocks in his fist and pulled the mostly featureless face close to his own. "Hey, Sleeping Beauty, it's your Prince Alarming here to awake you from your dreamless sleep. You eat a poison apple or something?" He looked up at Bunny. "I think I've got my fairy tales straight this time." The giant nodded impassively. "I've got just the remedy. Check this out, guys," he said and poured half the contents of the ice bucket on the man's ruined face.

The Rasta began sputtering and coughing, trying to spit out the salt water that had run into his raw, open nasal cavity. An odd-sounding hybrid between a scream and a gurgle came from his throat as his nerve endings regained sensation and he rolled weakly back over his side, moaning and shuddering from the pain.

"Is this bozo going to be able to tell us anything?" asked Bender, looking at Bunny and Ronno. He nudged the man's back with his slipper, bent over him, and said in a soft, intimate voice, "You know, my friend, despite you shooting me and killing a valued associate of mine, I've got to admit you showed a lot of chutzpah, cojones, couilles, whatever you want to call it, even taking this job. Did your employer tell you what was going to happen if you fucked this up? Were you informed of the risks?"

His voice rose. "Do you think that scumbag is going to take care of your family, if you have one, for taking this contract? One of the great luxuries in life is a good death, and that's no longer something you can hope for. What were you gonna get for this? A couple hundred Gs, maybe? Looks like chump change right about now, don't you think? Honestly, I'd like to hear your opinion on this subject." He cupped his ear and leaned closer to the Rasta, who was hovering on the edge of consciousness. "What's that? I can't hear you. Ronno, are you sure he's with us here? I'm not going to waste my breath on someone who's not listening to me."

Ronno reached over and backhanded the Jamaican, who murmured something inaudible. He looked down at his hand with disgust.

"This guy's leaking all over the place," he said, and bent down to wipe his hand on the drop cloth. "To tell you the truth, chief, I don't think you're getting through to him. But I'll tell you something. Alice told me about this new cocktail that's big right now in the Middle East for when they've absolutely got to know everything, and fast. I've heard that Saddam Hussein owes his life to this drug; it was the only thing that broke down a double agent, and he was able to get to his bunker hours before all the fireworks went off in Desert Storm. She brought some back with her. Anyway, aside from a couple of funny side effects, this stuff is supposed to really do the trick."

"What do you mean 'funny'? Funny like he's going to turn into Robin Williams or funny like he's going to grow another head?"

"Let's just say he's not going to be worth a whole lot to anyone afterwards. If he doesn't die, only vegetarians will want to eat him, if you get my drift."

"What the hell do you think I was going to do, send him to rehab? I don't care what happens after he spills. Let Bunny keep making brasiole out of him afterwards, for all I care. I don't give a shit. Is this Alice woman you've been talking about still around? Bring her here."

"I'll go get her," said Bunny, who stepped carefully around the gore so as not to mess up his loafers.

"Ronno, I'm disappointed. Growing up in a largely Jamaican neighborhood in Brooklyn, it hurts me to see this. I can't believe they'd try to muscle in on me. It's stupid, too. They wouldn't have a hope in hell of running my territory. Prop him up for me so he's sitting against the wall."

Ronno grabbed the would-be assassin under the arms and pulled him across the drop cloth until he was slumped against the paneled wall, his tattered pants trailing a brownish-red smear, a muted cry of pain barely escaping his lips. Bender turned around toward the antique English dartboard on the near wall and removed the three steel darts lodged in the center cork.

"I don't know what you can hear anymore, and I don't especially care, because you, my friend, have now reached the end of the line. You have one or two decisions left to make, and that's about it. Would you like a warrior's death? You can have one. I'll give it to you. One between the eyes, clean. You won't even know it happened. Otherwise, we can prolong this indefinitely. I have no other plans for a while. Come on. Talk to me."

Silence.

"Talk to me." He tossed a dart softly at the prone Jamaican. It struck him in the forehead, an inch above the left eye, and stuck. A thin ribbon of blood trickled from the small puncture hole, mingling with the other blood seeping from the myriad wounds inflicted upon the man like streams joining together to form a river.

"Who sent you?" Bender whispered through clenched teeth.

Silence again. Bender paused for a moment, uttered a low growl, wound up and fired the next dart. It embedded itself deep in the cheek of the semi-conscious man, this time just under the left eye. The dart stuck for a moment, drooped, and then fell to the ground, rejected by the cheekbone.

The door opened and Bunny strode back in accompanied by a tall, slender woman with long, straight, copper colored hair and an unusual makeup sense: partly erotic, partly kabuki, mostly insane. Finely detailed red and black diamond patterns with gold inlay trailed across the outer edge of her eyelids and down the sides of her nose. The right side continued further than the left, staggering from her nostril down to the corner of her full, sensual mouth as if it was a drop of blood that couldn't decide on a final resting place of coagulation.

Bender stared at her, immediately recognizing the power inherent in her features and carriage. She could seduce or execute with equal ease. She surveyed the room's occupants once through jade colored eyes and extracted a syringe from a pocket in her suede jacket.

"You understand what this is going to do to him?" she asked in a low, sultry voice, a hint of the deep south in the vowels. "Not that things are going to get too much worse, by the looks of this." She appeared unfazed by the carnage on the floor.

"Chief, this is Alice, the lady I was telling you about," said Ronno.

"Do you have any clue as to what you're doing, miss?" asked Bender. "Because if you don't, the repercussions will be more dramatic than your makeup." He pointed the dart in his hand toward her.

She turned her eyes toward Bender and responded with a frightening smile. "I think I like you already. I'm not often challenged and I always rise to the occasion. Do you?" She paced toward the Jamaican, lifted his right eyelid, looked at his staring eye, and said, "I do believe you might. But not to worry; I've seen this drug in action before. You're not going to have a large window of opportunity here, maybe sixty seconds or so, at best, before his brain will only be useful for scrubbing pots. But in those sixty seconds he'll tell you all his darkest, deepest secrets with enthusiasm. I wouldn't mind trying it out on Ronno first, just to make sure it works." She waved the syringe merrily in Ronno's direction and licked her lips.

"That might not be a bad idea," said Bender with a smile. Ronno's good eye widened. "Just kidding, there, bro. Actually, miss, I wouldn't mind knowing some of your secrets. How did you acquire this concoction?"

"It's an old family recipe, from the Borgia family." She pulled the stopper from the syringe, peeled one of the red tears from her right cheek, and placed it carefully in the solution already in the chamber. It dissolved in seconds. She leaned over the slumped Jamaican and said, "I don't think I have to bother disinfecting his skin," before depressing the syringe into the side of his neck. "This should take about fifteen seconds to kick in, so please have your questions ready."

Ten seconds later his head snapped back violently, making an audible thump against the wall. His eyes opened wide and bulged out ahead, unseeing, the breath rattling noisily from his ruined nose, tendrils of flesh appearing and disappearing from the aperture with each gasp. The tendons in his neck grew taut. The stuck dart quivered in his forehead, as if he was trying hard to pick up a radio station but couldn't decide what he wanted to listen to.

"You oughta try decaf next time, Alice," smirked Ronno.

The furious glare from Bender promptly wiped the smile from Ronno's face and he said, "You fucking idiot, don't waste time!" He bent down in front of the Rasta, who, judging by his expression, was completely oblivious to his presence, or anyone else's. He glanced over at Alice, who nodded, and said, "What's your name?"

"Lionel Logan," was the monotone reply. His voice sounded like the air was being forced through his vocal chords, though there was still a trace of the lilting Jamaican accent.

"Good, good. Alright," he said, a satisfied look on his face. "Lionel, who paid you to try and kill me?"

"Sal Cangelosi."

"Fuck, that's Baggio's capo," said Bunny.

"Shut up, Bunny. Time's short. Why you?" asked Bender.

Silence. Bender glanced over at Alice again.

"You've got to ask full and complete questions. He can't follow a train of conversation," said Alice.

"O.K. Why did Cangelosi send you, in particular, to kill me?

"He's trying to expand into your heroin business. They brought me up from Kingston to make it look like the posse was taking you out. Also, Sal knows you're doing his woman and he wants to make a statement."

"Ha! Those sons of bitches. Where are you supposed to meet Cangelosi after the hit?"

A gargling noise came from Logan's throat and pink foam began dribbling from between his lips.

"Not much time left," said Alice.

"Tell me. Where are you supposed to meet Cangelosi after the hit?" shouted Bender.

"Fesler's Diner, on Northern Boulevard." Logan's jaw was quivering and his eyes looked like they were about to leap out of their sockets. More pinkish drool dripped from his lips. His arms began twitching like he had stuck his finger in an electric light socket.

Bender, his face inches from Logan, grabbed a fistful of dreadlocks and, spraying his own saliva into the other man's face, growled, "How did you know where I'd be? How'd you know?"

"Inside," was the only word intelligible. Logan's spasms became violent. After five more seconds, he slammed his body back hard against the wall twice, straining every muscle, body completely rigid, lips pulled back from his broken teeth. With his nose and ears already gone, he resembled a live skull. A last strangled, hideous noise emitted from deep within his throat and he jerked back down, his head still quivering, a string of pink saliva connecting his chin to his chest and his eyes staring at something not in the room, perhaps not even in this universe. Whatever it was he saw, he was clearly not happy to be seeing it. Bender unclenched his fist, letting go of Logan's hair.

"Not bad." Bunny said after a moment of silence.

"I give him an 8.6. He had trouble with the dismount," intoned Ronno.

Bender glowered silently for a moment. At last, he lifted his head and said,

"I'm feeling hungry, guys. There's a diner in Queens I wouldn't mind paying a visit to. Cangelosi might get suspicious since he hasn't heard from Logan, so let's get there right away. We'll take him before the meeting's supposed to happen. Absolutely nobody takes a shot at me like that, fucking nobody. Besides his piece of ass ain't worth a piece of mine."

Alice laughed softly at the last remark, unsuccessfully covering her mirth. Bender turned to her, scowling initially, then started laughing, despite himself. Ronno and Bunny eyed each other discreetly and then joined in. It's always better to laugh when the boss is laughing. Soon the four of them were howling like hyenas, wiping tears away from their eyes. After a moment, Bender composed himself. He limped over to the door and opened it with a courtly gesture indicating that the others should pass first.

"Bunny, get someone in here to clean up this mess."

After the other three retreated into the anteroom, Bender, glanced back over his shoulder and, with a rapid flick of the wrist, flung the last dart still in his hand. It flew directly into the pupil of the Jamaican's unblinking left eye, burying itself until only the feathers showed. The eye ran like a one-minute egg. Bender winked at him with a jaunty smile, reached into the pocket of his robe, and tossed the bloody bullet that had, until recently, been a part of him in the direction of Logan. It bounced once and landed in his lap. Bender clapped twice, activating the circuit that extinguished the lights in the room, and closed the door.

6

"Hey there, guy, what's happening?" said a pie-eyed Pete Watts to his assistant, Greg, upon his arrival at Half Moon Bay studio. "Did I ever tell you that you do a bang-up job in keeping this place going when I'm not around? What I'm trying to say is that you are simply one utterly beautiful human being." He leaned against the doorway in an ungraceful manner somewhat approaching a slump.

"Pete, are you O.K.? You're not going to kiss me or anything, are you?" asked a concerned looking Greg. The assistant had been busy coiling microphone cables when his boss had lurched into Studio B. "What've you been up to? And, more importantly, why didn't you invite me?"

"Sorry, I didn't know you cared so much. To tell you the truth, I had some lunch of the liquid kind with my old father-in-law. That man is an absolute prince. He drinks Absolut Vodka, too. Do you think there's a tie-in somewhere there? It could be an X-File. What a pity I married his daughter instead of him, though he is a bit hairy for my taste. I wish he'd trim the stuff that's growing out of his ears. You'd think he was wearing cashmere headphones or something."

"Speaking of hairy, a rather large, bearded gentleman showed up here this morning," Greg said, wrapping the last cables and putting the spare microphones into their cases. "According to him, the quality of bathroom plumbing here leaves something to be desired, and the antique carpet business this fellow runs downstairs has suffered greatly from the streams of brown water flowing down the walls of his store last night. The guy's English wasn't the best, but no doubt his lawyer will have a better command of it, at least from what I could make out."

"Shit. Man, I'm glad I paid the insurance bill last week. You called a plumber, didn't you?"

"Yeah. He found four pairs of balled up socks that had been flushed down the crapper. It may just be a coincidence, but Pan Drippings were playing here last night in Studio A."

"Aren't those the strange guys who wear the weird togas and try to play hard-core punk with flutes and recorders? Did you notice if they were barefoot when they left?" Pete asked.

"I wasn't paying attention to their footwear, but who else could it be? It's not like we hold footsie conventions here."

"You know, I opened this place up 'cause I love music and thought it would be kind of cool to give bands a chance to get their acts together, but every problem I run into here is a result of people who belong in psychiatric wards! Why me?" He paused. "That's a good name for a band."

"'Psychiatric Wards'? That's a funky name," replied Greg, furrowing his brow.

"No, I meant 'Why Me?' Christ, I don't know what I'm saying anymore. I've got to get my own act together, let alone these bands." Pete looked around the room. "Is there any coffee left? I've got to meet Astrid in four hours and I'm not in good shape now. I've got a bad case of Gumbyitis."

"No problem. Three sugars?"

"Yeah. Pour it into a trough for me, will you?" Pete shuffled past Greg and sat down heavily on the drum stool behind the kit. "And get some drum sticks for me. I feel like John Henry Bonham himself right now. Another couple of shots and Neal Peart would be looking up at me, eating my dust."

"Only to see what was smelling the way you do. What kind of sticks do you want, the Vic Firths or the Pro Marks?" asked Greg.

"Hmm. I feel like some Japanese Oak this afternoon. Lord knows, I felt solid as a redwood last night. Send in the Pro Marks," Pete said with an imperious wave of his hand.

Greg chuckled and left the room. A Seattle native studying recording engineering at New York University, the opportunity to work with this relatively sophisticated sound gear was a perfect fit for his curriculum. He enjoyed the ambiance and eccentric camaraderie of the Greenwich Village music scene. Occasionally Greg would invite a band he particularly liked to play in one of the studios, recording their efforts on a second hand digital eight track machine he had found in a Ninth Avenue pawn shop, and, with Pete's assistance, nursed back to good health. He poured a steaming cup of coffee into a large Zabar's mug and walked back toward the studio, along with the specified pair of drumsticks.

"Here you go, dude. Play some 'Moby Dick' for me, if you will, sir," Greg said, invoking the legendary Led Zeppelin drum showcase. "Pete? Hey, where are you, man?" He looked around the room, but saw no one. A snoring sound drew his attention. He stepped up on the drum riser and peered behind the drums. There was Pete, curled up, with a ride cymbal for a pillow, dead to the world.

"Good thing I like my coffee this way too," Greg said, after having taken a sip from the cup. He left the room, turning off the lights as he left. "Don't worry, bud, I'll come get you in a couple of hours. No one's got this room 'til tonight, anyway." He called out to his unconscious boss and closed the door behind him.

Two and a half hours later, he poked his head in the door and said, "Hey Pete, you awake yet? There's a phone call for you."

A sound consisting mostly of consonants came from behind the drum kit.

"Dude, you should be getting up now. I got some good stuff for you, some Starbucks, not that east coast bong water you usually drink. The other coffee was getting kinda gnarly and was eating through the pot. It was saying bad things about your mom. I had to flush it down the now-working toilet. If it had gotten loose, I can't say what would have happened. I didn't want to take the responsibility if it ate Soho or something."

He moved behind the drum riser and shook Pete's shoulder, none too gently. "Not for nothing, as you New Yawkers say, but you've got a real penchant sometimes. I get the feeling you go on seek and destroy missions a little too often, dude. I mean, I sure as shit like to go out and catch a buzz, even tie one on, so to speak, every hither and yon. But with you, it's like you maneuver yourself into these situations and, while I say this with the utmost respect, you're not worth a whole hell of a lot when you come back. Actually, I don't say that with a whole lot of respect. I respect you, as a person and all that. It's just, aw shit, I don't know. Hey, wake the hell up!" Greg shouted the last five words into Pete's ear and was rewarded with a bloodshot eye slowly opening.

"You're definitely not the prettiest thing I've ever woken up to, but if I close my eyes and you blow me, I won't hold it against you," Pete said with a dry throat.

"Hi. My name is really Lorena and I don't much like men anymore. Me and my kitchen knife would like to have a chat with you, if you don't mind. I suggest you call the AAA shortly if you want to find your reproductive organs. C'mon man, get up. Someone's on the phone for you."

"Alright, alright. Give me a hand," Pete reached out a hand. Greg grabbed his wrist and yanked him into a standing position. "Whoa, don't dislocate my shoulder, guy. Wow," he said, holding his cranium. "What a head rush!" He ran his fingers through his disheveled hair, a few clumps stubbornly defying gravity, stretched, and asked, "You know who's on the line?"

Greg shook his head and Pete, rubbing his eyes, tottered out of the studio into the office. He opened a drawer in the desk and pulled out an ancient bottle of generic aspirin. He washed down three caplets, unfazed that none of the three were the remotely the same color, with the coffee, made a face, and picked up the phone.

"Sugar, you're a very hard man to get a hold of these days. Then again, I suppose a hard man is good to find. How are you, sweetheart?" cooed a lilting voice into his ear. He could picture those lips pursing, blowing into his ear. He then pictured the same lips brushing the ear of one ponytailed piece of shit poseur he'd seen last night and then, today at the police precinct.

"Just how hard is it to find a hard man these days, Angeline?"

"I can't genuinely say. The first entry I run into on the 'H' page of my little black book has your name and number on it."

"I just hope the rest of the page is blank."

"It's as naked as I will be when you come by my place now, though I have some red shoes I may throw on for the occasion. What time are you done at 'La Cour Des Miracles'?"

"What time am I done where? Are you making a bad joke about Smokey Robinson? I tell you, he's got the best falsetto I've ever had the pleasure of hearing." Pete liked the overall tone of the conversation, but always had trouble telling when she was pulling his leg, and his overall fuzzy-headedness wasn't helping him at all.

"Oh, Peter, promise me you'll never change. My God, it's so refreshing to talk to you after all the pretentious music industry people I've dealt with the last couple of weeks. They are such stuck-up assholes. The amount of air kisses I've had to endure, I can't tell you."

"So how'd the vocals go last night? No problems with the harmonies, I hope." said Pete, grateful she couldn't see the expression on his face.

"Everything went smoothly," she sighed, "though it took forever to get some of the higher notes right."

"I suppose all you need is the right inspiration to get them down perfectly."

"I don't know about that. I need to relax. It's one of the hardest things to do in a big studio like that. Everyone's watching the clock. It's not like at a show, where people only want to be entertained. Here, it's like, I don't know, it's like they're counting on you to feed them through a long, cold winter, and without you they'll starve or freeze. It's strange. I miss cutting demos with you. I talked to Richie about having you play on the record, but he said I have to use the studio drummer they hired. Pete, I'll tell you, he's no better than you are, and he's a real snot-rag."

"Ah, it's always who you know." said Pete. This conversation was becoming more and more surreal to him. He felt like a spectator in the theater of his own life, sitting in the cheap seats, his lines written by a bored playwright with a bad attitude.

"No, honestly, I'd love to have you on the project. I really would. But let's forget about that right now. It's boring. Listen, I've got a bottle of Pouilly Fuisee in the fridge. It's getting colder and colder as we speak, which, I don't mind telling you, is the opposite of what's happening with me right now. When will you be here?"

Pete wanted to look out the window to see if hell had frozen over or if he could spot some cows on their way home, but then noticed what a hypocrite he was being. After all, what had he been in the process of doing when he had seen her in the bar last night? Still, the picture of her cozying up with that dip-shit rankled. He had always thought of himself as an objective person and was now having trouble reconciling his tattered pride with the double-standard staring him in the face, not to mention he was due to pick up Astrid in a couple of hours.

After a titanic struggle lasting many a nanosecond, he replied, "In about four minutes."

"Oooh, I feel like I'm ready to ignite. I don't know if I can wait that long."

"I'd make it in three, but you know how bad cross-town traffic is."

"Just hurry, babe." The line disconnected.

Pete stared at the phone in his hand as if he'd never seen one before and hung up. His head was slowly clearing. He took another sip of the coffee that Greg had left for him and carried the cup back into the studio. He told his not very happy assistant that the place was his for the night, to check the fuse box before he left and went to a closet to retrieve his jacket. The phone rang when he was a step away from the door and he picked it up.

"Half Moon Bay Studios. Can I help you?"

"Yes. May I speak with Craven Moorehead?" intoned a familiar voice, albeit one that could only be a result of a nose pinched between fingers.

"Oh, man, I don't have the time for this now, Johnny. I'm on my way out the door."

"Alright, alright. Just tell me how it went last night. Without a doubt one of the more unusual soirees we've shared over the years, I'd have to say."

"You got that right, my friend. It ended on a high note, though. I've got to thank you for hooking me up with her. Astrid is a real doll, a beautiful sweetheart. We're going out again tonight. It's a pity she's leaving tomorrow."

"Good for you. I had a feeling you two would hit it off. They're both real friendly ladies. Kyra and I stuck around a little while longer at the club before going back to my place.

I introduced her to the concept of body shots. We found out tongues have virtually no effect on surface tension."

"A wonderful concept, I must admit. Someday we must drink a toast to its inventor."

"So where are you off to now?" asked Johnny.

"You're not going to believe it, but I'm heading over to Angeline's place."

"You're shitting me. After last night? Oh, baby!" Pete could hear his friend's laughter vibrating through the telephone wire. "That's absolutely perfect. This is the sweetest revenge possible. The one big advantage you have in this whole thing is you know about her and Daddy Slimeball last night, but she doesn't have the first idea about Astrid."

"Yeah, I know. To tell you the truth, though, I'm not into this game particularly. I feel like I'm being an asshole and I also feel like I'm being used, at the same time."

"A used asshole, huh, a pre-owned colon? That can't be a great feeling. At least I feel like a new asshole. A shiny sphincter, if you will."

"To describe you as useless would be an insult to people who serve no purpose at all. Can't you understand anything here? This isn't good."

"Understand yourself, scum puppy. You're on your way over to a woman who has rubbed your face in gorilla dung when later you'll be seeing a woman who, to quote Mick Jagger, would make a dead man come. What are you, a masochist or something? Guy, take a step back for a second. Get some perspective."

"What I'm going to do now is to take a step forward because that'll get me back to my desk so I can hang up the phone. This is crazy. You've never been in a relationship that's lasted more than a long weekend and you have the balls to think you can judge me and the way I handle my life."

Pete stayed true to his word and took the step, slamming the phone back into its cradle. He hopped into a cab and after a few minutes of listening to heavily distorted sitar music in the back seat, found himself at the stoop of Angeline's pre-war building. He was buzzed in through the front door and climbed the three flights of stairs to her flat.

The door was cracked open and, as he reached for the doorknob, he found himself thinking of the childhood riddle *When is a door not a door? When it's ajar.* He wasn't happy at all about his current state of mind and felt off-balance. He pushed the door open a little way. The only light he could see was the distant glow of a flickering candle in the back room. Angeline lived in a railroad flat, one room linking to another in a line through a series of doorways, and long shadows danced disconcertingly due to a strong breeze blowing through an open window at the back of the apartment.

When he had been a policeman, this circumstance would have called for a cautious entry, Beretta removed from ankle holster, sidling low from one doorframe to another, minimal exposure, clearing the apartment room by room. His adrenaline rush was telling him that this current situation wasn't so very far removed from ones he'd experienced in the past. He stepped into the lush carpeting of the living room. It was a plum color, resembling coagulated blood in the diffused candlelight. The large Vasarely print dominating the far wall was obscured in the dark. He could barely make out the white leather couch and futon nestled against the near wall, a star shaped glass table with a music magazine and a glass of murky liquid in front of it.

The magazine cover featured the emaciated face of Layne Staley, singer of the band Alice In Chains and, hopefully, now a recovering heroin addict, though the picture didn't offer much promise of recovery. Pete knew first hand that denial was not a river but a raging ocean, one he hoped the singer would be able to navigate, though he had his doubts, judging from the hollow-eyed expression on the vocalist's face.

He stepped into the sparse kitchen, past the refrigerator smothered with take-out menus of almost every type of food known to man, all held tenuously by magnets purchased at a myriad of flea markets throughout the city. Pete smiled, recollecting the impassioned haggling over prices between Angeline and vendors; she exerting every iota of feminine charm she possessed, while he wondered what the exact book value of a Scooby-Doo refrigerator magnet could be. On this one particular fridge, it was priceless, he thought.

"Could you open the wine in the fridge door? There's a couple of glasses on the tray next to the table," came a silky, disembodied voice from the back room.

"Sure," replied Pete.

He opened the refrigerator. The bottom shelf was a shrine to diet sodas, the middle to exotic cheeses, though Pete suspected some of them might not have been quite so exotic before they'd acquired their greenish pallor. The upper shelf housed a container of an indiscernible purple liquid, five rolls of film and a variety of makeup products. As can be imagined, the dominating odor was the cheeses, with the film, makeup and mysterious purple liquid vying for a distant, though still noticeable, second place. The diet sodas from a Brooklyn bottling company had retained their indie cool and hadn't even entered the competition. He fished around in a drawer next to the sink, found a corkscrew and deftly removed the cork from the bottle. Scooping up the glasses, their necks nestled between his fingers, he made his way into the back room.

A quick flicker of the candle caused her shadow to suddenly billow against the wall in back of the bed as a soft breeze blew through the grille of the open window. She was sitting on the edge of the comforter, one leg outstretched, the promised red shoe with a stiletto heel dangling from her toe. She flipped her ankle and the shoe slipped obediently back on her foot like a pet performing a well-practiced trick.

"I know what I said on the phone, but I got chilly and had to put something on. Do you like it? I bought it last weekend in that small boutique near St. Mark's I like, you know, across the street from Trash and Vaudeville."

She stood and twirled, the white lace of the gown swirling about her knees. A sash barely held the gown together and Pete followed the trail of flesh from the matching choker on her neck all the way down. White always looked good on her amber skin and contrasted beautifully with her jet black shoulder length hair. Her father was a mix of German and Italian, her mother Philippine and she had inherited the strength of her father's jaw and nose along with the softness and suppleness of her mother's eyes and cheekbones, a contrast that endlessly fascinated Pete. Candlelight certainly flattered the planes of her face.

With her vast range of expressions, he had always thought she would have been an excellent actress, but her first love was music and besides, as she had once told him, acting was more fun in everyday life. She had a fondness for creating drama where none existed, just to keep herself amused. At the same time, she would use comedy to defuse actual drama. Pete appreciated her approach as he, too, had been an actor in real life, a necessity for a detective deep under cover, though it had never been for his own amusement. They each had their own approach to the art, she the star and he the perfect character actor, and he sometimes suspected this was one of the reasons they went well together, as neither stepped on each other's lines much. He loved her exotic radiance while she valued his stability and the down to earth approach he brought to every situation.

He met her three years after finishing rehab and had just opened the rehearsal studio. Angeline came in with a scabrous looking and sounding group of musicians and, while the band was waiting for the drummer to show up, which he never did, they struck up a conversation and found out that they had a great deal in common concerning music and art. Pete sat in with the band and eventually became their regular drummer.

She had accepted his invitation to a concert by Joe Satriani, the brilliant electric guitarist. After the show, they spent the rest of the evening at a dive bar in Tribeca, recounting their lives with their mouths while their eyes held a more private conversation. Pete, sensing something special in his grasp for the first time in a long while, for once didn't rush it and merely kissed her softly at the top of the stoop of her apartment, promising to call her soon.

As a matter of fact, he called her when he had gotten home that very same night, just to tell her what a wonderful time he'd had. Though he'd awoken her from a sound sleep, she thought it was sweet, in addition to the eleven roses he had sent her the next day. Pete showed up unannounced two nights later with a bottle of champagne and a rose, saying there had been an unfortunate error on the part of the florist. He declared he wanted to rectify it immediately and hoped very much to make it up to her.

She suggested that a foot massage might get him back in her good graces and invited him in. He started with her feet and they had food delivered to her apartment for the next two days. For the last twenty-two months, they had enjoyed each other's company greatly, though commitment was a subject neither felt like broaching, both experiencing relationships sour on them through floods of expectations and droughts of communication.

She had always been a first class flirt, though, until recently, he assumed she was more talk than action. Now insecurity gnawed at him and he no longer knew where he stood. He'd been unfaithful on one occasion or two, make it three after last night, but the disparity in his standards wasn't registering with him at the moment.

"It looks great, Ange. I'll be damned if I can think of anything that doesn't look good on you. But do you know what always looks best?" He set the wine and glasses on a bed side table

"What's that, lover?" Even though her eyes were half-lidded, they shone.

"If I tell you, would you try it on?"

"If it fits."

"One size fits all." He came to her and ran his hands through her hair. He grazed her cheek gently and ran a finger down the narrow strip of flesh showing through the gown, deftly undoing the sash holding the robe together. The sash dropped to the floor without a sound. He reached around with his other hand and cupped a buttock, drawing her closer to him. Pete gave her a deep kiss, wrapping his arm around her as she melted into his frame. He recognized the subtle perfume she had daubed on her neck and ran his lips along her jaw line until he reached the source of the scent. She sighed gently. He slid the robe off her shoulder and blew softly on her skin.

"I can't believe how well you know my body," she whispered in his ear. Her tongue slid from between her lips and flicked his ear lobe. Prior to last night, he had considered this to be a major turn-on. Now he pictured a pony-tailed Lothario in his place and momentum ground to a halt, somewhat akin to the way someone riding a tricycle would feel if he hit a redwood tree. She sensed something amiss and cocked her head sideways to read his face.

"Baby, what's the matter? Are you O.K.?"

"Yeah, yeah, I'm fine. I think it's the meatball sub I had for lunch. It's decided to go on the offensive. I'll be right back." He knew he had to regroup and wisely decided that his favorite place for thinking would be the best possible refuge at the moment.

"You know you shouldn't eat that stuff. God knows where the meat comes from," she said to his back as he retreated from the room. "Don't forget to put the lid back down."

The bathroom was located off the living room, toward the front of the apartment. Feeling out of sorts, he locked the door behind him and sat down on the fluffy pink toilet seat cover. It sank a bit under his weight and discharged a slight hiss of air. He wondered why women bought seats made of foam rubber. Running his hands through his hair was no way to massage the barrage of thoughts stampeding through his head, but he tried it anyway.

He knew Johnny was at least partially right about the situation. He was due to meet Astrid in two hours and still had strong feelings for the woman waiting for him in the back room, even if he no longer had any idea how she felt about him. Nor was he confident there was any way to find out. She was capable of consummate performances and he doubted he could discern veracity from lie should he decide to make a stand. Pete desperately wanted to confront her and drag the truth out. His conscience was driving needles into his ego, reminding him of his dinner appointment and strongly questioning his right to be outraged.

He reached into the tissue box on the radiator next to the sink and wiped the sweat from his forehead. He didn't know if the perspiration came from the pressure he was feeling or was the last of his liquid lunch and, at this point, he didn't much care. He casually tossed the crumpled tissue at the circular wicker wastebasket under the sink. It hit the rim and bounced away. In high school he had missed an easy game tying shot at the end of a tight basketball game against his school's archival and had been a locker room pariah for a few weeks. This would prove to be a far worse miss.

He reached under the sink, retrieved the tissue and pulled the basket toward him with the intention of dunking the tissue. He heard a rattling sound as he put the wastebasket in motion and looked inside. A small glass vial rolled on the bottom. His heart sank as he held the vial up to the light for closer inspection. He uncapped the lid and passed it under his nose. Six years of undercover vice work made the identification of a crack vial a regrettably easy thing.

"Ohhh, shit," he said, not distinguishing whether he was referring to the current situation or the former contents of the vial. He dropped it in his shirt pocket, flushed the unused toilet, splashed some water on his face and made his way back to the bedroom.

"Hey, lover boy, you feeling better?" she said, "you're looking a little pale."

He showed her the vial and said,

"What's this, Ange?"

"What's what?" She squinted to see what was he was holding. He extended his arm and she took the vial. "Oh this," she laughed, "it's just a perfume tester from one of my magazines. I think it was in *Allure*. I thought I'd thrown it out. It smelled like raccoon piss."

"Ange, don't play with me here. This is serious."

"What's serious?" She frowned. "You think I should maybe recycle the glass?"

"You know what I mean."

"No, I don't. Do you go through everybody's garbage or are you just trying to make me feel special? You're not, you know."

"I'll tell you what. I'll make a bet with you. If I lose, it'll be well worth it. I'll take this to the precinct lab and have them do trace analysis on the vial. If it's perfume or raccoon piss or anything else than what I think it is, I'll fly us both to Aruba for a week."

"We don't need this stupid minor thing for us to make plans," she said and flung the vial out of the open window. She threw her arms around him. "You should do it anyway. We need to run off together, baby. I haven't had any time to relax with you in so long. All this bullshit seems to get in the way." She looked deep into his eyes.

"I'm the one who needs to get away," he said, extricating himself from her arms. "And bullshit is absolutely getting in the way here. Crack is no joke. My God, Ange, you know how I feel about drugs and this one is as nasty as it gets. Please, please listen to me. I've seen first-hand what this stuff can do to people." He held his hands out in an imploring gesture.

"Oh, come on. Just because you couldn't handle your own addiction doesn't mean everyone in the world is doing drugs." She put her hands on her hips and glared at him, her head tilted back.

"That's cold, Angeline. That's real cold. You know what I went through and now you're throwing it back in my face. If you're not going to be straight with me here, I'll talk to you some other time."

He spun on his heel and marched out of her apartment, slamming the door on his way out.

7

Pete hiked east, head bowed, in a straight line until he crossed over a narrow pedestrian bridge that extended over the FDR Drive to the walkway running parallel along the East River. He stood, staring at the river, which, had he been in the mood to appreciate symbolism, was an apt metaphor for his present state of mind, with its rushing currents, eddies and whirlpools. Symbolism wasn't high on his list of priorities at the moment, though. He was more into his current state of mind, with its rushing present, not to mention Angeline's future, both with him or without him, and wondered what part Richie Roeper played in it. Pete felt completely blindsided.

He'd never had an inkling she was into anything stronger than alcohol. She'd mentioned to him, in passing, that she'd smoked pot a few times when she was in high school. She'd also told him, while lying next to each other after a particularly tender love-making session, about the time, also in high school, when she had once stolen a couple of valiums from a medicine cabinet at a party to see what it felt like. She hadn't remembered much of the incident, apart from waking up next to the star forward of the soccer team shortly before dawn.

She had fully remembered in all its glory, however, the trip to the abortion clinic ten weeks later, and the raging emptiness that relentlessly followed her and set in for the last half of her junior year. It culminated in an attempt at cutting her left wrist open with a letter opener at another party, before being subdued and rescued by the goalie of the same soccer team. What this said about the importance of offense versus defense was a subject debated for the rest of the semester among the more jaded students.

He watched the Circle Line boat putter unhurriedly past him on its way around Manhattan, its load of camera toting tourists causing the boat to list slightly to the side facing the island.

He'd once taken a young cousin on the boat tour around Manhattan a few years back, one brutally hot New York summer. Already having begun his heroin usage, he'd drunk two beers before boarding and nodded out in a deck chair twenty minutes into the cruise. The cousin had awoken him moments before docking, after having spent over three hours baking in the sun. Pete remembered the voyage distinctly as the little fiend had stuck a creamsickle stick on his forehead as he slumbered, insuring that Pete's suntan line would be unique. All in all, it was a fairly unique summer, but that's another story, one Pete suppressed to the best of his abilities, though ghosts of it periodically jumped out at him, such as last night in the men's room of the Pyramid Club.

An elderly woman wearing a large, floppy hat and a yellow dress with a loud floral print approached and sat on a bench across from where he stood at the railing. She dug out a pair of wraparound mirrored sunglasses from the beach bag slung over her shoulder and carefully polished them with the hem of her dress before putting them on. She gazed out straight ahead of her and withdrew a large plastic sandwich bag filled with chunks of old Italian bread. She crumbled and carefully arranged the bread on the pavement in a pattern only she could discern, a semi-circle covering the immediate area in front of her. The woman sat back, folded her arms and said, a satisfied expression on her face,

"Now we set a feast in our father's name."

Pete, though clearly not in the mood for this, nevertheless had a New Yorker's natural proclivity for observing this type of scene, and turned his head toward the old lady, who lifted a gnarled finger and admonished Pete.

"Just you watch, sonny. They'll be here in a minute or two. It never fails, and they're the biggest damn things you've ever seen."

"What are?" he asked reticently.

"You've never seen a Delaware sparrow before, huh?" she said with a hoarse chuckle. "You might mistake them for something far, far bigger. They always show up right around now, when the sun is hanging over the horizon."

"The sun's on the other side of the city, over there. Shouldn't you be hanging out by the Hudson river instead?" Pete said, looking west, over the skyscrapers.

"They don't care which side the horizon is on, sonny. Do you?"

"I'm not sure." The question threw him a little.

"It's there. And there. And there, too." She faced each direction of the compass. "Everywhere you look. How can you miss a horizon? You sure you don't see it? It's everywhere!" She stood up, threw her head back and lifted a finger straight ahead of her before executing a near-perfect pirouette and sitting back down heavily on the bench.

"I guess it's kind of hard to miss, if you know where to look."

"You'd be surprised how many people refuse to look straight ahead."

"You're probably right," said Pete, becoming sorry he'd engaged this woman in conversation.

"And if you think everything is going your way, it just means you're driving on the wrong side of the road," she responded.

Pete couldn't help but laugh at this last observation. His smile waned, though, and he directed his attention toward the water and watched a pair of young men in wet suits jet-skiing up the East River, zigzagging against the strong downtown currents until they were out of sight around the next bend, heading toward the Fifty-Ninth Street bridge. He turned back to the woman, about to ask her something clever about the migratory habits of the Delaware sparrow, when he saw that she was scooping the crumbs back off of the pavement and eating them by the handful. She twisted toward him, her expression intense, and said something, though nothing comprehensible came out.

He sighed, turned north, and made his way towards Astrid's hotel, never once spotting the famed Delaware sparrow. Despite his leisurely pace, after walking over twenty blocks, more than a mile, he still arrived at the hotel over half an hour early. He bought a newspaper and sank into one of the overstuffed lobby armchairs. Always an avid fan, he purveyed the statistics of all the teams in the National Hockey League, though it was only a month into the season. After perusing statistics from the Anaheim Mighty Ducks to the Washington Capitals, he had slaked his thirst for goals, assists and penalty killing percentage and felt somewhat renewed. It must be a guy thing, he thought, but somehow this truly helped him. Statistics are something easily measured, not like points of views, eddies and swirls, mental states or other perspectives, and, in their totalitarianism, are somewhat reassuring. He left the newspaper on a side table next to the armchair for another prospective reader, introduced himself to the front desk clerk, a perky brunette, and asked her to ring up Ms. Hedberg's room.

"Ms. Hedberg left a message. She's running a little late and asked if you could meet her in her room."

Pete thanked the desk clerk and took the elevator up to the thirty-eighth floor. Running his fingers through his hair, he did a minor primp in the mirror adjacent to the elevator before lifting and releasing the knocker on the door of Astrid's room. The door opened.

"Hi, there. It's so nice to see you again," she said with a warm smile, letting him in.

"I've got some nice memories of this place, and they're pretty fresh. I might add that you're kind of fresh yourself," Pete said. He kissed her, slowly at first, and then, tongues on the loose, more fervently. "Easy, darling, we'll never make it to dinner this way."

"You make for a tasty appetizer. Is there some sauce with this?"

"You are very, very bad and that is very, very good," Pete answered with a big smile. "You don't know how much I've been looking forward to seeing you. You can't imagine."

"You want to see the proofs from today?" She produced a leather-bound folder, extracting photographs of her posing suggestively in leopard and tiger striped bikinis while caged animals lolled listlessly in back of her.

"I don't know. This lion doesn't look too interested." He pointed to one photo featuring Astrid spread-eagled against the cage bars, only to have the lion bury his head in his paws in the background. In fact, the only remote sign of activity from the feline was the emphatic way his tail had swatted a fly that had gotten too comfortable on his hindquarters. "It must have been kind of warm at the zoo today."

"It's not the heat, but the humidity," replied Astrid, looking askance at Pete when he burst out laughing at the cliché.

"I'm sorry, I've had a long day and I'm feeling punchy right now. Put a glass or seven of a nice vintage Bordeaux in me and I'll be my usual abnormal self. I should take this moment to observe that these mangy animals behind you in the pictures only serve to accentuate your radiance. Had they just been fed?"

"What's that smell?" she asked, sniffing the air, "It must be the shovel full of bullshit you're hiding behind your back. Oh, I know these pictures didn't come out too well. I only hope the bikini company has a bit of a sense of humor or that Johnny's advertising firm can somehow make this work for them. I'd hate to have to redo this shoot. There's a lot of strange people who stand around and watch you when you work in this city, you know. There was one man wearing a raincoat and short pants who was exceptionally intense in his attention." She knit her brow. "You know, I hope he was wearing shorts. Now that I think about it for a moment, I'm not sure anymore."

"I imagine you attract tons of attention wherever you go, even when you don't want to, and I'm sure Johnny's agency will try to turn whatever happened today into something positive. I sure hope they don't use one of his horrendous poems to try to sell it. He's got a good head for promotion, but his rhymes can cause a lot of commotion."

Astrid laughed merrily and reached up to give Pete a kiss.

"You are everything I've ever wanted to meet in an American, sir, do you know that? Except perhaps one thing: you didn't ride up to the hotel on a white stallion, by any chance, did you?"

"My God, Astrid, you could no doubt do a whole lot better than me. You're every guy's fantasy come true, that much I'm sure of."

"You're very sweet."

"You ready to go?" Pete opened the door, and with a sweeping motion of his arm, saluted her as she strode through the doorway.

When they exited the lobby, a horse driven carriage was waiting in front of the hotel. Coincidentally, the horse was white. Astrid looked at Pete with wide eyes. He waved at the carriage driver and said,

"Take the rest of the night off. But have my steed ready in the morning, James."

He turned immediately to avoid the carriage driver's somewhat rude hand gesture and they crossed the street. They took a bus, as Astrid wanted to look at the streets in a more leisurely fashion, and, after twenty minutes, stepped off in front a quaint French bistro. The facade was painted dark red and an agitated looking rooster adorned the wooden plaque hanging over the front door. Once inside, a maitre d' with a firmly waxed mustache ushered them to a quiet, secluded table toward the back of the restaurant. When the waiter appeared shortly after, Pete, no oenophile, ordered a bottle of Bordeaux he'd recently developed a fondness for.

The waiter soon returned, complimenting Pete on his choice, opened the bottle and lit a candle set in an ornate floral centerpiece on the vermillion colored tablecloth. He left them alone to pore over the menu. When he returned, seemingly out of thin air, he poured a dollop of the wine into Pete's glass. Pete sniffed the glass and sipped the wine, though, in truth, had it been vinegar, with some sugar added to take the edge off, would have still concurred and indicated their glasses should be filled.

"I'd like to impress you and order our dinners in French," Pete said as he sipped the wine, "but the last time I tried that, I ordered broiled tractor, so I think I'll stick to my native tongue this time. You need more than a toothpick to get the gear shaft out from between your teeth."

"I'd like to stick you to my native tongue, but I'll try to remain civil for the moment," Astrid replied with a saucy expression. "What do you recommend?"

"There are a few things I'd like to recommend that you won't find on any menu, in any restaurant, but all the south-western French specialties are delicious here. The cassoulet and the bouillabaisse are both excellent."

The waiter returned and took their orders. Pete ordered coq au vin and Astrid a salad Nicoise, a delectable combination of sardines and fresh vegetables. While they were waiting for their main courses, the waiter came along with a sampling of different pates, which they enjoyed with fresh baguettes served in a country-style basket.

"Peter, this is wonderful. I've never eaten such food in my life, and certainly not with such magnificent company!" said Astrid, between bites.

"French restaurants aren't very popular in Sweden?" he asked.

"They are, but a lot of them are simply Swedish versions of French food, and it's not the same."

"You're beautiful, you know that?" said Pete, a look not too far from love in his eyes.

"Thanks," said Astrid. She sipped her wine and closed her eyes for a moment. "I get compliments a lot, sometimes from desperate men who want the prestige of being seen with a model." She made a face when saying the word 'prestige'. "It's so incredibly stupid. Think about it for a moment. Do you only want to be known as the sum parts of your physical appearance? After all, it's only a question of genetics, a fortunate accident of birth. If my genes had dictated otherwise, a millimeter or two here or there, I wouldn't be considered beautiful and would have to fend for myself in other ways. Two hundred years ago I would've been considered too thin. Sometimes, I almost wish this were the case. I've been forced to focus on superficial things for much too long. You're a good looking man. Would you want to be treated that way? Would you like to feel like an ornament?"

"Fantasy-wise, I probably wouldn't mind. But, if you think about it for more than a minute, it would suck. No one would take me seriously, not that anyone does now. I think I know what you mean. I suppose it's sort of flattering, but only up to a certain point. After all, aside from magazines, how many people care what the latest super-model is thinking about?"

The waiter reappeared, bearing the main courses on beautiful pieces of Limoges porcelain and uncovering them with the subtle flourish all good French waiters possess. They tucked into their dinners, offering forkfuls from each other's dishes. Conversation temporarily halted until the plates were three quarters empty, when they simultaneously let out contented sighs and Pete refilled their wine glasses.

"So, Peter, how have you come to this place in your life now? Last night, you tried to save someone's life, and it was a natural, instinctive act for you, like you'd done this before, many times. You spoke of explosions, dead bodies and other things. These are not daily occurrences."

"You don't want me to ruin a wonderful dinner with nasty stories like that. Tell me about yourself instead."

"I was born a poor black child," she said, giggling. "I'm sorry. This wine is delicious and must be affecting me. I just want to know things about you. You don't have to tell me unpleasant details, if you'd rather not. You were a policeman once?"

"Yeah, for about six years. It seems like ages ago, like it happened to another person. I worked narcotics, undercover. I was so naive, very into the job. When you're young you think you can really make a difference, and I didn't care what I sacrificed to close a case. It was only after I'd lost almost everything that meant anything to me that I learned." Pete absently scratched at the label on the wine bottle.

"You can't clean everything up. There'll always be another scumbag taking the place of whoever you put away. Some are worse than others, but it's the same thing, every single goddamn time. I once read about a study some researcher did. People who have jobs that can't be completed suffer much more stress than people who do. Look, if you're, let's say, a landscaper, you have a property to work on. You do your thing, you plant or trim some hedges, you do stuff with flowers, make everything look nice. Maybe put in a Japanese rock garden, I don't know. But anyway, at one point, you stand back, pick up the last couple of leaves, and say 'this is done'. There's nothing else to add. It looks right. Then you get paid and move on to the next project. I've never liked the word 'closure', but there's a sense of completion there. What I was doing was like trying to exterminate every cockroach in the world. In the end, I was completely obsessed and my sanity started to get away from me. I became a junkie and wrecked my marriage. To this day I still don't understand how I lost my way."

He stopped, looked down and saw the wine label was shredded and his fingernails were trying to dig into the glass of the bottle. "Jesus, Astrid, I understand you want to get to know me, but this is something I especially hate to talk about. You have no idea how I've disappointed myself. Can't I tell you about something else, instead?" A fragile smile flicked across his face. She reached out, took his hand from the wine bottle and held it in both of hers.

"You know, I wasn't a bad drummer when I was a kid, and I was hoping for a while I was going to make a name for myself, earn my living that way. It always makes me feel good when I sit down behind my kit. It's just me and the music and I can lose myself in a good way. One of the reasons I have this rehearsal studio is it gives me the chance to get back some of my innocence. I see myself in so many of the young bands coming in there."

"I'm sorry, Pete. I don't want to bring up bad memories for you. It just seems like such an exciting life, looking at undercover work from the outside. Maybe I've seen too many American TV shows." She smiled, and said in a bad imitation of Telly Savalas, "Who loves ya?"

"I hope you do tonight, many times. And you won't have to worry about the lollipop, either."

"I'm not surprised you're a good drummer. I've noticed your sense of rhythm is exceptional."

"I'm glad all those years of practice in my parents' basement paid off in some way," Pete said with a smile. He removed his hand from hers and motioned toward his plate with his fork. "Would you like some more?"

"Sure." She accepted the proffered fork and daintily placed it in her mouth. Astrid exaggeratedly rolled her eyes and exclaimed, "Mmmm. Your coq is delicious."

"You're incorrigible."

"You just try corriging me. You'll live to regret it," Astrid answered, waving his captured fork, a defiant look in her eyes.

"I wouldn't dream of it. And give it back to me before you fork yourself," he replied.

"No. It's mine now. You can't have it. Use your spoon," Astrid replied petulantly.

"Now, Astrid, you know I don't just give a fork like that."

"You still have your salad fork."

"You want that, too? You know, I don't give two forks."

"Oh, you're just forking around. Here's your fucking fork," she said and haughtily returned his purloined silverware.

"You're something else," Pete said. He reached across the table to take her other hand.

"And you are certainly something. What's the difference between something and something else? And, most importantly, are they compatible?"

"Something and something else. Hmmm," Pete pursed his lips in an effort to look thoughtful. "I suppose they could be compatible, in a ying-yang kind of way."

"As opposed to a ping-pong kind of way?"

"More like the King Kong kind of way, if you must know. As a matter of fact, after dinner, I was gonna climb up the side of the Empire State Building in an effort to impress you."

"What if I decide to take in the sights from the Chrysler building, instead?"

"Might be a problem. O.K. Scratch that."

"Scratch what?"

"No, I mean scratch that idea. Do you like blues music?"

"Are you intending to play the blues while climbing up the Empire State Building? I never knew you had so many talents."

"I have talents you've never dreamed of. However, I was thinking of something in a more observational mode. The Blue Knights are playing at Manny's Car Wash tonight and they can play a slow twelve bars like nobody's business."

"Forgive me for not understanding what you're saying here. There's a place in New York where people in suits
of colored armor go to get them cleaned and waxed? And
the part about all the drinking establishments with laggard
barkeeps going bankrupt is entirely beyond me," she said,
charmingly feigning ignorance.

"No, no, no. We're encountering a cultural barrier
here," Pete said, his face flushed from the wine. The waiter,
who clearly possessed some sort of extrasensory perception,
appeared and asked if monsieur would like another bottle of
the same. Compared to other decisions Pete was currently
facing in his life, this one was a no-brainer. Soon another
bottle was breathing on the table and the waiter took their
dessert orders after refilling their glasses. Astrid indulged in
a crème brulee and Pete ordered profiteroles, puff pastries
filled with vanilla ice cream and covered with a hot chocolate
sauce.

They talked easily, naturally, the subject of conversation running from her childhood crushes (Robert Vaughan
in *The Man from U.N.C.L.E.*) to movies to music. They found
themselves in the beautifully unselfconscious mood one ar-
rives at when the company is perfect and the liquor and the
food are complements to the moment, fully satisfying but
not overpowering. The laughter between them grew louder as the level of the second bottle of wine descended from
above the label to below and shortly the waiter divided the
remnants into their two glasses. Pete raised an eyebrow aris-
tocratically and asked him for the bill,

"L'attrition, s'il vous plait."

"Certainement, monsieur. Tout de suite." The waiter
tweaked the curl of his mustache, winked at Astrid and re-

treated behind the curtain separating the dining room from the kitchen.

After the bill had been paid, Pete led Astrid out into the street and looked to hail a taxi. It was a beautiful evening, warm with a light breeze and, with a little imagination, one could almost imagine there were stars in the sky, high above the lights and pollution. The half moon could be seen clearly, though, and there were still the millions of lights the city produced itself. Pete and Astrid were relishing the moment, the knowledge she would be departing the next day serving only to sweeten it. A situation like this can sometimes create desperation, the need to squeeze every emotion, every sensation from the night. They knew to simply savor it. They arrived at the club, the sound of a weeping slide guitar wafting through the open door.

Once at bar, Pete ordered two shots of tequila, presenting one to Astrid. She took her little finger, dipped it daintily in the glass, daubed herself behind each ear, and downed the shot.

"Just in case you get thirsty later," she explained.

"What happens if I get hungry?"

"Oh, I'm sure we'll find something for you to eat," she replied. Pete luckily had the tequila in his hand, close to his mouth, and, barely, just barely, the presence of mind to rapidly down it and slam the glass back down on the bar with an audible *thwack*. The liquid burned almost as much as the look with which she had just favored him, and at that moment his fascination with the blues was strictly limited to the color of her eyes.

"You want another?" he rasped.

"Sure," she replied. As with a lot of women, when a display of femininity is followed by such calculatingly devastating results, Astrid took pity on Pete and gave him a chance to collect himself. "I like this music. What's the fellow over in the corner playing? It looks like he's ironing something, but it sounds so beautiful."

"Oh, him, uh, yeah. That's a pedal steel guitar. I've always liked that instrument." He thought of the beautiful tones he'd heard Rusty Young coax from the guitar in concert with the group Poco a long time ago at a free concert in Central Park. "There's so much soul in that instrument. It sounds like it's singing for a lost love somewhere."

After the moment in which they recognized the pedal steel could be singing about them as soon as tomorrow, their eyes locked and the rest of the universe fell away. Pete took her into his arms and kissed her, hard, their passion cresting and rolling over them with the fury of a tsunami. The moment melted, dripping into timelessness, pooling beneath them as all else disappeared in the friction between their lips. Gradually, inevitably, they separated, though still holding each other close. Astrid whispered huskily,

"I will never forget you, Pete. Never. Never." She buried her face in his neck.

"God, me neither." Pete whispered into her ear. He gripped her tight, hoping the tear welling in his eye wouldn't roll its way down his cheek and rubbed his face into her hair to remove the evidence. He could feel the way her arms gripped him tightly around his waist and his back. He could feel her hand on his shoulder. He paused, frowning, and realized this was too many hands for one person to have.

"Hey dude, how's it going?" came a voice from behind him.

He turned and looked over his shoulder to find Greg's face inches away from his. If looks could kill, Pete would have had to place an ad in a local trade paper the next day for an assistant to work in a rehearsal studio.

"Bitchin' band, man. The dude can totally wail on his axe. Rad!" shouted Greg with enthusiasm.

"Uh, Greg, this isn't the best time." Pete gave Greg the universal "Get lost" look, but wasn't sure the venom streaming from his eyes was having the desired effect, as the oblivious Greg continued talking.

"Hey, sure, man. No prob. I'm here to record the opening band, the Kahunatics. They play this Hawaiian surf blues and it cooks in a major way. And talking about cooking, they also brought some outrageous Hawaiian herb, bright green with red hairs, with them on their tour. Jesus, two hits and I'm on some kind of surfing safari, riding the tidal wave from *Deep Impact*. Hey, man, did you ever see that movie? Cool special effects, kind of dumb otherwise." He looked past Pete's shoulder and finally caught a glimpse of Astrid's head, looking at him quizzically. "Oh hey, man, I didn't see you were busy. Sorry." He made a vague salutary gesture in her direction. "Nice to meet you. I'm Greg." Pete's intensified glare stifled further formalities. "Oh yeah, one more thing. After you left today, this dude called up, funny sounding voice, but he sounded real serious. He said his name was Walter Woodlenacker, I think. He left a number."

"C'mon, Greg. That must have been Styx with another one of his bullshit calls."

"I don't know, man. I don't think so. The dude sounded mighty official. You know, kind of constipated."

"That Johnny, what a pain in the ass." Pete shook his
head, then lowered his voice to a stage whisper. "Hey, can
you make like a tree and leave? I've got something good going on here and momentum is slipping away with every second I'm talking to you." He motioned dramatically sideways
with his eyes at Astrid for emphasis on the off chance that
Greg was a total dolt, the odds being slightly less than fifty-
fifty at the time. From the murky recesses of his mind, Greg
reached out and made the connection.

"Yeah, I can see you're working a good sitch. Hey, good
luck, dude. See you tomorrow."

Greg saluted Astrid again, more crisply this time,
turned and melted into the crowd, much to Pete's relief.

"I'm sorry about that." Pete said. "He was left on
my doorstep in a bassinet and I had to take him in. How
they ever fit him in that bassinet last week, I'll never
know."

Astrid looked at him strangely for a moment and then,
getting the joke, burst out laughing and gave him a hug,
though not nearly as intense as the last one. The band then
kicked into "Red House". The guitarist deftly ran through
different styles with each subsequent lead he played, starting
off by imitating Jimi Hendrix, then moving on to Buddy
Guy and eventually Eric Johnson, before ending with a rave-
up in his own style, bending notes with vehemence and fiery
abandon. It was a spectacular performance and the audience
erupted at the end of the song. The guitarist wiped his brow
with a towel and took a deep pull from a bottle of beer sit-

ting on his amp. He sauntered over to the microphone and drawled,

"Man, the amp got so hot, it boiled my beer. Anyone got a cold one for me?"

Eight or ten bottles were thrust at him from the front of the stage. The guitarist looked for the fullest one, exchanged a guitar pick and a high five for it, and drained the balance of the bottle. He belched into the microphone, grinned, pushed back his hat, and used the empty bottle as a slide intro into the Allman Brothers' nugget "Statesboro Blues", the band kicking in on his head signal.

"I can't think of a better night than this one, unless you count last night, and my mind is still digesting that one." Pete said. "When I die and wind up wherever it is I'm going to go, I don't want to hear angels playing harps or anything like that. Just put me wherever Robert Johnson wound up and I'll have myself one very happy eternity."

She smiled at him and her hug got closer to the intensity of the first one. They stood there, basking in the music, holding each other and swaying to the rhythm. There wasn't much to say, the shine in their eyes and the shared glances accounting for the conversation. A half hour later, the guitarist came up to the microphone.

"You know, I've always loved the way the good people of Great Britain picked up the blues from the United States and made it their's for a while. Some great things happened 'cause of that," The crowd roared its approval. "One band that never got enough credit as a blues band, though they sure made a fortune off of it, is Led Zeppelin. This is called 'Since I've Been Loving You.'"

"Oh, I know this one! My big brother has all their re-cords," said Astrid. She launched into the chorus of the song: "Since I've been loving you, I'm about to lose my worried mind."

Pete thought that Robert Plant didn't have to worry about his job too much, but was so touched by this woman that he swept her up in his arms and twirled her deliriously around. Luckily, the crowd had thinned just enough so he didn't cause any serious damage. Drink spillage is never considered serious damage unless the clothing is of high quality, and anyone who wears something high priced to a blues bar is almost certainly lost and asking for directions, anyway.

"Let's go back to the hotel," suggested Astrid, after the song was over.

Pete pursed his lips and pretended to consider it for a moment. He then broke out in a big smile and, with an "after you" sweeping gesture of his arm, which he put around her as she passed, followed her out of the club.

"It's such a beautiful night. Do you mind if we walk for a while? This is such a lovely city," she asked.

"Sure. I've always liked Park Avenue for a stroll, or would you prefer Madison? There are lots of stores and galleries. I always like to take ladies to Madison Avenue after the stores have closed. It's a lot cheaper that way."

"So I'm getting the same tour as all your other out of town floozies?"

"No. No, please don't get me wrong," he said, raising his hands defensively, "I do this with my New York women too."

"Good. I don't want you to be nationalistic with me. And I certainly don't want to pry, but while we're on the subject, do you have a girlfriend, or a wife, or a significant other, as you Americans say, not counting pets?"

"You know, Astrid, I honestly don't know right now." He put his hands in his pockets.

They stopped and faced each other. Pete took her hand and kissed it before lowering it.

"I don't know what to tell you. You've arrived in my life these last couple of days when," he smiled wryly, "this sounds like a line from a TV movie, my heart's been in turmoil. I guess the best way to put it is that until recently, and this has nothing to do with you, or us, I thought I was in a relationship. If you don't mind," he said, looking at her sadly, "there are again details I'd rather not go into right now, a lot of very fresh pain. I know I sound like some guy on the make, but please believe me, this is legit. I need to get some sense of perspective. I should tell you, too, that you've really helped me. If it wasn't for you....." he trailed off, running his hand through his hair.

"Pete, I'm sorry I asked. I don't have the right to, though I'd like to know." She smiled. "I'm not asking for anything from you now. I was trying to be cute and I don't want to put a damper on this wonderful night. Besides I won't force you into a decision. You can have both."

"What?" The word fairly burst out of his mouth and landed on the sidewalk in front of them, quivering, complete with the quotations and question mark.

"Of course, there's no problem. I'm not an unreasonable woman. We can walk down Park Avenue for a few blocks, and then move over to Madison." She playfully punched his shoulder. Pete rolled his eyes.

They turned the corner and strolled arm in arm down Park Avenue, past the lavish residences looming one after another in a procession. Uniformed doormen hurried out from beneath green and beige canopies to open taxi and limousine doors for the residents of their respective buildings.

They passed one well-dressed lady berating a young homeless man for having the temerity to ask her for some change, telling him there was nothing stopping him from going out and getting a job like the rest of the world. When he asked her what it was she did for a living, she snapped at him, saying it was none of his business, and hastily turned into the lobby of her building, wrenching the neck of the small dog she was walking. Pete and Astrid glanced at each other and crossed the street at the next corner, choosing instead to take in the sights of Madison Avenue. There they passed galleries featuring a riot of styles ranging from classical portraits to a sculpture consisting of a wooden rack with green spray painted rubber bands stretched across the frame, anchored by rusted nails. They tried in vain to read the price tag dangling from the contraption. Neither could quite make it out, but both could see it contained quite a few digits.

As they moved further south, Astrid stopped and looked into some of the tonier boutiques, admiring the fashions and easily identifying the designers to Pete, relaying her experiences working with some of them, and dishing significant dirt on each. He'd always figured there were eccentricities in the fashion world, but had assumed that sex and drugs belonged mostly to rock and roll, or sex and rock and roll belonged mostly to drugs, or whatever. In any case, it wasn't hard for Pete to see why rock stars and models frequently made good, though temporary, couples. Each thrived on visibility, and, as the axiom states, any publicity is good publicity, as long as they spell your name right, and often. Astrid had a good way with a story and, coupled with her droll delivery and facial expressions, had Pete doubled up with laughter.

Further south, they crossed Fifty-Seventh Street. Pete, a native of the city, believed the incorporation of streets of character such as Fifty-Seventh and Forty-Second had robbed them of much of their individuality and charm. To think that the "deuce", as New Yorkers are wont to call the Times Square area of Forty-Second Street, had become nothing more than a large advertising opportunity for mega-corporations sickened him. Granted, it had formerly been a seedy, crime-infested sea of filth, but at least it had personality.

He hated to see the massive Middle America mall mentality sink its hooks into his beloved city. Besides, when he had been a cop, the deuce had been a wonderful point of entry for an undercover cop looking to infiltrate lower rungs in the hierarchy of drug gangs. He understood the city was cleaning up its image to globally attract tourists, but something was being diminished.

They passed majestic Saint Patrick's Cathedral and then Rockefeller Center. In a couple of weeks, the skating rink would be installed. One of Pete's favorite pastimes was to watch the tourists watching the skaters.

Eventually, the office buildings took over from the stores and they turned back towards Lexington Avenue, and soon found themselves in front of Astrid's hotel.

"I would invite you upstairs, but I'm afraid you wouldn't respect me in the morning," said Astrid, demurely batting her eyelashes.

"What makes you think I respect you now?" responded Pete.

"Oh. In that case, come on up." She kissed him quickly and passed through the lobby door held open by the smiling doorman, who had overheard the exchange. When they arrived at her suite, Pete paused.

"Aren't you going to carry me across the threshold?"

"I don't know if I can manage it in one trip. Maybe piece by piece?"

Pete's expression of consternation swiftly dissolved when he saw what she had in mind. Her fingers deftly undid the zipper of his pants and slipped in under the band of his underwear.

"Hey, where it leads, I usually follow. Just don't start running," he said with a big grin as she guided him into the room.

"I want to keep you on a short leash," she said. Looking down, she added, "However, this leash seems to have some ideas of its own."

"It certainly has its own agenda, and you seem to be on top of the program."

"I definitely want to be on top of the program."

She turned him around and pushed him back on the bed. Pete quickly learned that she had not bothered donning undergarments this particular evening. She pounced on him like one of the lions she had been working with during the afternoon, hoisting her skirt up, straddling him, and sliding what had, at one time, been considered a leash and now had become a billy club, deep inside herself.

"Oh my God," she moaned. "I've been waiting for this all night."

Her rhythm and breathing grew frantic and it was all he could do to not fall off the edge of the bed as she made love to him like a woman possessed. Her final cry of passion came from a place she never knew had existed before this night, and built to a piercing crescendo and at last she fell, sobbing, into his arms. He held her trembling shoulders for a moment, caressing her hair with his free hand. His passion, though, wasn't to be denied either. He promptly turned her over on her back and thrust hard three, four times until he felt the massive release surge throughout his body. Astrid wiped her eyes and smiled, though he could still see a look that burned as hot as the guitars they had just listened to.

"I swear this won't be the last time we see other," she said to him as he rolled off her and lay on the bedspread. "I almost want to be sad, because I thoroughly hate good-byes. But this feels so much more like a beginning than an end, that I can't."

"I know what you mean," Pete replied, but he wasn't sure what anything meant right now. He was going through too many peaks and valleys in rapid succession to feel very sure of his emotional footing. It seemed to him that inner peace was close at hand but somehow would slip away the moment he grasped it. Every time he had his soldiers lined up in order, they started moshing. He had to chuckle to himself at this piece of mental imagery.

"What's so funny?" Astrid asked, still vulnerable.

"Nothing. Everything. Just the way things work out, you know."

She nestled in the crook of his shoulder. They lay in this position for a few minutes, neither wanting to ruin the moment by saying something banal or trite. Gradually, though, the smell of her skin close to him cut through Pete's haze and he began stroking her thighs. It didn't take long for things to heat up again, though not to the frantic boil of their last coupling. This was a very pleasant simmer they had a chance to savor. Afterwards, they lay facing each other, limbs loosely intertwined, and each soon drifted off into a deep sleep with the face of their lover as their last waking thought. While they slumbered, dark clouds slowly gathered over Manhattan until an intense thunderstorm drenched the city, spikes of lightning sliced the night, illuminating the skyline. This impressive display, however, was lost on the lovers, who were content to simply ride the waves of their dreams. After a while, the thunderstorm, realizing it had no audience, dissipated into first a drizzle, then a few random drops of rain, and finally simply turned the stage over to the morning.

8

The next morning began with the shrill ring of the telephone. Pete rolled over and searched blindly with his hand on the bedside table for the offending noisemaker. He backhanded the clock radio to the floor with a crash, eventually locating the telephone and silencing the ring. He tried to say "Hello" into the receiver, though it sounded more like a Wookie mating call than anything resembling English. Apparently, the man at the front desk lobby was multi-lingual, and told Pete in a cheerful voice,

"Good morning. Miss Hedberg's limousine is ready to take her to the airport. Will you be requiring assistance with your luggage?"

Pete looked at the bedside table, expecting to see the clock, which, until recently, had resided there and now was in pieces on the floor. Astrid stirred and opened one sleepy eye.

"What time is it?" Pete asked.

"It's 10:15, sir," Astutely judging the situation, the voice on the phone said, "Shall I tell the driver you'll be needing more time?"

"Yeah. We'll be down in a few." He hung up the phone, sat up groggily and rubbed his eyes. "Christ. I feel like an armadillo spent the night in my mouth, dancing the Macarena in stilettos."

"Oh, my head. I love red wine, but I don't think the feeling is mutual." Astrid got to her feet and staggered toward the bathroom, bracing herself with her hand against the wall for support.

"You look a little pale," said Pete.

"I feel a little pale," she said and lurched into the bathroom. Gagging and retching noises ensued. Pete thought of the line in a song "Something's coming up and it ain't the sun." but didn't dwell on it too long as he wasn't feeling at his best, either.

They dressed hurriedly. Astrid shoved her clothes and toiletries into a large overnight bag, put on an oversized pair of sunglasses and smiled wanly at Pete.

"This isn't how I wanted to say good-bye to you."

"I wouldn't want to say good-bye to anyone this way, and I don't want to say good-bye to you at all, in any way." Pete replied, taking her in his arms and kissing her tenderly. A realization dawned on him. "Hey, I don't even have your phone number." She reached for the pad on the desk and wrote her phone number down on a sheet while Pete jotted his on another.

"Don't lose it," she said, pushing the paper against his chest with a serious look that quickly dissolved into a grin. "Or I'll have to come back here and give it to you again."

They rode down the elevator in silence. When the doors opened, the driver was waiting to take her bag to the long white stretch. She turned to Pete and said,

"You know, I hate these things. Give me a Mustang convertible anytime."

They shared one last kiss before she climbed in and the chauffeur closed the door behind her. The back door window slid down silently. Pete leaned on the roof of the car and saw her smile, though he couldn't see her eyes behind the sunglasses.

"Hey, take care of yourself. I'll talk to you soon," he said.

"Peter, I can't think of two better days I've ever spent. You're a wonderful man and I'll miss you."

"Astrid, you're something else. I'll miss you too, a lot."

"Did we finally decide last night if something's and something else's were compatible?"

"I think we proved that beyond a doubt."

Pete would've given a lot to stop time right then. He didn't have enough. The limo's engine started up. Astrid's face crumpled momentarily and then her composure returned. She blew him a kiss.

"See you soon, I hope," she said.

"Me too. Get home safe." He stood back as the limousine pulled out into the traffic, Astrid's hand waving back to him from the window.

Pete swallowed hard to dissolve the lump in his throat. The problem with fantasies, he thought, is that even if they become real for a while, they always recede and the mundane comes roaring back with a relentless and grim expression. As if in agreement, a stiff wind suddenly gusted and reminded him that winter wasn't so far away. He wasn't due at Half Moon Bay for a couple of hours and thought a nice walk would clear his hangover. He leisurely strolled downtown, wondering how he could ever live in a city like Los Angeles, where it seemed that everyone drove everywhere they had to go, whether from one side of town to the other, or simply to go three blocks to get a container of milk.

The rhythm of his own stride was relaxing and he couldn't imagine how driving could be as calming. Christ, without a doubt not in this city, he thought, watching four cars negotiate into three lanes as the traffic light turned yellow at an intersection. Had the cars tuned their horns to each other, they would have played a nice harmonic chord, as opposed to the dissonant clash assaulting his ears when all simultaneously honked their displeasure. The horn of the car left behind, stuck at the red light, trailed off plaintively longer than the rest. It was a vehicular version of musical chairs.

Pete allowed himself a small chuckle and stepped from the curb. Luckily, he had been watching the automotive ballet for a moment. If he hadn't, he would have been creamed by an onrushing white stretch limousine, which had swerved in front of him in an attempt to gain a parking space by the curb. For a moment Pete's heart leapt. He envisioned Astrid jumping out of the back seat telling him she never, ever wanted to be away from him. He even took a tentative step towards the car, a smile forming on his lips. The rear door didn't open, however. The driver's side did and a burly gnome wearing an ill-fitting suit and a brush cut emerged from it. He rounded the car in a threatening manner, eyes bulging and fists clenched.

"Hey, shitheel, get away from the car," he snarled. Pete thought he resembled an angry hedgehog.

"I'm sorry, did you mean to park on the sidewalk? Maybe we can all move into a doorway and give you some room," Pete replied, motioning to the gathering of people standing at the corner, waiting for the light to turn.

"You think you're funny? You're gonna look real funny in a couple of minutes, when I'm done," growled the hedgehog. He stepped up in front of Pete, his snout in Pete's chest. The light turned green, but only one or two pedestrians crossed. The rest lingered, anticipating some entertainment. At that moment, the rear door opened and an impeccable looking man stepped out. Everyone in the immediate area stopped and stared, as if some higher being had pushed a pause button on a remote control somewhere. The man needlessly adjusted the cuff on his tailored gray suit jacket and addressed the driver in a cultured voice,

"Mr. Snedli, I don't think belligerence is necessary at this moment."

Pete guessed that Mr. Snedli wasn't too sure what belligerence was, but in the way a dog doesn't necessarily understand its master's commands, but more the tone of his voice, responded by taking a step back.

"Down, boy. Be a good Snedli," Pete said, patting his pockets. "I'm all out of doggie biscuits."

This garnered a few snickers from the onlookers. There is an unconscious way a group of watchers can subliminally influence the outcome of a situation. It was clear they wanted to see some action and weren't far away from egging on the principals. Pete was fairly certain the hedgehog was carrying something concealed in his left jacket pocket, though it looked more like a blackjack than a gun, judging by its shape. Of course, Pete's advantage would be Mr. Snedli underestimating him.

"Mr. Snedli, I don't want to get a summons for being parked illegally. Please find other accommodations for the car. Thank you," the silver haired man said to his chauffeur, gesturing to a fire hydrant the limousine was parked directly in front of. The hedgehog, realizing he was being pulled back on his leash and that nothing further was going to happen, glared once more at Pete. He made a gesture, backhanding his fingers under his chin and then out away from his face, recircled the car and stood before his still-open door.

"Maybe his flea collar's a little tight." Pete grinned. "That's probably why he parked so close to the hydrant." He made a small leg-lifting movement in the direction of the hydrant. The man smiled benevolently at him, and soundlessly clapped his hands twice in derision. He said,

"In another situation,......." spreading his hands while tilting his large head slightly to one side before striding across the sidewalk into the building. A uniformed security guard held the door open for him. Snedli hurried around the back of the car to close the rear door before running back to his side of the car and climbing in. He glowered at Pete and pulled away from the curb to parts unknown, though a nearby garage would be a reasonable guess.

The man stared expressionlessly out through the thick shaded glass doors he had recently passed through and watched Pete cross the street on his way downtown, then turned towards a long bank of elevators. He strode straight to the end of the bank and into an elevator, which had only one button on its interior panel, with a keyhole located underneath it. He withdrew a key chain containing four keys from his finely tailored pants and inserted a key into the hole. The button lit, revealing a ying-yang symbol of a deep crimson color, and the man pushed it. The doors closed, revealing the name "Magma" etched into the steel, and the elevator accelerated upward.

Seconds later, the doors hissed open again and he stepped out into a very large, spacious office, the main feature being a spectacular view of downtown Manhattan visible along the back wall, consisting entirely of smoked glass. The office itself was sparsely furnished, though still retaining an air of opulence. A large auburn lacquered desk with a swiveling leather chair was positioned in a corner near the glass wall. A long black leather couch occupied the far side of the room. Framed gold and platinum records lined the wall over the couch in rows of three. Once at the desk, he sat in the reclining chair and lingered a moment before pressing the intercom button built into the desk.

"I have arrived."

A minute passed and a door next to the couch opened. A strikingly attractive, efficient looking blonde woman wearing a powder blue Thierry Mugler suit entered with a tray containing a steaming pot of coffee, a mug decorated with the same ying-yang symbol as in the elevator, and a large croissant stuffed with almond paste.

"Good morning, Mr. Morgan," she said and placed the tray in front of him.

"Thank you, Irene," he replied, and poured himself a cup of coffee.

"Sir, Mr. Roeper is already here for his 11:00 meeting. You've got lunch at Lutece at 1:00 and the major shareholders will be in video conference room E at 4:00, as per your instructions. Your wife phoned a half hour ago to tell you she was having some rug samples delivered here for your perusal. I took the liberty of setting up your accommodations and flight to London tomorrow for the further merger discussions." She placed a stack of papers on the corner of the desk. "Here are some documents ready for you to sign, as well."

"Thank you, Irene."

She made to go back through the door to her desk, but stopped when she heard him clear his throat. She turned again to face him.

"Irene," he said, his face expressionless, and swiveled his chair so as to face the view of the city.

She came around the desk and kneeled between his parted legs, wrapping her long blonde hair speedily into a bun. Unzipping his suit pants, she slid his member out and proceeded, once again with great efficiency, to deliver an excellent blowjob. Gazing out at the Manhattan skyline, he sighed gently as he ejaculated into her mouth. She got back up off her knees and he rezipped his pants.

"Thank you, Irene," he said, as she walked to the door. "Send Mr. Roeper in fifteen minutes, please."

Sixteen minutes later the door reopened. A pony-tailed man wearing granny sunglasses, dressed in a black Armani suit and an open necked red silk shirt entered the office.

"Ian, so good to see you again."

"Hello, Richie, how are you?"

"Couldn't be better."

Irene came in and took the tray from the desk without looking at either man before leaving.

"Please hold all my calls, Irene."

"Yes, Mr. Morgan," she said, and closed the door behind her.

"Very nice," said Roeper with a salacious grin. "Where'd you find her?"

"I use an agency. Would you like to try her? She's quite good."

"Maybe in a little while."

"You've unquestionably earned a perk or two," said Morgan. "Sales have been booming. The Patterson disc is flying off the shelves, from what I'm given to understand. You were masterful in creating a huge underground buzz on him. I'll be meeting with the board later this afternoon and there should be many smiles on their well-fed faces."

"Always glad to hear it."

"Do you have anything new cooking up?" he asked, with a hopeful expression.

"As a matter of fact, I believe I do. This could be big. She's quite beautiful, and talented to boot. I want to guide her along gradually."

"In any case, Richie, I've learned to trust your instincts in these matters."

"I'll bring her around to meet you soon, when the time is right. I have a CD of some rough mixes we've been working on, if you'd like to hear it."

"Oh, that's not necessary," replied Morgan, looking at his watch, "but, why not? Let's hear it. What demographic are we targeting this time? The shareholders always like to know these things."

"It looks like female fifteen to twenty-two, though I think we'll get a fair amount of male across the board, especially on the young end. As I said, she's a looker."

"Wonderful."

Morgan reached into the center drawer of the desk and took out a remote control. He pointed it at the adjacent wall, pressing a button. A large section of paneling slid back to reveal a state of the art stereo. Simultaneously, four other panels opened, one high in each wall, revealing speakers, with small sub-woofers next to each. Roeper reached into his jacket pocket and handed Morgan a compact disk, which he placed in the stereo. From his key chain he selected an ornately carved key, and unlocked a small teak cabinet discretely placed beneath the stereo. Inside the cabinet were many small drawers. Roeper eyed the cabinet hungrily.

"You favor Peruvian, if memory serves me," Morgan offered.

"I do, Ian, though anything you've got in that happy cabinet of curiosities of yours will do just fine, I'm sure. How about a little taste test?"

"If you prefer, Richie, if you prefer." He randomly selected a mixture of cellophane packets from different drawers inside the cabinet. All were labeled with typewritten adhesive labels, each describing a different country and make. He tossed them onto his desk and said,

"Go to town. Do you need a straw?"

"No thanks, Ian. I always try to be prepared for these types of circumstances. It's my Boy Scout background. I never outgrew it, I guess." Roeper said. He took off the sunglasses from his hawk-shaped nose and placed them in the breast pocket of his jacket. From an interior pocket he removed a hard red leather satchel. He unzipped it and spread out the contents on the desk: a small rectangular mirror, a five-inch sterling silver straw and a razor blade. His smile grew wider as he surveyed the packets and took a mental inventory of their contents.

"Would you like to ride the horse, Richie?" asked Morgan, holding out another packet, this one with brown powder, aloft in his hand. "This came in yesterday from Afghanistan."

"It's tempting, Ian, very tempting, but that's a loser's game I reserve for others. Dale had some trouble gauging purity and look where it got him." His beady eyes narrowed to slits as he pulled his attention away from the feast awaiting him on the desk. "You don't know how sometimes I'd like to join them on their merry descent into hell, even if only for a small part of the journey. But," he added with a dry laugh, "I must draw the line somewhere. And this looks like as good a place as any."

With that, he emptied some of the contents of the packet labeled "Medellin—offwhite—high grade" onto his mirror and began breaking up the larger chunks into powder, and then four lines running the length of the mirror. He inhaled the left one, then the right up the respective nostrils in his nose. He paused for a moment, repeated the act, and then, eyes wide as saucers, gasped,

"Oh my God. Sweet Jesus. Ian, Ian, where did you ever come up with this? This is the nectar of Olympus."

"This company has its share of Colombian investors, if you'll remember, Richie. You'd be amazed at the creative financing involved. Do you remember the Vanilla Ice comeback tour we sponsored last year? It made me think of the wonderful Mel Brooks movie 'The Producers', in which an attempt was made to lose as much money as possible, for insurance purposes it was, I believe. Sometimes it's quite to our advantage to produce the vilest dreck imaginable. And, do you know what the funniest part about it is?" he said, his face suddenly animated, though his clear grey eyes betrayed no mirth. When Roeper shook his head, he took it for a negative expression and not a drug-induced spasm, and continued, "Some of those intentional disasters have become our most massive hits! Oh, how I laugh, how I laugh when this happens. Can you imagine explaining to the accountants of some of the most nefarious businessmen in the world that they've made four hundred million dollars when they were trying to lose fifty million? On one hand, as accountants, they are initially happy for a moment, and then, as they grasp that these profits in fact go against their employer's wishes, the change in their expressions is most amusing to observe. They are unable to launder their money and have to engage in even more preposterous investments in order to justify all the cash rolling in. Richie, these meetings become the very height of absurdity. I would gladly videotape them for posterity if the potential repercussions weren't so severe."

During Morgan's discourse, Roeper had sorted through more of the packets, eventually settling on one labeled "Ecuador - pink — untested", another labeled "Hong Kong—crystal—fuhgetaboutit" and was in the process of creating a mini four-lane highway on his mirror. Being American, he stayed in the right lane and plowed through the Ecuadorian sample first, before moving into the passing lane. He whistled softly, and daubed the leftover pink powder from the mirror with his index finger and rubbing it against his gums.

"Damn, that's nice. Ian, you're something else. I can't wait to try out this Hong Kong packet, but I just want to chill for a couple of seconds and enjoy the buzz. You want me to chop a couple for you? This is some toot uncommon." He motioned at the mirror.

"No, no, Richie. Thanks," Morgan waved a hand. "I've got an important lunch in an hour or two and I want to have an appetite left for it. If I were to join you now, I would leave a full plate of some excellent French food and act like a chatterbox when in fact, all I want to do is listen. It's possibly what I do best. Speaking of which, let's hear what your latest songbird sounds like. Does she write her own material?"

"Yeah and her publishing contract, like Patterson's, rewards us quite favorably," he wiped his nose. "Dumb bitch even asked me if I knew a good lawyer. The first song on the tape seems like an obvious single to me, though the next one's not shabby, either. You know, she's genuinely good," he laughed. "Her singing is, too. Check it out."

Morgan pressed the play button on the remote control. A sinuous bass line emanated from the speakers, at first solely accompanied by a closed high-hat cymbal keeping eighth note time. A sultry female voice began singing. South American percussion kicked in, along with a synthesized string section. As the music began its crescendo toward the chorus, shimmering guitars chimed in and the vocal grew impassioned, the lyrics urging a lost love to please, please come back. Morgan looked at Roeper, pursed his lips and arched his eyebrows. A solid snare and kick drum joined the mix for the second verse to provide a dynamic backbeat. The singer rested, letting the rhythm establish itself, before admonishing the lost love that he was missing more loving than he could afford to, all the while maintaining her vulnerability. It sounded completely irresistible and, as the last chorus faded out, over a flanged guitar solo, Morgan looked at Roeper and made the same soft clapping motion he had made towards Pete an hour before, though with sincerity this time.

"Not bad at all. Is this your arrangement?"

"I'd take credit for it, if I could. And, you know, I just might, if I can." Once again, Roeper's reptilian smile emerged. "She's got, or should I say, had a boyfriend who's helped her out on a lot of the material. I don't think he's going to prove to have much of a shelf-life, if you get my drift." After emptying half the packet and lining up some of Hong Kong's finest onto his no longer cleanly polished mirror, he bent his head and inhaled the drug in a fashion to make a vacuum cleaner proud. "My, oh my. Ian, this stuff is rocket fuel!" he said, and wiped a tear from the corner of his eye.

"Why don't you take the rest of the packet with you?" said Morgan, palm outstretched.

"I love these labels, too," Roeper said, waving his hand at the assortment of packets on the desk. "I can picture your secretary typing these up and wondering what the hell's going on. And while we're on the subject, does your offer to take her for a test drive still hold?" His eyes glistened.

"Definitely, Richie, of course. Have a seat at my desk. May I also suggest that you turn the chair toward the view? It's quite an uplifting experience."

"Ian, you sure know how to treat a guy right."

Roeper sprawled on the chair after undoing his pants and dropping them around his ankles. He wasn't wearing underwear and stroked himself until half-erect. He took a random packet from the pile and sprinkled some of the contents on his organ and said, in a guttural voice, "I'm ready."

Morgan pressed the intercom button and said,

"Irene, please step into my office. I have some further dictation for you."

"I'll be right in, sir," came the disembodied voice from the speaker.

"Thank you, Irene."

9

Pete sat in a coffee shop down the block from Half Moon Bay and made his way slowly through scrambled eggs, bacon, toast and hash brown potatoes while reading the sports pages of a local tabloid. He accepted a third cup of coffee from a smiling waitress and acknowledged her with a wink.

"Why can't the Rangers get a decent wing for Gretzky," he muttered.

He read quickly through the rest of the paper, wondering if he should put his meager savings into internet stocks. He scanned the financial section on his way to the front page, proclaiming, in bold headlines, the death of Dale Patterson. "R&R OD in Alphabet City" was this particular tabloid's attempt at cleverness. Radio stations had promised to play tributes to this fallen "hero". Childhood abuse was insinuated, making young Dale's demise a proper American tragedy. A picture of him, culled from his high school yearbook, showed him in happier times, albeit with a nerdy haircut.

Lab tests had shown his last high to be a real doozy. According to forensic experts, he had injected an almost uncut dose of heroin into his veins and the newspaper speculated he couldn't have been aware of the drug's purity. The usual parade of rock stars that had performed this type of supernova was listed. Pete couldn't believe he was reading Patterson's name in the same sentence with such icons as

Hendrix, Joplin, Bolin et al, especially after having witnessed the less than garage band quality of Patterson's last
performance with End Over End. He was even more amazed
to find how many discs the public was purchasing. It was
speculated his record would enter the Billboard charts in the
top five when sales were tabulated at the end of the week.

On one of the interior pages of the newspaper, Pete
stopped at an article describing the murders in his neighborhood that the Reaper had asked him about. One of the
burnt bodies had been identified through dental records
as Yorkis "Liquid" Nasciamento, formerly of the Bronx
Nasciamentos.

"You know, I think that was Pepe's youngest brother.
He was always running around with a toy gun, trying to act
tough," he said to himself, remembering the teenage boy
he knew. Armando "Pepe" Nasciamento had been a lieutenant in a violent drug gang known as Las Panteras d'Oro.
Pete had managed to bring down several members, posing
as a Canadian heroin importer, though he had been unable
to capture the unidentified leader, who had fled to South
America by way of Toronto, ironically enough.

Pepe had died in a bloody shoot-out with the police
in a condemned tenement serving as a drop-off and cutting
house for the gang. The members all had tattoos of a gold
panther in a springing position on their chests covering their
hearts. Pepe had been hit by a shotgun blast at such close
range that only the tip of the tail of his panther had been
left.

Pete found the seemingly endless plight of these gangs
depressing. It was a vicious, self-perpetuating cycle. In the
midst of hideous poverty, a few individuals are able to flash

expensive jewelry and cars, and the neighborhood children come to view these people as heroes, despite some of their parents' concerned warnings. Pete had also seen parents actively pushing their children into gangs and thought these people were among the lowest scum in the universe. Once, his goal in life had been to rid the world of these predators, but, after a while, he felt as if he was defending a sandcastle at high tide.

One of the main reasons he operated the rehearsal studio was to be around optimistic people. Musicians, talented or not, are usually aspiring to higher things, always hoping the next show would be their big break, their next recording heard by a record company executive who would understand what they were trying to do, sign them to a label and enable them to spend their days creating. Ninety-nine percent never reach their aspirations, but reality has little to do with dreams. Besides, creativity in itself is a statement of optimism, a healthy outlet for self-expression.

Pete had burnt himself out dealing with the dreck preying upon people's addictions and this was redemption for him, even if on a small scale. He'd almost drowned in the sea of shit he'd tried to sail on. In an effort to "stay in character" and impress a gang he was infiltrating, he'd started snorting the drugs he'd spent so much effort to take off of the streets. Pete had broken the first law of the undercover narcotics cop. Now, like some old gunslinger who'd escaped with his life after many showdowns, he wanted no part whatsoever of his former life.

In the westerns he had loved to watch as a kid, the gunslinger was invariably dragged back into action against his wishes to save the town from threatening desperadoes.

Pete prayed this would never come to pass for him, but was certain what would happen if his convictions were ever truly challenged. Which life is an illusion, he wondered: The one where idealists reached for stars only to find white paint speckled on a cold, black ceiling, or the one in which savage drug dealers were lionized by the very communities they raped? If neurotics build castles in the sky and psychotics live in them, Pete supposed he must be a janitor.

He asked the waitress for the check, left a healthy tip and paid at the counter. He crossed the street to the studio and took the elevator upstairs. While cleaning the rehearsal rooms, he noticed a ukulele with single coil electric guitar pickups added to it, sitting in the corner of the room set up for recording. He smiled to himself, picturing his assistant bringing the Hawaiian blues band back to the studio for an impromptu jam last night, all of them stoned and wearing brightly flowered shirts, playing "Tiny Bubbles" a la Johnny Winter. He thought of asking Greg, when he came in later that afternoon, if he'd gotten leied the night before, but decided against it. The bad pun police might be watching, and one can never be too careful with them.

He was paying bills at his desk and attempting to balance the studio checkbook without much success, when the telephone rang.

"Half Moon Bay Studios. Can I help you?" he answered.

"Hello. This is Walter Woodlenacker of Woodlenacker, Visconti & Childers Associates. I represent Mr. Aziz," said a nasal voice.

"Oh, Christ, Styx, give me a break. I'm not in the mood for this crap. Would you grow up already?" he responded testily, tempted to hang up the phone. He was still annoyed with his friend after yesterday's conversation. "How many times are you going to make these jackass gag phone intros? Don't you ever get tired of this?"

"Sir, I honestly have no idea who you think you're speaking to. I'm calling on behalf of my client, Mr. Ali ben Aziz, the rug merchant on the third floor of the building in which your, ahem, musical venture is located on the fourth floor. He is presently retaining the services of my law firm. I assume you are Mr. Peter Watts, the proprietor of this establishment?"

"Oh, heh, heh, sorry about that. I have this friend, you see. Sometimes he makes these prank phone calls. Never mind." Pete felt like an idiot.

"There has been extensive damage done to his business and Mr. Aziz is expecting immediate restitution. He cannot do any business as long as his antique carpets have water stains and smell like feces."

"No, I can imagine it would be tough. Would airing out the rugs get rid of the odor?" Pete asked hopefully.

"I sincerely doubt the solution would be so simple, Mr. Watts. Mr. Aziz has also suffered a great deal of emotional trauma in addition to the damage done to his business."

"Emotional trauma?" replied Pete "Are you sure you haven't been standing too close to his carpets, 'cause you're starting to have that fecal feeling yourself?"

"Recriminations are unnecessary, Mr. Watts. I just want to make sure my client gets his due,"

Pete, sensing the bad pun police might still be on patrol, didn't make the due-due/doo-doo joke that seemed like such a lay-up to him at the moment. Still, he was having problems taking this conversation seriously.

"Look, Mr. Noodlewacker, or whatever your name is, why don't you call my insurance company and maybe we can work out something to everyone's satisfaction? Unless you feel it would further contribute to Mr. Aziz's fragile emotional state. I would hate to upset the gentleman."

Pete read off the telephone number of his insurance agent. "You got it?" he asked. When he received an affirmative response, he added, "I hope to not have the pleasure of speaking with you again, you miserable bloodsucker." and hung up the phone.

The next band scheduled to rehearse, Afternoon Delight, wasn't due to arrive at the studio for another hour and a half. This band was an offshoot of a religious cult who refused to go outdoors after the sun set. They rehearsed during the daytime and played lunchtime concerts at colleges and coffeehouses. Pete puttered around, checking the tubes and transistors in the amplifiers and making sure none of the speakers had been fried by over enthusiastic Van Halen wannabes. The equipment in all the rooms was constantly put through the paces by the various bands and breakdowns were a fact of life.

Pete found minimal damage, a cracked crash cymbal in one of the drum kits. He was foraging around in the storage room for a replacement when the phone rang again.

"Half Moon Bay Studios. Can I help you?"

"Yeah, is Barry McCockiner there?"

"Styx, I'm not going to believe you graduated from kindergarten until I see the diploma," Pete replied exasperatedly.

"Does it matter to you if it was written with crayons?" replied Johnny.

"Not if the frame was made with play-doh. What's up?"

"Not much. I hate to have us pissed off at each other. Besides I picked up the tab at Electric Willie's and you owe me a couple of rounds, which I intend to collect, and soon."

"A peculiar place, to say the least," said Pete. "Who would think of a decor like that? Undeniably the product of a twisted mind. It wouldn't surprise me if you had been somehow involved in the planning stages."

"You think that was bad? Oooh, boy, have I got a place for you! You ever been to the Sandpaper Diaper Club? Most likely not, I guess. You free tonight?"

"Sadly, yes."

"I don't want you to think I'm some sort of decadent individual."

"The thought never crossed my mind. You're far too stupid to be truly decadent."

"Coming from the oral majority, I'll take that as a compliment. This time I'll appeal to your more prurient instincts. You want a more respectable establishment? A touch of class, perhaps? Petey, my boy, I think you're ready to go a little more upscale. Now, what could be more respectable than a bank? And I don't mean an S & L."

"A bank, Johnny? We're going to have fun, fun, fun 'till daddy takes her ATM card away? Not only are your screws loose, my friend, but the threads have been stripped."

"No, no. You're not very "au courant", are you?"

"You calling me a fruit?"

"Maybe a dumquat. But no, I'm not doubting your sexuality, what little you have."

"Where exactly do you intersect with reality?"

"You heard of this new club down in Chinatown called The Depository, just off of Mott Street? It used to be First Federal, or something along those lines, before management was involved in some big embezzlement scandal and the whole thing went belly-up. They liquidated their remaining assets and some downtown promoter bought the Chinatown branch to turn it into a club. Very funky clientele."

"Sure, why not? Let's check it out. I've got nothing to lose. You know, you ought to be one of those guys like Speed Levitch, giving these bizarre walking tours of the city."

"Anyone who gives a good tour of this city and doesn't point out the more outrageous aspects of it is kinda bizarre in his own right," replied Johnny.

Pete smiled, accurately picturing the expression of righteous indignation on his friend's face. Johnny shared Pete's love for the city, but in a different way. Pete just appreciated it as it came to him, on his own terms, but Johnny loved to dig into it, to discover the otherwise unknown areas, the nooks and crannies, and in these streets, the terrain constantly evolves. If Pete ever wanted to know the newest 'in' spot, the information was always just a phone call away.

Johnny, though, instantly abandoned interest as soon as the media caught on to the establishment and the promoters and publicists initiated their feeding frenzies. He had no desire whatsoever in being one of 'the beautiful people'. On the contrary, he felt contempt for their shallowness. He simply reveled in the act of discovery.

"We don't want to be the first ones there," said Johnny. "Why don't you meet me around 11:30 at Pearl and Roy's around the corner, on Bayard Street?"

"Sounds like a plan. It should be easy to find. See you then." Pete hung up the phone.

He stared at it for a moment, debating whether to call Angeline. After a few moments, he decided against it, though throughout the rest of the afternoon, whenever he passed the phone, he could feel its silent seduction. Every time his resolve started to weaken, though, he remembered the callous fashion in which she had treated him before he had stormed out of her apartment.

The afternoon passed quietly. Greg showed up around three o'clock, wearing sunglasses and a Seattle Mariners baseball cap, not having much to say. Afternoon Delight arrived on time, played for two hours, left a few dozen pamphlets on the bulletin board Pete hung up for bands searching for drummers or singers, or who wanted to inform the world of their upcoming gigs, and left.

A five-piece Goth rock band arrived around 8:00 in the evening to play in Studio A. Pete didn't notice anything out of the ordinary about them at first, but when he came into the room a few minutes later to adjust the microphone levels, he saw the lead singer had a very large snake wrapped around his/her neck, stretching from one arm to the other. This band had rehearsed at Half Moon Bay three or four times before, and it had been an ongoing discussion between Pete and Greg as to what sex, let alone what sexuality, the lead singer was, not that either of them was particularly interested, one way or the other.

Pete hadn't thought of putting up a "No Pets Allowed" sign up, but nevertheless told the band it was standard studio policy not to allow animals into the rehearsal rooms. The singer promised, in a sultry voice, that the reptile was harmless, having been recently fed, and they would never bring it in again, but could they please, please stay, just this once. Pete relented, but was shortly to regret it. An hour later, a sheepish looking bass player emerged from the rehearsal room. Actually, goatish was a better description, as he was wearing a Viking helmet with an aggressive looking pair of horns protruding from the front.

"We've got a slight problem. Roger's passed out and the snake climbed up the speaker cabinets and is hanging from the light fixture."

Pete and Greg exchanged a quick glance. Glumly, Greg reached into his pocket, took out a five dollar bill, and handed it to Pete.

"Damn, I could've sworn it was a chick."

Pete, although happy for the sawbuck, didn't relish what awaited, and trod into studio A. The singer of the band was slumped face-down on the floor in front of the microphone stand, the three quarters empty bottle of Jack Daniels more upright than he was. This was a minor consideration compared to the large mass of reptile coiled around one of the heavy spot lights, its head undulating, eyes glinting and forked tongue periodically slipping between its lips.

"Does anyone here know anything about snakes?" Pete asked. The band had gathered on the other side of the room, behind the keyboards, as far away from the snake as possible, while still trying to give off an air of detachment, as if some of the sound patches on the synthesizer had suddenly become fascinating, and merited immediate band discussion. They shrugged in unison.

"Uh, I don't think it's poisonous." One of the band members offered. "I doubt that Roger would've been carrying a poisonous snake around, you know."

"You're probably right. Any ideas on how to get it down from the lights, fellas?"

More unison shrugs. Pete thought that if they sang together as well as they shrugged, these guys might have a future in the business, though they'd have to ditch the lead singer, who, at this point, looked like he belonged in a ditch somewhere.

"In any case, we've got to do something here. Where's Marlon Perkins when you need him?" Pete said. He sidled up cautiously to where the snake was hanging, reached over to the guitar stand, picked up the guitar, and thrust the neck toward the snake, hoping it would grab onto it and leave his light fixture alone.

"Hey, man, watch what you're doing! That's a '61 Strat. Are you out of your mind?" screamed the guitarist.

Pete looked at the head of the guitar, and then derisively back at the guitarist.

"61? What's that, your IQ? Do you see any serial numbers on this instrument, Captain Crunch?" His voice was heavy with sarcasm.

"I know what it is. Listen, I paid over three grand for this axe," the guitarist replied sullenly.

"How much have you spent on lessons?" replied Pete, and regretted saying it immediately.

He made a point not to comment unfavorably on the lesser bands that played in his studio. After all, they all essentially paid his rent for him, whether talented or not. Sometimes, though, when he heard pure cacophony issuing from his rehearsal rooms, he fought the urge to hand the "musicians" their money back, ask them to please, please sell their instruments and take up something else, maybe mac-ramé or stamp collecting.

But these people were, in many cases, living out their fantasies and the two or three hours they purchased to use Pete's sound equipment were very precious to them. Maybe this guitarist he had just insulted worked in some degrading job, and this was his one chance to shine a little, to tell his friends, "Yeah, my job sucks, but my band really cooks, and we're going someplace. Come down to our next show."

Besides, Pete knew his opinion of someone's musical talent was worth as much as the next guy's, and who was to say what might succeed and what wouldn't? You sure couldn't tell by looking at the charts. He certainly didn't want to be a determining factor in someone's failure, only their success. He turned toward the guitarist.

"Sorry about that, man. Look, I've had a bad day and you can imagine I don't want to deal with this right now. I just want to get the goddamn snake out of here. What does this thing usually eat?"

"Roger usually feeds Sadie a couple of mice every week," offered the drummer. Pete noted to himself, some-what proudly, that drummers are usually the most useful members of any band.

"Sadie? What a lovely name," said Pete to the snake. "Sadie, I'm sorry to say we're short on mice here right now. I might be able to scare up a cockroach or two, if that would be of interest to you."

Sadie, clearly a reptile of comfort, flicked her tongue disdainfully at the mere mention of a cockroach.

"Uh, Roger usually puts some peanut butter on the mice before he feeds them to her. She loves peanut butter," said the bassist.

"You're kidding, aren't you?" Pete glanced over at him.

"No, really. Roger usually covers them up in it. Sadie's got a real thing for peanut butter. Sometimes he puts it on places you can't imagine."

"I think I'm learning more about Roger and Sadie than I need to know right here. But we might be on to something, though." He called out to Greg, who was hovering near the doorway, taking in the scene. "Hey, guy, bring me the jar of Skippy from the fridge."

Greg presently returned with the jar and handed it to Pete, who took one of the microphone stands and liberally smeared peanut butter on the top half of it. He had Sadie's rapt attention from the moment he twisted the lid.

"I know I can't use your axe," Pete said to the guitarist, "but do you mind if we use the case to hold the snake?"

The guitarist assented and Pete set the jar on its side toward the back end of the case, where the guitar's head and tuning pegs would be. He held up the microphone stand toward the snake and Sadie raptly slid towards it, entwining herself around the stand. In a short time, she had vacated the lighting fixture and Pete gently laid the stand into the guitar case. Sadie immediately spied the open container, disengaged herself from the stand and wriggled towards it. Just as she left the stand and her tail cleared the back end of the case, Pete quickly snatched the jar and shut the guitar case, immediately closing the fasteners.

"I suggest you let Roger deal with Sadie whenever he's sobered up. I have a feeling she might not be too happy about this."

"Hey, no problem," said the guitarist, "I can carry my guitar home tonight. Stan, can you give me a ride? We'll drop Roger off on the way."

The bassist consented. The guitar case started to shake around on the floor as if it were alive. The guitarist gingerly picked it up and carried it out the door. They paid and, as they walked out toward the elevator, Pete called out after them, "Hey, you guys bring me a jar of peanut butter next time."

The elevator door opened and the band filed in. Roger, the singer, was carried in by two of his band mates, his knees dragging. The guitarist, the last to enter, waved at Pete. Just then the guitar case lurched violently and fell from his arms into the elevator, where the latches sprang open. The doors shut behind them and Pete could hear muffled screams originating from inside the elevator as it descended.

"I'm kinda glad I'm not in there." Greg said.

"I hope the lawyer from that tapestry guy downstairs is waiting in the lobby for the elevator right now," Pete smirked.

The rest of the evening at the studio passed unremarkably, by comparison. Pete left around 10:00 after giving Greg some last instructions in tube replacement for a couple of the more worn-out amplifiers. He went home, showered, shaved and changed clothes. He wasn't too sure what to wear to a club that used to be a bank, but he went by the old Manhattan rule: if it's below 14th Street, wear black. It may not be very adventurous, but it usually works.

After taking the subway a couple of stops to Canal Street, in the Chinatown section of New York, he ambled a couple of blocks north and rounded the corner to find himself on a relatively empty block. Halfway up the street was a dilapidated establishment with a neon sign in the process of giving up the ghost, only the apostrophe between the *Pearl and Roy* and the *s* showing an occasional firefly-like flicker. He entered and a slurred voice from the back got his attention,

"Hey, jackass, close the door! You're letting all the smoke out."

Pete took two steps toward the bar, situated on the left, and his eyes adjusted to the dim light coming from track lights set into the ceiling. He ordered a beer from the ancient Irish bartender and found the nearest vacant stool, about halfway up the shabby bar. On the right, a pinball machine was wedged between the wall and a jukebox, currently playing a Roy Orbison weeper. The raucous bells of the machine were oddly in tune to the music, though not to the mood of the song.

"Buddy, good to see ya." Johnny said, turning from the pinball machine. "Check this out. I'm only a million points away from the high score."

"And you're only about a million cells away from having a brain, too. Don't tell me this place is one of your main hangouts."

"It's the only place I know of that still has the old Terminator machine. You'd think in a big city like this, you could find some good places to play pinball, but nooooo, not one."

"Kids are staying home and playing on their computers, I guess. We're going to have a generation full of great jet fighter pilots soon."

Pete watched Johnny play his last ball. All of the body English and machine shaking in the world, though, couldn't get him close to the high score. The ball drained down the side despite making one last valiant attempt to keep it in play, slapping the side of the machine with a loud *thunk*. The tilt light glowed yellow against the backdrop. His score was still good enough for the top ten, and so Johnny typed in "STX", and saw at least he held seventh place.

"I don't think I'll be telling my grandchildren about this one, but I'll drink to it."

He went to the bar and asked for a vodka and orange juice. Pete ordered the same and they sat on two of the less worn barstools. The jukebox switched to Kenny Rogers's "You Picked a Fine Time to Leave Me, Lucille".

Johnny laughed when he heard the song.

"You ever notice how bar jukeboxes always seem to play the soundtrack to your life? No matter what place you step into." He took a healthy swallow, draining half his glass. "So how's it going with your harem these days?"

"For one thing, there's a little lady named Sadie who thinks I'm quite irresistible, just as long as I keep a jar of peanut butter handy." Pete waggled his brows suggestively in Groucho Marx fashion. Johnny grinned in anticipation of a lewd story. Pete laughed and described his serpentine adventure. His mood darkened, though, when he recounted his last meeting with Angeline.

Johnny whistled softly between his teeth, "Wow. Are you sure, absolutely sure, it was a crack vial?"

Pete looked sadly at Johnny, who put his hand on Pete's shoulder.

"Yeah. That line of bullshit of hers might have fooled me, probably would've, 'cause I'd want to believe her, but you've been in the field way too long not to know what's what. Man, I'm so sorry to hear that. You know, if it was only a case of her being a slut or something," he grimaced, "Ah, that's a crappy way of putting it, but this is a lot closer to home for you than it should be."

"You're telling me, pal. I hope to God she finds her way off that road before it's too late. I want to talk to her. I really do, but I don't know what to say without it sounding like a lecture."

"I can't believe she'd invent that story."

"The road to hell is paved with good inventions."

They stayed at the bar for another hour and a half, Pete switching from his customary beer to join Johnny's screw-driver parade, reeling raggedly along its route. Pete's mood lifted for a while as he and Johnny took a trip down memory lane, reminiscing about some of their escapades in the old neighborhood. Pete paid the tab. They got up somewhat un-steadily from the rickety bar stools and made the mercifully short journey to the Depository.

A very large bouncer dressed up unconvincingly as a bank guard was stationed in front of the revolving door. He seemed to vaguely recognize Johnny as they made their way through the small crowd waiting to get in, and waved them in with his nightstick. They wandered into an enormous room with a domed ceiling three stories high. The sound of Brazilian music resonated off the white concrete walls. The lighting was multi-colored, but subdued.

The first bar they spotted, on the right, was situated behind the rows of the tellers' windows. The kiosks in the middle of the room, previously used by bank patrons to fill out deposit and withdrawal forms, were still there, even down to the Plexiglas slots. Groups of well-dressed, well-heeled young people milled around, chatting and sipping their drinks.

"Interesting place," remarked Pete.

"Hmm. Looks like most of them never left the bank when it closed down," replied Johnny. "I say, Peter, old boy, let's mingle."

They stopped first at a teller's window, withdrew a couple of fresh screwdrivers from their accounts, and looked around. The crowd was aloof, mostly people wanting to be seen.

"I forgot to let my publicist know I was going to be here tonight. The gossip tabloids should've been all over me like a cheap suit by now. And I'm having a good hair day, too." Johnny pretended to pout.

"There, there, dear. Don't get upset. I'm sure Leo and his posse will be here any minute," Pete said consolingly, and brushed some imaginary dust from Johnny's shoulder.

"Hi fellas, what's happening tonight?" asked a voice from behind them.

They turned around to face a tall, dapper blonde young man wearing a tuxedo and red clown's nose.

"Don't tell me. Your name is Rudolph," said Pete.

The young man clucked his tongue.

"If I had a dollar for every time I've heard that," he said, waving his hand. His manner was effete and Pete immediately regretted having brushed Johnny's shoulder in the fashion he just had.

"Just call me Beep." He stuck out his hand, which both reluctantly shook. "I've got the candy concession here tonight, gentlemen."

"Christ," muttered Pete.

"I've got X. I've got Y. I've got some shit they use to get elephants in the mating mood. Pachyderm Viagra. For you old timers, I still have blow and hash. All reasonably priced to sell. I've even got some placebos, if you only want to be conspicuous."

"Placebos? Wow! I haven't done those in ages!" enthused Johnny.

"Hey, you'd be surprised how many people just want to look like they're doing something, act silly for a while, and go home, knowing there's no price to pay the next day."

At times like this, Pete wished he still had his policeman's shield. He would've liked nothing more than to pull the rubber nose back and let the elastic do its thing when he let go. Without the badge, though, it would only be an invitation to a mauling from the bouncers. Beep was surely kicking back some profits to the club in exchange for the exclusive rights to sell his wares on the premises.

"I think we'll pass, thanks," he said darkly. Beep waved and made his way toward another group gathered at what would have been the new accounts desk.

"I wish sometimes I could be in some sort of vigilante movie. I'd force every one of those scum bags to O.D. on something nasty, or, better yet, watch their loved ones go through it."

"I know. I know. C'mon, don't let that moron ruin your evening. Let's get another drink and talk about something more pleasant. So, how are the Rangers doing? Oops," said Johnny, needling Pete about his favorite hockey team's position, mired near the bottom of its division.

"I don't think I really need another drink, bud. Thanks for the offer, but I'm going to go home and crash. This place is a little sterile for my tastes, though it's kind of an interesting idea. They should turn other stuff into bars instead of banks, though. I mean, the Limelight's pretty cool," he said, speaking of the legendary Manhattan club that had been converted from a church. "I'd rather see maybe a butcher's shop, a zoo or a library or something. I don't know. Anyway, it's been a long day. You gonna stick around here?"

"Yeah. I don't have much to do tomorrow. The bathing suit people were happy with what we put together for them. My boss, therefore, is happy with me, and wants to put me on some other projects, though he doesn't quite know what yet. All I'm going to do tomorrow is drink lots of coffee and screw around on the internet."

"Alright, Styx, take it easy, my friend. Don't take any wooden placebos," Pete said, giving his friend a brief hug before strolling towards the revolving doors.

"Hey, man!" called Johnny, and Pete turned around, "remember one thing, guy." Pete inclined his head and his friend looked at him seriously. "You can pick your friends, and you can pick your nose. But you can't pick your friend's nose."

Pete waved a dismissive hand on his way through the doors and hailed himself a cab.

Johnny sighed and went to the teller's window for one last drink. To make it count, he ordered a double and gave the bartender a nice tip. He prowled around for a while, looking for a stray female to catch his eye. Seeing nothing that struck his fancy, he went to the back, in search of the men's room. He found it, next to a stairway. After putting some of the screwdrivers back into a porcelain toolbox, he went down a staircase he had noticed other patrons descending.

It was the lower level of the bank, formerly housing administrative offices along with the safety deposit vault. Johnny was intrigued. With his modest upbringing, he had never seen the inside of a bank vault, aside from movies and television shows. He marveled at the thickness of the open steel vault door and imagined himself as a bank robber, gauging where to place the dynamite, or sensitizing his fingertips with a nail file in order to figure out the combination.

The interior of the vault had been converted into a lounge, low sofas set in the corners. The lighting was even more subdued, the music somewhat muffled, and Johnny liked the feel. The rows of safety deposit boxes seemed endless and he wondered if anyone had forgotten anything inside any of them. He stopped at one row and was idly trying to pry one of the boxes open when a low voice caught his attention,

"You could go to jail for that. An attractive fellow like yourself would make lots of new friends in jail."

Johnny turned around. At the end of the row, he caught sight of the silhouette of a tall, slender woman, but couldn't distinguish her features in the shadows. "A guy can never have enough friends, but I prefer to keep mine in front of me, if you get my gist."

"I think I do," the response was followed by a soft laugh. "What's your name, handsome fellow?"

"John." Her silhouette looked sensuous and he wished she would step out of the shadows so he could get a better look at her.

"John, as in John Doe? Or John as in John Deere?" She took a step closer, but he still couldn't make her face out, though a glint of light glanced off her hair, revealing a deep copper color. She started singing, "Doe, a deer, a female deer. Ray, a drop of golden sun. Me, a name I call myself. Fa, a long, long way to run. Actually, me isn't my real name. It's Alice."

With that she stepped out of the shadow and into the light. Johnny's eyes widened. Her makeup had changed somewhat. The diamond pattern she had worn during the Rasta's interrogation had been replaced with tears, red-tinged with blue and green centers. They trailed down the outer edges of her face, outlining the contours of her cheekbones, the left one stopping at the corner of her mouth. She wore a long sleeved, flowing blue dress that clung to the outlines of her slender figure.

"Do you feel like running, John?" she said, gazing into his eyes.

Johnny, in fact, felt somewhat frozen, like a white rabbit remaining motionless in the snow, praying that the wolf a short distance away wouldn't catch his scent. After a second, he regained his equilibrium and laughed. He beamed the "bring it on home" smile, which worked with more than a fair amount of regularity on women.

"Only if it means I'm racing you back to your place."

"Oh dear, John, you're a most forward person! Are you a gentleman?"

"Forgive me. I left my manners in a glass about a half hour ago."

"I'm not looking for a gentle man tonight," she replied.

"It's O.K. I have no idea where that glass went, anyway. I'm sure it's already in the dishwasher."

She took another two steps closer.

"Are you sad?" Johnny asked, gazing at her with an expression that he was certain looked longing. "I'd love to kiss those tears away."

She threw her head back and laughed, not very kindly. Johnny didn't know if he liked her too much, but man, there was definitely something about her. A night with her would surely be interestingly spent. He was about to find out, the hard way.

"That's not a request I get very often," she said.

"I find that hard to believe."

"O.K, dear John, then why don't you choose one, and only one? Be careful of your choice, though. This could be the most important decision you'll ever make," she said, challenging him with her eyes.

"I guess that eeny-meeny-miney-mo would be kind of inappropriate, then." He leaned over and kissed the second blue tear coming down from the right eye. When he lifted his head, he was surprised to see that the tear was no longer on her face. He touched his lips, felt a cool dampness and then looked up at her. Fire seemed to dance in her hair. She looked even stranger with the gap in her makeup.

"Good choice, John, my doe."

"What?"

The word echoed in his head once, twice, and then began ping ponging back and forth between his ears like some outrageous stereo effect.

"We're going to walk out of here now and go back to my place, and there won't be any need to race. Oh, I rhymed," she laughed and clapped her hands. "Do you like rhymes, John?"

"Yes," he replied woodenly. If she told him to rip off one of his own ears and eat it right then, he would have had no choice but to comply.

"I wish sometimes it would leave them with a little more spirit," she sighed, "still, it could've been a lot worse for you. If you'd tried the green tear just above the one you kissed, all your blood and urine would have mixed together in your veins by now, and that, from what I've seen, is not a pleasant experience. But don't you worry, John Doe, all I'm going to do is turn you into John Buck, or maybe John Steed, tonight. You're going to give 'til it hurts, and then quite a bit more. Put down the drink and follow me."

Johnny let the glass drop from his hand and it shattered on the tile floor. Alice passed the rows of safety deposit boxes and up the stairs, Johnny in tow. Casually they walked toward the front door, Alice murmuring to him softly and ignoring his vacant stare. Beep did a double take when he saw them approach the revolving door. He nudged the portly, bearded man next to him.

"Hey, Sal, I think I've seen that bitch with Bender's guy, Ronno! Can't be too many people running around looking like that."

The man with the beard lowered his sunglasses and looked at the couple departing.

"The cop got me some more info. Bender's crew is gonna be at a funeral tomorrow. Maybe we can work out some sort of package deal for them," he said, traces of Sicily evident in his voice.

He motioned to another man dressed in urban cowboy chic who was lounging in the corner. The cowboy looked up as the bearded man gave him a quick series of hand gestures meaning: "Follow, but don't interfere". He quickly stepped out of the club and jumped into a limousine waiting outside, parked directly in back of the taxi that Alice and Johnny had just entered. Both cars pulled out into the night.

10

Late Friday night Pete woke up from a dream in which he found himself in the shower of Astrid's hotel room. The bathroom was heavily steamed in and the shower door dimly outlined in the haze. Subconsciously, he knew Astrid would soon be entering and parting the mist with her lithe naked body. He felt very aroused with anticipation, but nothing happened. The steam grew thicker and thicker. He began to have trouble breathing and after a while the very sound of the water felt tinny, artificial and oppressive. He reached through the scalding water and pushed in the metal faucet, stopping the flow. The puddle on the floor of the shower was sluicing in a small vortex on its way down the drain when he heard the sound of a small glass container shattering on the tile.

"Astrid? Are you O.K., babe?" he called out.

No reply came from the shroud of steam. Pete wiped the water from his eyes and opened the shower door. The steam swirled around the motion of the door, but refused to show anything. He stepped out tentatively with his left foot. The Cheap Trick song he'd been humming in the shower that existed in the waking world came back to mind and he finally remembered the title: "I Want You to Want Me".

He took another step and his right foot landed on a shard of glass. He gritted his teeth, but felt no immediate pain. He lifted his foot and looked at it in what seemed like stop motion photography, the way a strobe light seems to halt action. He finally was able to grip his heel and extract half of a small glass vial from it. A few drops of blood welled and a trickle ran toward his outer ankle before giving in to gravity and daubing the white tile on the floor. He cursed silently, but was enthralled by the crimson pattern spreading out before him. Only a few drops actually hit the floor, but they extended to the grout between the tiles and eventually outlined a path, five tiles wide, toward the far side of the bathroom. The mist cleared faintly over this path and a duller crimson shape emerged on the ground a few feet ahead of him. He hopped gingerly on his left foot down the red tiled road.

"Toto, we're not in Soho anymore," he commented to no one in particular, though he was in no position to click his heels.

Drawing closer to the shape, he recognized the pair of red leather boots Dale Patterson was wearing the night he had checked out of the Needle Arms hotel. He also recognized the long, slender legs leading up from the boots. He stood on one leg, rooted, as the steam lifted to reveal, not the wicked witch of the west under a house, but Angeline sprawled on top of the toilet seat. She was wearing the white lace gown he had last seen her in, and her head lolled back from her shoulders. A syringe was buried in her right arm, the plunger depressed. He gasped and took a step toward her, the pain in his heel suddenly shooting up his leg. Just as he reached out to touch her face, her head snapped forward. He recoiled in horror as her almond shaped eyes opened to reveal glowing, molten red pupils. She smiled sweetly before a cruel expression overtook her face. Her mouth worked, opening and closing twice before she finally turned toward him and shouted,

"It's a power play goal!"

Pete's eyes flew open and he jolted awake with a start, sitting abruptly upright on his couch. This caused the half eaten slice of pizza to fall from its resting place, a paper plate on his lap, onto the floor, liberally scattering all ingredients not fastened to the thick crust by the now epoxy-like cheese. He looked dejectedly at the fallen slice, which had, of course, landed face down, and then back up at the late night ESPN hockey game on TV.

There he saw what appeared to be a variety of Mighty Duck, the kind from Anaheim, though, for just a moment, he could have sworn they were Delaware sparrows, mobbing each other in front of a dejected looking goalie. It's hard to get a good read on a goalie's emotions beneath the mask and all that equipment. Still, body language says a lot, and Pete's initial impression was reinforced when the goalie swung his stick and smashed it against the crossbar of his goal, nearly beheading a linesman who had stooped to retrieve the puck from the net. The incensed linesman was agitatedly gesticulating at the goalie when Pete found the television's remote control in a crack between the cushions of his couch and shut it off.

"Christ, what time is it?" he muttered and craned his head to look at the clock on the microwave in the kitchen. The blue LED flashed 1:48 A.M. He sighed heavily and reached down to rescue the fallen slice of pizza. The throw rug in front of his couch initially offered resistance but eventually let go of its prize. Pete shuffled to his kitchen and deposited the remnant into an already overflowing plastic trash bag. He opened the refrigerator door and, after his sight adjusted to the sudden light, selected a long necked bottle of beer from a six-pack crouched alone on the bottom shelf.

Pete's refrigerator held the standard contents of the 'single guy living alone' fridge. The obligatory leftover rice from a Chinese restaurant delivery and a wax paper wrapper containing some sort of mystery meat graced the top shelf. He would have had some sour milk in the door rack, but didn't put milk in his coffee. Scattered plastic wrapped slices of processed American cheese and a pair of petrified English muffins dominated the middle shelf.

Pete wasn't sure what the muffins were so scared of, perhaps the mystery meat, but he wasn't taking any chances. He tossed them on his kitchen counter. One landed with a crack and broke in half. The other one alit more with a heavy thud. He reached into a drawer underneath the sink for a spatula. He twisted open the beer bottle, took a swallow and proceeded to stick handle the muffin with the spatula one-handed around a coffee mug and past some silverware to the far edge of the counter. The kitchen window was open about five inches. He pulled back the spatula and cried out,

"Leetch is open at the point. He takes the pass from Gretzky and shoots!" He swung the spatula hard, recreating a hockey slap shot. The muffin survived the impact with the spatula, but not with the window frame. It broke into a thousand crumbs, some landing on the sill, most on the floor. He found a broom in a closet and swept up the mess.

Hydration giving him energy, Pete slipped into cleaning mode, sweeping through the rest of his apartment. He pondered whether to tackle some of the electronic repair jobs piled up on the living room table and decided to wax the floors instead. An hour later, he slumped back on the couch, the floors gleaming and the fourth beer almost halfway done.

He thought how he used to infuriate and confuse Rose, his ex-wife, by getting up in the middle of the night to perform household chores. Some people just work on different internal clocks, he used to tell her. It wasn't that he was particularly into cleanliness, but Pete found it was, like walking, a way of getting into a rhythm where his mind could free itself and sort things out. Drummers have a thing about rhythm, and find it in the strangest places. Doing the laundry at four o'clock in the morning was particularly liberating, something about the noise of the dryer rotating the clothes.

Rose was a solid, devoted woman, but without many diverse interests of her own. She had placed him in the center of her universe, but once he'd gotten embroiled deeper and deeper in undercover police work, there were huge sections of his life he couldn't, and, after a while, wouldn't want to share with her. He didn't want to pollute her psyche with the sordid details. And, as in physics, if the sun doesn't hold the planets in its gravitational field, they start to drift.

Rose's friends had always thought that Pete was the perfect husband, strong and sweet, providing for her, always doing house chores, but they didn't know what was building up inside him and that he found it impossible to confide in his wife. It wasn't just her, either. He had no place to unburden himself. He'd tried tentatively with Johnny first, then a police psychiatrist, but although both tried to understand, they couldn't see inside him. His silences became louder than his words. Both suggested he take some time off, maybe even look into a different line of police work, but Pete was on a mission he wasn't about to let go of. The simple things that had once attracted Pete and Rose to each other no longer held the same meaning, the same importance. After a few months of heavy undercover work, when he would only show up for a few odd hours at a time, a shower and a quick meal, perhaps a stab at lovemaking, they arrived at the mutual conclusion that they had become loving strangers to each other.

Though there was still a great deal of respect and affection, they had grown apart to the point where it wasn't possible to maintain a real marriage. Since there were no children, the ties that bind weren't quite as hard to cut. Pete blamed himself entirely for the eventual divorce, knowing it was the changes he had undergone that had led to the break up. Rose blamed herself entirely for the divorce, thinking her inability to stand by her man was the cause of their ultimate separation.

All in all, it was as amicable a divorce as one could hope for. They agreed to go their separate ways, licking their wounds, and try to move on as best they could. Time doesn't really heal, it just eventually dulls the pain, and one day you wake up and something else than a state of despair urges you on to better things.

It was getting close to four o'clock in the morning and Pete was starting to think that it might be nice to hear Rose's voice. It had been a long while and he just wanted to see how she was doing. Although at first he thought she would be devastated when they had broken up, he had soon revised his thinking and rationalized that she was the strong one in the relationship and would get over him fast enough.

In truth, her fragile self-confidence was completely shattered, and she spent her frequent sleepless nights questioning whether there had been something, anything, she could have done to rescue her marriage. She endlessly replayed conversations, especially the ones close to the end, which had occurred when his grip on reality became tenuous and it looked like nothing could stop the downward momentum.

Compounding the problem was that Rose's father worked in the same precinct as Pete. In fact, Charlie had introduced the two to each other at one of his family barbeques. Charlie, knowing the two were having problems, tried to be the good in-law and not interfere, but it was plain that Pete was going down the tubes professionally at the same time as personally. Pete would sporadically show up at the precinct, looking strung out and mangy, and intermittently deliver reports of varying coherence. Word got around the department rapidly. Desperate, Charlie sat him down and read Pete the riot act. Through the haze, Pete understood he was losing himself and decided to try and rectify the situation in one fell swoop. It didn't work and almost literally blew up in his face.

He stared at the phone, wishing there was someone he could talk to, and came to the conclusion that to call Rose right now, at this time of the morning, wasn't the right thing to do. Suddenly, another idea dawned on him, and he ran to the bedroom to rummage through his jacket pockets. He returned to the living room with a crumpled piece of paper.

"It's got to be, what, ten o'clock in Sweden," he mumbled, doing some quick math.

He dialed the number Astrid had given him and waited a few seconds for the different sounding ring of a European telephone.

"God morgen," answered a deep male voice. Pete almost dropped the phone. He hadn't considered for an instant that she would be involved, but who was he kidding? A
beautiful, intelligent woman like Astrid would have guys all
over her and it was insane to think she wouldn't have some-
body in her life. He'd noticed right away she wasn't wearing
a ring, but that didn't mean she wasn't spoken for.

"Uh, I think I might have the wrong number here," he
stammered, "is Astrid there?"

"Astrid? Nej inne," was the response. Pete's command
of the Swedish language was nonexistent and he had no idea
what had been said or what to say. Feeling like an idiot, he
said,

"I guess it must be a wrong number, then. Sorry about
that." and quickly hung up the phone. He hit himself in the
forehead with his palm.

"Oh boy. Way to go, idiot," he sighed and finished off
the last of the beer in one long swig. The late hour and all
the cleaning caught up with him all of a sudden, and his only
desire was to go to sleep. Pete went into the bedroom and got
undressed, throwing his clothes into the open closet serving
as his laundry bin.

He awoke seven hours later, daylight streaming
through the dusty blinds of his window. Last night's events
were mercifully cloudy in his mind, though he remembered
the timbre of the man's voice who answered the phone number Astrid had given him.

He set the coffee machine on and stepped into his shower, cursing it loudly as a wide variety of water temperatures assaulted his skin. He wondered why the superintendent of his building had ever bothered putting an "H" and a "C" on the two shower knobs, as neither had anything remotely to do with the temperature of the water.

It was a warm day so he dressed in jeans and a loose fitting dark green shirt. He threw on a beat-up baseball cap and left his apartment to go to the subway station. After changing lines twice, he exited the train on an elevated platform in Queens and walked the remaining five blocks to Officer Mike Tippins's two-family house. Mike lived on the bottom floor with his wife and two young sons, ages five and two. Pete pushed through the low gate next to the garage and stepped into a small, fenced in back yard. A can of beer hurtled toward him. He caught it two and a half inches in front of his face and popped the top in one motion.

"Good to see you ain't lost your reflexes. The eyes are the usually the first thing to go," said Mike Tippins with a crooked grin. He was wearing a pair of paint stained cutoff jeans, a tank top, a chef's hat, and an apron embroidered with the words, "Kiss the Butcher".

"Then how do you explain what happened to your brain and your dick?" replied Pete.

"Hey, his dick still works, at least every other weekend. The brain, well, we don't know if it ever worked in the first place. I should've maybe checked for a warranty, but it was too late by then," said a voice from behind him.

"Oh, hi Eileen. Didn't see you there," Pete turned with a smile and saw Mike's wife emerge from a screen door at the side of the house, carrying a heaping platter of hamburger patties. "Need a hand with anything?" he asked.

"No thanks, Pete. Give me a sec and I'll give you a hug." She put the platter down on a picnic table in the yard, next to the grill, came over and threw her arms around him. She was an attractive, petite brunette with warm eyes and a generous mouth that made her look like she was always about to smile, which she did frequently. "How are you?" she asked, pulling away and looking at him. "Are you taking care of yourself? Better yet, is someone taking care of you?" Pete shook his head. "No? You know, my sister Cathy'll be here in a couple of hours."

"Good Lord, woman, at least get them drunk before you unleash your sister on them," said Mike. He came over and threw a muscular arm around Pete's shoulders. "We're going to slip roofies to all the eligible guys here and then let Cathy take her choice of which one she wants to feed on first. It's relatively painless, after the initial sting. She just wraps you up in her web and slowly digests you."

"How dare you talk about my sister that way?" said Eileen and punched Mike in the chest. She turned back to Pete. "She really is a wonderful girl."

"I'm sure she's real nice, Eileen. If she's half the woman you are, she's already too good for me."

"Oh, you silver tongue," she gushed, "why don't you teach my husband to talk romantically to me like that?"

"He tried a couple of times, hun," said Mike, "but it got a little intense and we had to break it off."

Pete winced. "I thought we'd agreed never to tell her about that." Eileen glared at the two men. "Hey, is anyone else coming to this barbeque or are all these burgers for me?

I hate to be the first one to show up. I tried to be fashionably late, but I guess it didn't work."

"We can be reasonably sure Eileen's sister'll be stopping by," answered Mike, casting a sidelong glance at his wife, "the rest of the guys should be here soon. It'll be like old times, Petey. Hey, look who's here! My big guys!" His sons sidled up to their father and stood shyly behind his legs. "Jeez, Pete, last time you saw Sean, he must've still been in a stroller. And Mikey was just a gleam in his daddy's eye. Say 'Hi' to Pete, fellas." Mike tried ushering the boys out from behind his legs, but they were having no part of it, though the younger one, a red headed tyke, gave Pete a shy smile.

"Mike, these kids are way too good looking for you to be their father." Pete crouched down to say hello to the youngsters.

"I thought we'd agreed never to tell him," said Eileen to Pete with a big grin, as her husband shot her a look. "You've met Sean already. The little guy is Mike junior. You're looking at the Mets' double-play combination in the year 2020."

"At least we won't have to buy season tickets anymore," said Mike. "Those goddamn things cost an arm and a leg."

"Hey, Mikey, you didn't have that addition to the house last time I was here, did you?" asked Pete, pointing to the L-shaped extension of the house that jutted into the yard. "And this deck looks great, too. You hit the lottery, or what?"

"Got to have some room for a growing family, my friend. I redid the basement, too, built up the workshop. Want to check it out?"

"Oooh, you're going to get a guided tour of the dungeon, you lucky man," said Eileen.

"Yeah, I'm gonna show him the vat of boiling wax that I'm preparing for you, hun. You'll always keep your looks this way."

"Pete, unless it's my sister, don't get married again. It has a way of ruining men," replied Eileen with a giggle.

The men pushed through the screen door and turned left, away from the kitchen and descended the flight of stairs into a well-lit low-ceilinged basement. They passed through a storage room into Mike's workshop, a long rectangular room whose far wall was entirely covered with a mounted peg board, a vast array of tools hanging from hooks.

"Man, this place brings back some memories," said Pete. "You've really added a lot of stuff. You still designing gadgets? Those retractable sleeve harnesses you made for me saved my ass in a big way once."

"Not as much now that I'm out of vice and back in uniform, but I still tinker around."

"What's that on the work bench?" Pete pointed at an odd looking object hanging from a table vice. Two leather shoulder straps held a fat, snub-nosed shotgun barrel. The trigger to the device was situated on the side of a steel ring that circled the barrel. "It looks like something you could attach a strap-on dildo onto. You must be the life of the precinct parties."

Mike snorted with laughter. "I never thought of that. Not a bad idea at all. Shit, Petey, I've missed you. You are the sickest bastard I've ever known."

"I'll take that as a compliment, coming from you."

"You should. Anyway, it's something I've been putting together for a pal who's working undercover target detail.

This is gonna give some mugger one hell of a surprise during a hold-up."

Eileen's voice wafted down to the basement. "Mike, I think the charcoal is about ready."

"Be right up, hun."

They remounted the stairs back to the yard. Mike inspected the barbeque.

"You wanna be the guinea pig, Petey?"

"It's the least I could do."

Mike threw one of the patties on the grill. It fell through a gap in the grill and landed on the charcoal. He grinned and fished it out with a fork. Mike nonchalantly flipped it backwards over his shoulder and the high wooden fence into an adjacent yard where the sound of an overjoyed dog devouring a treat soon emitted. Mike took another patty from the pile and had more success with his next toss. After a few minutes, he flipped it over and put a slice of American cheese on it. Soon it was piled high with raw onion, mushrooms and ketchup on a bun and making its way toward Pete's awaiting mouth. Mike turned on a portable radio to a rock station.

"Whaddaya think?" asked Mike, after watching Pete inhale the burger.

"It sucked. Make me a better one."

"Everyone's a critic," Mike sighed. This time he tossed a patty up in the air and snapped his head forward like a soccer player, heading the meat on to the grill. A small grease stain was visible on his chef's hat where he had made contact with the patty. "A little Irish grease always tenderizes the meat just right. I even popped a big zit on my forehead this morning just for your dining pleasure. I'd been saving it for a special occasion."

"Michael Tippins, you're an ill man," said Eileen with a shudder.

"I may be illin', but I sure be chillin'." He reached into a large garbage can filled with equal parts ice, water, cans of beer and soft drinks. He fished out a beer. "All this cooking makes for a thirsty man. And speaking of thirsty men..."

Through the gate strolled officers Impeliterri and Weaver with their wives. Mike took beef and beer orders while Eileen returned to the house to bring out the rest of the food: salad, hot dogs, chicken and foil-wrapped potatoes, which, except for the salad, all found their way on the barbecue. Mike demonstrated all the ways food could be placed on a grill: the burger behind the back toss, the chicken breast spin toss, the roll the potato off the biceps launch toss. The guests, now numbering an even dozen, egged him on to more and more elaborate methods, but Eileen cut him short before he climbed on the roof of the house to lower hot dogs onto the grill using a clothesline.

Eileen's sister showed up and turned out to be very nice, despite being painfully shy. Food and beer were copiously consumed and the group was highly entertained by Weaver's hilarious impersonations of Charlie Grimson, who'd been invited, but couldn't attend. Weaver was such a gifted impressionist that even the people who had never met Charlie were in stitches. During a rare lull in the conversation, an aggressive, eerie sounding song playing on the radio faded out.

"Yeah, there's the new one climbing the charts, up to the big number three in just one week!" said the DJ. "Dale Patterson, what a tragedy! What a future! What a song! That's 'You Never Know', the first single from this disc. Stay tuned to the Dale Patterson retrospective tonight at ten o'clock."

"A Dale Patterson retrospective? Oh, come on," said Pete. "How the hell do you do a retrospective on a guy who put out one record two weeks ago? I don't believe this!"

The non-law enforcement guests looked strangely at Pete, thinking him to be insensitive.

"Ah, Pete, don't let it get to you. Forget about it," said Impeliterri. "Anything to make a buck, that's how it goes." He patted him on the shoulder, opened a beer and took a sip. "Oh shit, Pete I didn't tell you! You remember Tex Rothstein, don't ya? You musta busted him three times. They found him this morning in a lot in Brooklyn, his throat cut wide and all this weird makeup on him."

"Tex? Damn. He wasn't too bad a guy, for a crook. Funny as hell. He'd have this shtick he'd run past me, while he was in the back seat of the patrol car. I always told him he'd make more as a stand-up comic. He told me 'If I was a stand-up guy, I wouldn't be doing what I'm doing now.'" Pete laughed at the memory. "He was this Jewish guy from the Bronx who always liked to dress like he was working on a ranch. He once told me he'd seen the movie *Urban Cowboy* thirty-eight times. I tried to get him to rat and turn evidence each time, but he never would. I guess he knew he'd be out of jail quick each time."

"Word was he was working for Cangelosi's crew, a real nasty bunch. Some bad ass dudes," added Weaver.

"What's this about the makeup, Vinnie? I thought Rothstein was straight," Pete asked.

"I don't know. I wasn't there. I heard the report coming in before I left. Maybe he had a side job as a rodeo clown," replied Impeliterri. Weaver let out a loud guffaw.

"Speaking of clowns, did you guys ever figure out who's dealing the bag that Patterson was carrying when he died?"

"Not yet, but that was some high octane cocktail he spiked. That crap tested close to eighty-five percent. It's like he was asking for an overdose."

"I guess you never can tell about some people," said Pete.

"Tell me something I don't know. I mean, look at Tippins," Weaver motioned toward Mike, who was trying to balance a hot dog on the tip of his nose. "Is this the kind of person the American public wants defending it against the scum of the earth?"

"That's a scary thought. Can't you guys get him a desk job?"

"We're trying to get him transferred to the firing range. Maybe as a target changer or something."

"Not a bad idea, John," said Impelliteri to Weaver. "I was thinking he'd be good for vice squad decoy duty. Maybe try to infiltrate one of those transvestite prostitution rings."

The three of them, picturing Tippins's stout body and mug in drag, exploded into laughter and clinked their beer cans together. Mike saw the commotion, came over and said,

"Hey, there'll be none of that here. If you all want to have a good time, go somewhere else. I knew I never should have invited any of you. And Petey, I'll tell you, you disappoint me the most out of all of youse. I thought your time away from this kind of element would have taught you some maturity."

"I'm sorry, Mike. I don't know what came over us. We were trying to plan your future career moves. You know, buddy, we only have your best interests at heart," said Pete in a sincere tone.

"I don't know, guys. I don't think they make high heel pumps in sizes that big." Impelliteri said, regarding Mike's bare legs.

"What the hell are you guys talking about?" growled Tippins as the others doubled over in laughter.

"Uh, nothing, man," said Weaver. Sniffing the air, he added. "Hey, I think the chicken's starting to burn. You ought to check it out. Get me another beer, too, while you're there. Thanks."

Mike regarded them suspiciously and returned to his grilling duties. In another hour, all the guests were reclining in lawn chairs, stuffed to the gills and lethargic from the beer. The women began cleaning up while the men gathered to discuss the fortunes of New York's two football teams.

Shortly before six o'clock Pete got to his feet and declared he had to go to the rehearsal studio. He'd promised Greg the night off and wanted to catch up on some paperwork. After many hugs and promises to get together in the near future, he left. At the gate, Eileen rushed to him with a bulging plastic bag containing grilled chicken and salad, insisting he take it. Pete thought that after a couple of weeks in his fridge, it might be able to take on the mystery meat for supremacy of the domain, but he thanked Eileen and took the bag.

On the subway home, he saw a bedraggled, barefoot homeless woman curled up on the end of a row of seats and placed the bag in front of her. She initially cowered and shrank back upon his approach, but after he left to return to his seat, she furrowed into the bag and came out with a drumstick. She glanced at Pete for a moment and smiled before ravenously eating it. The smile transformed her face and he realized that under different circumstances, she might have been considered an attractive lady, but the hand life had dealt her had long since etched itself into an expression of pain and despair.

He arrived an hour later at the studio. It looked to be a slow evening for a Saturday night, only five bands booked into the three rooms, the longest session being two hours. He realized he'd be able to get out of there relatively early. He finished some odd jobs and paperwork. One of the bands complained about not having enough room in the studio to work on their choreographed dance steps. Pete promised to knock out a wall by the time they returned. At 11:30, all the rooms were clean and he locked up.

Upon arriving at home, he found his answering machine blinking. The first message was from a dazed sounding Johnny.

"Hey, guy. I guess you must be at the studio. I feel like shit warmed over, man. Did I have that much to drink with you on Thursday? I don't even remember going home. Gimme a buzz whenever you get back, if it's before midnight. Later."

Pete chuckled and waited for the next message.

"Hi, Peter. It's Astrid. I miss you already. Did you try calling earlier today? My father said some strange man called, asking for me in English. Well, even if it wasn't you, I hope you haven't forgotten me already. By the way, I'm pregnant. Just kidding," she giggled. "In any case, call me when you can. I miss you so much. Bye."

Pete's smile threatened to tear his face in half. He pumped his fist three times into the air and let out a whoop. He did a Chuck Berry style duck walk across the living room into the kitchen, reached into the fridge and pulled out a beer, wondering for a second if the cheese hadn't been on another row when he'd last looked. He decided to end the mystery meat's ugly reign of terror and threw it emphatically into the trash. Back into the living room, he plopped down on the couch, taking the phone with him. Pete wanted to share the good news with someone and it was still a few minutes before the witching hour. He was singing Iron Maiden's song "Two Minutes To Midnight" as he dialed Johnny's number.

"Hello," came a muffled voice.

"I'd like to speak with Dick Holden, please," said Pete, relishing the moment.

"Oh, aren't we the amusing one this evening,"

"I've always wanted to do that. Do I sound as stupid as you do?"

"You've mastered the nuances quickly. What's up?" said Johnny.

"I'm returning your call, dummy. But, listen, I just got a message on my answering machine from Astrid."

"Hey, great. She wanted to tell you that's she's got crabs?"

"Very funny, Styx," Pete replied and recounted the previous night's phone call.

"Yeah, I can see how you'd be relieved. You talk to Angeline since the other day?"

"Nah. I don't really know what to say to her right now. So what's up with you? You sound like hell."

"Jeez, man, I don't know. I guess I'm hung over like a rat, but it's weird. Was I with anyone when you left?" Johnny sounded perplexed.

"No. You said you were going to hang out for a while, but you weren't with anyone when I split. You were feeling no pain, I'm sure, but were in reasonable condition. Maybe you took too many placebos from that guy and he had his way with you."

"Well, someone sure did."

"What do you mean?" asked Pete.

"I don't know. It feels like I was in a fight or something. My muscles ache and I've got all these small cuts and bruises over my body. I don't remember a goddamned thing, though."

"Maybe you fell down some stairs," Pete suggested.

"Yeah, maybe. But there's something weird, too. You promise not to laugh?"

"I promise to laugh like a hyena if it's good enough."

"I guess it figures. It's funny, but I feel like I balled my brains out. You know the feeling? That nice kind of soreness?"

"I know it well, my friend. It's a not so distant memory."

"The thing is, I have no idea what happened or who I was with, if anybody. It's a freaky feeling, like something out of a movie. You know where the guy wakes up in a strange hotel room with a dead woman he doesn't know next to him, with no idea how he got there?"

"You're into dead women now?"

"No. No. No," Johnny said exasperatedly.

"You know, I used to be into necrophilia, but I got the cold shoulder and she split on me."

"You're having a great time with this, aren't you?"

"I feel your pain," said Pete, doing a bad Bill Clinton imitation. "Seriously, though, are your hands banged up, bloody knuckles? Maybe you got into a fight and suffered a concussion.

"Guy, I'm not bullshitting you," said Johnny quietly, "but it looks like I have rope burns of some sort on my wrists and ankles."

"I suppose that rules out alien abduction. They usually use force fields to keep their subjects subdued while they perform their experiments. I saw it on *The X-Files* a while ago." Pete paused. "This may sound strange, but it's a legit question. You didn't stagger into some S & M club or bar on your way home, did you?"

"Christ, I hope not. Still, it would account for some of this. God, that would be totally fucked up. But I tell you, I wasn't hammered. You saw me. For that to happen, I'd have to be completely incoherent and not know what was going on. I know it sounds funny to you, but this is creeping me out."

"Yeah, I remember getting you home a couple of times when you were totally out of it. Remember your twenty-first birthday party?" Pete asked with a laugh.

"Not too much of it, I have to admit," Johnny laughed too. "I know we had a hell of a time for a while. Man, remember the raunchy strip club and the Tuesday Two-Dollar Tit Special they had going back then?"

"I also remember some drunken idiot getting up on the strippers' runway and running headfirst into the pole they were swinging around."

"Oh? Those details seem to escape me," Johnny said innocently.

"Do you remember the bouncers and my desperate pleas that they not pound you to a bloody pulp? I should've let them. They might've knocked some sense into you."

"Did I ever thank you?"

"I believe you promised everlasting servitude. Now iron my shirts, bitch, and not so much starch this time," Pete ordered.

"I think the power has gone to your head, not that there's much to block it from going straight to the top of your skull. And speaking of which, I'm going to take some more aspirin and try to get some sleep. My head is killing me."

"Alright, guy. Sweet dreams. I just hope your phone number and address aren't written on the bathroom wall of whatever S & M club you wound up in. Mistress Roxanne might be paying you a visit when you least expect it, and she won't be so kind this time."

"Thanks, buddy, I appreciate the sentiment," said Johnny. "Let's get together next week. I hope to be feeling a little more human by then."

"Later."

"Later."

Pete hung up and snickered at the idea of Johnny going home one night and finding a leather clad dominatrix waiting for him at his doorstep, slapping a riding crop into her gloved fist. He debated whether to read or watch some television, but decided to go to sleep instead. He drifted off immediately once his head hit the pillow.

11

"He's a cockroach! A goddamned cock-a-roach. I can't wait to get my heel on him!" roared Frank Bender as he flung a heavy glass tumbler against the wall. It shattered and left an indentation in the dark oak paneling. Anger enabled the working class Brooklyn accent that he'd tried to leave behind on his uphill climb into society to creep back into his voice. He took another glass and filled it with mineral water and ice from the bar. He promptly downed it and paced the room, glaring at Alice, who was sitting calmly in an overstuffed armchair, her legs crossed. She looked pensively at the bits of glass scattered on the parquet floor, which, a couple of days before, had been covered with a drop cloth during the interrogation of the recently deceased Lionel Logan.

"They look like frozen tears, don't you think?" she asked dreamily.

"Frozen tears?" He could barely contain himself. "Frozen tears? This is no time for symbolism, miss. Maybe you could go and help Ronno take care of Bunny."

"Bunny'll be fine, I'm sure. It's only a flesh wound, though it looks messy. The bullet went right through him. Ronno's got it under control."

"I can't believe Cangelosi would try something like this at a funeral, for God's sake." He shook his head.

"All in all, I'd say you were lucky the wind was gusting the way it was. From a long distance, it's so important to take wind currents into account." She held a finger out and blew across the top of it, then waved it slowly back and forth as if admonishing a recalcitrant child.

"True, it could have been a lot worse. What disturbs me here is I'm a step behind; I'm reacting instead of initiating. No one in the organization has been able to tell me where that bastard is." He struck his forehead in frustration, and then cracked his knuckles behind his head.

"Perhaps I was a trifle quick with the cowboy fellow who followed me the other night. My blood was up, the thrill of the chase and all that. If I'd taken my time, I'm sure I could've gotten something out of him. You know, at first, I thought he was a mugger. How many people in New York City get mugged by cowboys, do you think?" She laughed softly, before turning towards Bender with a look of steely resolve. "But do you know what I hate most of all about this? That poor gravedigger standing on your left, I'm sure he didn't make it. Half of his head was gone. I can't stand when civilians have to pay the ultimate price in the wars we wage! It's one thing when soldiers die. It's sad, but it comes with the territory. But when the bystanders, the innocent...." she trailed off, buried her face in her hands and sobbed.

Bender, astounded by her rapid mood changes, almost wanted to laugh, but didn't dare to at the moment. After a brief moment, Alice looked up at him, a vacant expression on her face. She reached down to the floor and picked up one of the larger pieces of the shattered tumbler, turning it in her hand, her head cocked to the side. She lifted up her thin sweater. She wasn't wearing a bra. Bender could see a web of crisscrossing scars, some old, some fresher. She cradled her left breast in one hand and sliced it open with the piece of glass. A look of religious ecstasy crossed her face. She sighed and pulled down the sweater, its yellow color staining to a dark orange where she had cut herself.

"Miss?" said Bender.

"Oh, that's much better," Alice replied in a throaty voice, her eyes closed. "Much, much better. Mmmmm." Her eyes opened to slits and she licked her lips. "I would love it right now if you would fuck me hard while I lay on the glass. Would you do that for me now, please? Come on, take me. I know you want to."

Bender was quite happy to see Ronno and Bunny come through the door at that moment. Bunny's left arm was in a makeshift sling and the big man looked haggard, though a defiant glare burned in his eyes. Bender walked in back of the bar, took out a bottle of Sauza Hornitos tequila and filled half of an old fashioned glass. He handed it to Bunny, who downed it in one swallow. He put the glass down and wiped his eyes.

"The bastard must have been set up on the roof of a building across the avenue from the graveyard, couldn't see it with the naked eye." he growled. The pain in his voice made him sound even more bearish than usual.

"I took Richie and Stan up to check out the roofs. The one on top of the deli had some sniper rifle casings and cigarette butts near the ledge. It was a long way, but he had a clean line of fire," said Ronno. "Judging by the casings, they were 308s. You're lucky you still have an arm, buddy. Another inch and it would have shattered the bone."

"I'm only going to need one hand to break that guy's neck when I find him," Bunny glowered.

"This brings me to the main issue here," said Bender, immediately capturing everyone's attention. "We need to find Cangelosi so as to avoid further incidents of this kind. We missed him at the diner and Alice went overboard with Rothstein. Admittedly, she's new to this area and didn't know who he was, so she can be excused. Still, in the future, miss, if someone's tailing you, exercise some restraint."

She nodded, apparently having regained her composure. Ronno noticed the blood stain on her sweater and said, "Shit, did you get hit too?"

"No, Ronno, I'm fine. It's only a scratch. I'll go and disinfect it."

"I could take a look at it, if you like," he replied, a leer forming on his distorted features.

"Some other time, Ronno," she said and left the room.

"Hey boss, do you have any of that Hawaiian weed of yours around?" asked Bunny, a little sheepishly. An extremely proud man, he never liked to ask anyone for anything.

"Sure, Bunny. Your arm must be killing you." Bender reached in his jacket and took out a slim silver cigarette case. He opened it and withdrew a neatly rolled joint that could have easily passed for an unfiltered cigarette. He lit it, took a deep drag, and handed it to the man who towered over him. Bunny drew in some smoke and coughed it out.

"Damn, I'm not used to this stuff anymore." An awkward smile creased the giant's face. "I feel like some kid taking his first hit."

"Maybe you ought to sit down, big man. You've lost a lot of blood and that stuff will go to your head in a hurry," suggested Ronno.

"Sounds like a good idea, Bunny," echoed Bender. "Doctor's orders. Right, Ronno?"

"Right, boss."

Bunny collapsed into the chair Alice had recently vacated, the joint drooping between his lips.

"Ronno, remind me again where we brought Alice in from and who recommended her to the organization?" asked Bender, fixing Ronno with a stare.

"She came very highly recommended from the Molinari family in Denver. She solved a few of their internal problems, if you get my drift."

"Really? It seems to me she carries quite a bit of extra baggage with her." Bender steepled his fingers.

"Yeah, I know. Alice ain't the tightest wrapped chick I've ever met, for sure, but she's deadly effective. She's been around the block, from what I've heard. She was in the army for a while, in one of their 'special service' squads, mostly wet work, and then hired herself out as a merc to some very unpleasant internationals when that didn't pan out."

"Didn't pan out?" Bender asked, spitting the words out. "What the hell do you mean, didn't pan out?" He took a step toward Ronno.

"Hey, boss, I never got the whole story, and sure as shit didn't get it from her," said Ronno, lifting his hands in a placating gesture. "Word is she iced the platoon leader after he ignored her warnings and ordered the shelling of what the army thought was a munitions center. It turned out to be an orphanage. She sliced the guy to ribbons with a pen knife."

Bender winced as he thought of her scarred chest.

"Anyway, the P.R. would've been horrible, if the media had ever gotten a hold of that bit of news," continued Ronno, "so the army let her go with a discharge. She even got a couple of medals and they kept the whole thing as quiet as they could."

"Alright, Ronno, if you say so. I can't say I'm happy about the way she handled Rothstein, though. You know, he used to work for me a long way back. She almost took his head off. There's no need to leave a body in a state like that unless you're leaving a message for someone, and I'm the only one who decides if and when messages are to be given. Ronno, you'll relay this to her?"

"S-sure. I'll tell her," Ronno didn't want to be on the bad side of either Bender or Alice, and wasn't certain how to handle this situation.

"Now!" Bender snapped. Ronno quickly left.

Bender paced back to the bar and poured himself some more ice water. He looked over at Bunny, whose eyes were becoming droopy.

"The Hawaiian helping any?"

"This hits the spot, boss, pure and easy. Thanks." He waved the joint, now halfway finished.

"Be careful with the ash. There's an ashtray right next to you, on the end table." He pointed to Bunny's left.

"Oh, sure. This furniture's most likely worth more than I am," Bunny chuckled, then grimaced when he twisted in order to deposit the joint in the ashtray.

"Bunny, we go back a while, and I've always valued your opinion. What's your take on all this?" Bender leaned his arms on the polished mahogany slab serving as the top of the bar.

"It's not my money, but I think we should put a bunch of it on the street and see what we can catch. There'll be a leak in Cangelosi's operation somewhere, and cash is the best bait. Even if we don't land the big fish that way, we can find someone who could lead us to him." Bunny's eyes no longer drooped, though the lids were pinkish.

"You may be right. It surely wouldn't hurt to try. Take care of it for me, will you?" said Bender. The big man nodded. "Something else that concerns me is what Logan said while under that weird drug of Alice's. I couldn't make it out completely, it was near the end and there was more foam coming out of his mouth than words, but the one word I heard for sure was "inside". There aren't many people who can pinpoint my location at all times. Alice is a logical suspect, but she's also smart enough to know I'd ask Logan how he knew where I'd be. This tends to rule her out, but you never know. If Julius Caesar had paid more attention to what was going on around him, he might have stuck around a bit longer as emperor." Bender paced across the room.

"She absolutely marches to another drummer. I don't claim to understand her but, and this is only going on gut, I wouldn't peg her as a snitch, though I can't explain why. There's a hell of a lot I wouldn't put past her, but I'd be surprised." Bunny shifted in the chair, trying unsuccessfully to find a comfortable position to rest his shoulder.

"I have to be honest, Bunny, she worries me. Taking someone out isn't performance art. What the hell was she doing with the makeup job she put on Rothstein? For God sakes, the guy looked like a court jester on a bad acid trip by the time she was done with him. Make it look like a hit, or a mugging, or something normal. This only attracts attention. Do you have any idea what she had in mind, what she was doing?"

Bunny shook his head. Bender paced and stared at a print of horses jumping over a fence hanging on the near wall.

"Look, whether or not she has other loyalties, I want this to be the last association we have with her. She is a loose cannon. I don't want her to survive this war." He turned towards Bunny. "But don't do it too soon. I think she can still be of use to us, in some way. Make sure she's the last casualty. And do it with honor, she's earned that much. Two to the back of the head; you know the routine by now." He made a pistol of his hand and simulated pulling the trigger twice.

"She should worry you, boss. I've talked to her a couple of times. She does the dirty jobs and knows more about killing than any man I've ever met."

"Any idea what's with the tears?"

"Not really. I've heard a couple of second hand stories about some goings-on in South America, but they're too strange to be true. I know in some prison gangs, guys tattoo a tear near their eyes for each person they've offed. If that was the case with her, she'd be knee-deep in a river of them."

"Another thing worries me, too. Ronno seems to have taken a liking to her. Don't let him get in the way of what you have to do."

"He knows which side of the bread is buttered. Don't worry about him," said Bunny.

But inside he knew how fixated Ronno could become. He remembered an incident involving a barmaid in the Hell's Kitchen section of Manhattan that had degenerated badly one bloody evening, ending with Bunny and Ronno burying the bodies of the woman and her husband in oil drums in New Jersey. Ronno was most in his element when bathing in the blood of his victims; the more sanguine the situation, the better. Bunny didn't shy from violence, enjoyed inflicting it, but emotionally volatile situations made him nervous.

He killed or maimed dispassionately, taking pride in brutal effectiveness. He had never even been arrested for any crime, a tribute to his care in thoroughly cleansing any crime scene he was involved with, never leaving witnesses. Consequently, he'd never been fingerprinted, though his prints had shown up sporadically throughout the years on recovered murder weapons, never to be identified.

In contrast, Ronno seemed to relish his work, as if the life he was taking from someone else was somehow added to his own. All the professional killers that Bunny had known, he reflected, had a kind of signature, from Bunny's professional dispassion, to Ronno's lust, even to Alice's psychosis. He'd even known one guy, during a stint in Philadelphia, a real wacko who called himself Mad Max, who carved an "M" into the sole of each foot of his victims.

Needless to say, Max did not last long in the business. For one thing, he nearly got caught as a result of attempting to remove a thigh high boot from a straying prostitute. The boot wouldn't budge and Max was still trying to get it off as the police car pulled into the alley where he had recently dispatched her. Bunny had seen to Max's dismissal personally. He didn't want the same thing to happen with Ronno, whom he genuinely liked and had worked with for the last three years. But a job, to Bunny, was always a job.

"I know I can count on you," said Bender and crunched loudly on one of the ice cubes dissolving in his glass. The popping sound was like bones cracking.

12

"Sounds good, Angie. You want to take a break and listen to what we've got so far?"

Angeline smiled, waved through the half-inch thick glass window at the portly man with the salt and pepper handlebar mustache and mutton chop sideburns, and took her headphones off. She placed them on a rack that held seven other pairs and stepped out of the vocal booth, running her fingers through her dark locks to get rid of the "headphone hair" effect. She cat-strolled across the large room with the paneled ceiling set at diverse angles. This room was used to record most of the musicians. She skirted the baffles strategically placed to provide isolation for the different instruments and into the control room, where Hunter, the engineer, was adjusting levels on the massive forty-eight track recording console per the producer's instructions.

The man who had spoken into her headphones, producer Paul "Poppa" Stevens, turned and smiled broadly at her as she sat in one of the swivel chairs in front of the console. She pushed off hard with her feet and spun around quickly in it.

"Whoa, easy there, rocket queen," said Stevens, as her knees hit him in the rear end. She giggled and Hunter smiled. Hunter was a tall, lanky man with a large unkempt mass of curly red hair who wore dark tinted glasses.

"Take another hair or two off the midrange and don't leave it sounding too wet." Paul said. "Too much reverb makes her sound like she's singing in a subway tunnel. We still have a lot of tracks to build and, as much as I like their sound, I don't want our back-up vocals to sound like some Def Leppard song. Try it now."

Hunter, she still didn't know if it was his first or last name, pressed a button and the chorus of the song flew from the monitor speakers in the control room. It was an up tempo song and, despite the amount of times they'd all heard it by now, no one in the room could keep from tapping their feet to the infectious beat.

When the chorus reached its crescendo, Paul pointed to the fluctuating black needles of the sound meters, and caught Angeline's attention.

"There, you see? Hit the high note right there, and it's gonna bring the house down, believe me. The other backup vocals are layered and lead right up into it, right up to that one moment, and all the tension will be released. I know you don't care too much about the theoretical end of music, but this is the beauty of a suspended chord. It makes your ears beg for release. And when it resolves, you feel like everything's alright in the world again."

"An eargasm?" Angeline said coyly.

"Something like that. Yeah, right. Just like that," said Paul with a loud guffaw. "So how does your voice feel now? Can you give me those big notes tonight or do you want to take it up later? It's no big deal either way. I've blocked out time here all weekend long. We've gotten a lot done tonight already and I've got a guy coming in to do some percussion overdubs soon. If you feel tired, just go home and get some rest. You don't want to strain that beautiful instrument sitting in your throat."

"Let's see what I've got left in the tank, Poppa. If it doesn't happen in three or four takes, we can call it a night. Do you have any more of that good tea of yours left?"

"We'll brew it until Central Park is bare, Angie."

"Ah. I always wondered where the secret ingredients came from. Two spoons of honey and a little lemon, please."

"Hunter, could you fetch mademoiselle her usual?"

Hunter left the room to boil some more water. Paul felt like lighting up a cigarette but decided to hold off until Angeline was back in the vocal booth. Singers are notoriously skittish artists and he wanted to keep the vibe perfect.

"So what's new with you these days, Angie?" he asked innocuously.

"Not much, Poppa, and nothing good. I had this very bad, nasty fight with my boyfriend, or maybe I think ex-boyfriend. I'm not sure what to think of him, now."

"Great," thought Paul to himself, "way to keep the positive vibes going, you old idiot."

"Yeah, he's the one you were telling me about; the guy with the rehearsal studio who plays the drums, right? Hunter's gone to a couple of hockey games with him, I think," he said.

"Pete's his name. He's a sweetheart, I guess. I don't know. Sometimes it seems to me like he's just a lost soul. I get the feeling our lives are going in separate directions, you know? We're becoming different people as time goes on."

"Not everything is permanent, hon, but then again, not everything is temporary, either."

She laughed softly, steepled her hands together and bowed gracefully.

"Sensei Poppa, this humble grasshopper will try and follow your learned and sacred path."

"Have you attempted the drunken penguin stance yet, young one?" said Paul in a bad fake Chinese accent. She shook her head rigorously, though a smile played on her lips. Hunter returned with three cups of tea and placed them on a short metal table away from the console. "Ah, Won Hung Lo has brought the tea. Thank you, apprentice."

The two men turned and bowed ceremoniously to each other, barely avoiding knocking foreheads. Paul reached into a cabinet next to the mixing console and pulled out a bottle of dark Jamaican rum. After pouring a healthy dollop into each cup, he handed one to Angeline.

"This will lead you down the path of the drunken penguin, my daughter." They clinked teacups and took sips of the hot tea. Paul got up and said, "Observe, grasshopper." He then waddled around the control room, flapping his arms and lurching from side to side, his eyes rolling in his head.

Angeline laughed so hard that she almost fell off of her chair. Paul breathed an internal sigh of relief. Possibly the most important part of a producer's job is to make sure the artist is in the right frame of mind to create, and he didn't want her to be thinking bad thoughts about a rocky relationship when she was in the vocal booth singing fiery love songs. A buzzer sounded from the wall, and when Hunter pushed a button, the studio receptionist's voice was heard from a small speaker under the console,

"Paul, Edgardo Rincon is here."

Hunter looked at Paul, who nodded. "That's the percussionist. Wait till you hear him. This guy has played with everyone who's anyone. He's an absolute master. Send him in, please."

A couple of minutes later, the door to the studio opened and a handsome dark haired man wearing jeans and a dark cobalt peasant shirt arrived, carrying a large trap case, which he lugged, with considerable effort, to the side of the room where other different sized cases were stacked. Hunter arrived with an assortment of microphones attached to cords slung over his forearm. The two men chatted briefly while Rincon removed the assorted percussion instruments from the case.

"Wow, check out all the stuff he's got!" exclaimed Angeline as Rincon laid out some exotic African and South American instruments on a long rectangular table set up on the left side of the studio. "How on earth do you know what to use on each song?"

"To tell you the truth, even I don't know what every last one of them sounds like," replied Paul with a laugh. "Edgardo is truly one of the best in the business. There are a few songs I think would benefit from some out of the ordinary sounds, and I want to keep them warm and organic sounding, not just use a synthesizer and some samples. Old-timers like me still have a fondness for the analog, you know. I'll play the tapes for him and see what he thinks might work for each song. It could be a touch of something here or there, some ear candy, or it could really add a lot to the pulse of the tune. It's why I always like to work with creative people. Most of the best musicians don't need a boatload of instruction. You just point them in the right direction, wind them up, hit the record button, and let 'em go."

"Do I still have time to do those vocal tracks while they're preparing? I feel pumped up and ready to go."

"Sure, sweetheart, knock 'em dead. You won't hear them setting up at all when you're in the vocal booth. Do you need a lyric sheet or can you remember the word 'oooooo'?" asked Paul.

"Oooooo? I think I can handle that. You spell it with an 'o' or a 'u'?" Angeline responded with such a sweet smile that Paul hoped her boyfriend would soon come to his senses and not let this one get away. She put down her tea and returned to the vocal booth, where she donned the headphones and planted her feet at the tape mark set ten inches in front of the small circular mesh screen placed in front of the microphone to catch any spit, pops or sibilance.

"O.K., I'm going to let it roll now." Paul said into her headphones. "All I need is one good one from you. I can copy and splice it around the song if I get a good take. Ready, darling? Get your breathing lined up."

She winked, gave him a thumbs up sign and closed her eyes to focus her concentration. A good musician knows when they are locked in to the music and Angeline was in the moment. The music started softly in her headphones and built inexorably to its crescendo. She heard the other background tracks she had recorded earlier blend seamlessly and gain momentum as the drummer hammered an urgent roll across the tom toms to lead into the chorus.

She instinctively took in a deep breath and let loose a ferocious note of such power, passion and intensity that her knees almost buckled with the emotion released by her own voice. She let it trail off with the smallest of trills at the very end of the note and hung her head for a moment before lifting it up and opening her eyes. She couldn't hear Paul's reaction in the control room, but could see his beaming smile and hands clapping. He clasped his fists together at his chest and blew her a kiss. She smiled modestly for a moment before getting caught up and let loose a big grin.

"Want me to try it again?" she whispered coyly into the microphone.

"Nope. After that, I'm going to have to replace the monitor speakers in here as it is. I don't think they can take another blast like that. Very nicely done, Angie. There's a couple of touch-ups on two or three other songs I wouldn't mind doing while I have you in the booth, if you're still feeling up to it." Paul bent over the console, pushed a few buttons, and lined up another song they had been working on earlier in the day.

"Sure, but afterwards I want to party. I think Richie'll be stopping by before long."

Since he was still hunched over the console, she wasn't able to see the grimace cross Paul's face when she mentioned Roeper's name. Hunter took a break from setting up the percussionist's microphones to return to the control room and help him adjust sound levels for the tracks of another song. Soon everything was set and Paul cued Angeline to come in on some harmony vocals he felt needed touching up. After about ten minutes, they were almost finished.

The buzzer in the control room sounded again and the receptionist announced that Richie Roeper was there. Paul asked if he could please wait five minutes as they were almost done. Fifteen seconds later the door to the studio flew open and slammed against the wall. Roeper stormed into the room, shouting and gesticulating wildly in the direction of the control room, which he soon reached. His open leather coat billowed around him like a cape in a heavy wind. He flung the door open and shouted at Paul, spit spraying from his lips.

"You fucking jive-shit motherfucker, don't you ever, ever try and tell me when I can come into the studio! This is my fucking project! Do you understand, you old sack of shit? I can't believe you think that you matter in this world. If this wasn't so close to the finish line, I'd throw your ass out of here right now. You work for me, asshole, and you'll do what I tell you, and when I tell you. Goddamn, but shitheels like you piss me off! You're just an old parasite trying to hang on in a business that passed you by a long time ago." His finger was pointed about two inches away from Paul's nose. Paul's face grew pale and there was a steely glint in his eyes, but still he spoke calmly.

"Do you have any idea what you've accomplished by roaring in here like this? Take a look at the vocal booth, if you know where it is."

Roeper turned in time to see a wide-eyed Angeline rushing out of the booth, a concerned expression on her face.

"Richie, baby, what's wrong? Are you O.K.?" She came over to him and put her hands on his shoulders.

"Nothing. It's nothing I can't handle. I'm fine," he said blackly. He sat down hard on Paul's leather chair, a sullen expression on his face. "Go back and finish whatever you were doing, Ange."

She looked at him with a questioning expression, started to say something, and then thought better of it. Lightly shrugging her shoulders, she strolled past the now almost completed percussion set-up and back into the vocal booth.

Once she had readjusted her headphones, she looked up at the control room for guidance.

"Ready to roll, Angie?" Paul asked.

She gave a thumbs-up and Paul ran the tape. When the first chorus came by, she sang it well, but didn't hold the note quite long enough to match the rest of the vocals.

"Can I try it again?"

"Sure. No problemo," replied Paul.

This time, when the chorus came around, she inhaled and coughed explosively instead of singing.

"Whoa, easy there, Angie! You O.K.?" asked a concerned Paul into the console microphone.

She looked up tentatively, took a sip from a water bottle and cleared her throat.

"I'm going to try one more time. Let's take it from the same spot in the song."

Paul rewound the tape to a few measures before the chorus and hit the record button. At the chorus, Angeline came in on time, but her voice sounded ragged and lacked the force of her earlier attempts.

"How'd that sound, Poppa?" she asked into the microphone.

"I think we ought to shut you down for the night, honey. Give your voice a rest and take it up tomorrow afternoon. You did great today. We're not far from the end."

"I think you're pushing her too hard," said Roeper, folding his arms. "There's nothing left of her voice by the end of the night."

"Everything was fine until these last couple of takes. You ought to take care of the business end of the proceedings and stay out of what you know nothing about. Every time you're in the studio, you bring this bad, edgy vibe with you and nothing gets done," responded Paul.

"O.K. fuckhead, that's it. Get the hell out of here right now. You're through with this project. And if you're not out of here in two minutes, I can also guarantee you some hospital time in the very near future," Roeper snarled and waved the back of his hand dismissively toward Paul.

He swiveled his chair to the right. "You, uh, Hunter's your name, right?" The engineer gulped and nodded, his eyes darting back and forth between Stevens and Roeper. "You'll finish this up with me now." He swiveled the chair back and said to a now red-faced Paul Stevens, "You're still here, asshole? I'm warning you for the last time, you fucking fossil, be out of here before she gets back from the vocal booth, unless your Medicare is all paid up." Angeline was in the process of taking off her headphones and gathering up some lyric sheets she had been using throughout the session from a music stand.

"You'll be hearing from my lawyer, you vampire. That poor girl in there is going to regret she ever met you. I know I do," Paul said through clenched teeth. He exited the control room and marched out of the studio before Angeline could pull open the door of the vocal booth.

Shocked, Hunter watched as Roeper pulled a slim cell phone out of the inner pocket of his jacket and pressed a number programmed into the speed dialer. Angeline entered the control room, saw the look on Hunter's face and was about to speak when Roeper lifted one finger in her direction. When a voice answered the phone, Roeper said, "Hello, is this the den of iniquity?"

The faint tinny sound of laughter could be heard through the earpiece of the phone. "Hey, Beep, bring your traveling road show, with a full suitcase," Roeper said, giving him the address of the studio. He flipped the phone closed and announced, with a gleeful grin, "I think it's time for a little party to celebrate my new career as a producer."

"What happened to Paul, Richie?" asked a wide-eyed Angeline.

"How do the music papers usually put it?" He waved his hands expansively. "There was an amicable split due to musical differences. Ange, that old fart was dragging down the whole process. You shouldn't have some ancient relic trying to give you a modern sound. Besides, this way I can oversee your career properly. Did you know that I brought some of the rough mixes to Ian Morgan himself a couple of days ago? He loves what we're doing, and right now is seeing how big an advance he can get for us. All aboard the gravy train! His lawyers are working on the papers and we'll be going in to his office for the big signing in a few days. Climb aboard, ladies and gentlemen, the USS Angeline is about to boldly go where no star has gone before!"

"Richie, oh my God. Are you for real?" Angeline shrieked. "This is so incredible! Oh, baby! You are the best!" She ran around the console, threw her arms around him and gave him a big hard kiss.

Hunter stared at this surreal scene with disbelief and shook his head. He quickly stopped when Richie turned toward him.

"Hey, Hunter, there's a liquor store on Second Avenue open until midnight. That gives you about fifteen minutes to run in there and buy us a bunch of stuff."

He pulled out a massive silver bill clip with an "R" insignia from his pants pocket. He casually took a half-inch wide chunk out of the middle and handed it to Hunter, who riffed through the edges, noting that no bill was less than three digits in denomination, estimating it at somewhere over five thousand dollars.

"Make sure there's at least a couple of cases of chilled Dom Perignon, some Johnny Walker Blue, some Stolichnaya Crystal vodka and use your fucking imagination for the rest. There's got to be a twenty-four hour deli around here that delivers, too. Make sure we've got enough mixers and beer, cups and ice, you know, whatever bullshit we need to get this place rocking tonight. For crissakes, it's a goddamned mausoleum in here and I got rid of the mummy just now. C'mon, Hunter, that liquor store better not close before you get to it, if you know what's good for you. You can keep whatever's left over from this wad if I have a good time tonight."

Hunter hurried out of the studio to begin his career as a caterer. At that point, Edgardo Rincon, who had been waiting patiently by his percussion while watching the situation pan out in the control room, stuck his head in through the door.

"I'm ready whenever you guys are," he said

"Who the fuck are you?" asked Roeper.

"My name is Edgardo Rincon. Paul asked me to come down and play percussion on a few songs."

"Well, as you can see, Paul's not on the project anymore. I'm running this show," Roeper replied. He paused to think for a moment. He was tempted to throw Rincon out of the studio based simply on the fact that it had been Paul's idea to have a percussionist. However, if he really wanted to produce a record, he had to get used to making musical decisions.

"Alright, we might as well put you to work then. Studio time's expensive." He stood and looked around the studio through the glass partition. "O.K., on the first song, I wanna hear some, uh, tambourine. You've got one over there, in all that crap, don't you?" he asked, motioning vaguely toward the table where the percussion had been arranged.

"Sure, I brought five of them. Which one do you want me to play?" asked Rincon.

"Oh, play the biggest one."

"Do you want me to play through the verses in addition to the chorus?"

"Yeah, sure, whatever you like," Roeper was getting annoyed by the questions.

"Quarter notes?"

"Just hit the fucking thing!" Roeper exploded. "I've gotta tell you everything? Jesus, I might as well be playing the goddamn thing myself."

"No problem." Rincon said. He'd dealt capably with flaky individuals throughout his career; one of the reasons, aside from his excellent and intuitive sense of rhythm, he was always in demand. "You're the boss."

"Yeah, I am," replied a mollified Roeper with a flinty smile. "As long as everyone remembers that, we're going to do just fine."

He sat back down and looked at the console while the percussionist went back to his area in the studio to pick up his largest tambourine and get ready. Roeper, who found the cassette deck in his car a challenge to manipulate, let

alone the forty-eight track board in front of him, realized
he'd be far better off if he kept himself to giving orders and
left Hunter, who he had just sent out for supplies, with the
actual button pushing. He did, however, manage to find the
button on the board that activated the console to studio microphone.

"There are a few levels I want to check with the engineer before we get rolling. So why don't you take a ten
minute break?"

Rincon shrugged and smiled. He couldn't care less.
This was his last session for a couple of days, and if it ran
overtime, as it was surely looking like it would, who was he
to turn down time and half pay, when he was making three
hundred dollars an hour?

Twenty minutes later, Hunter came back through the
door with a burly deliveryman from the liquor store in tow,
pushing a heavily laden hand truck onto the parquet floor
of the studio. On it were four cases of liquor and a large tub
half filled with ice. Hunter and the deliveryman broke open
the case containing the champagne and shoved bottles deep
into the ice. Hunter went into a closet and pulled out a long
folding table similar to the one that Rincon had laid out his
percussion on.

Roeper rose from the swiveling leather chair to inspect
what the deliveryman was removing from the other cases.
Hunter phoned a twenty-four hour deli that delivered and
began ordering supplies. Roeper looked on approvingly and
marched into the studio, reached into the ice tub, pulled out
a bottle and popped the cork. He returned to the control
room, took a big pull from the bottle and turned toward

Angeline, who was still glowing from the prospect of a large recording contract. He handed her the bottle.

"You see this?" he spread his hands. "Now this is how I've always envisioned recording sessions should be. I've read stories about what sessions with the Stones, Led Zeppelin, and the other big rock bands were like. I'm surprised Stevens didn't try to bring Mother Theresa into the studio to play bass. You've got to fuel creative ability, and darlin', tonight is high octane night! We're gonna prime the pumps."

She smiled tentatively. She had come to trust Richie's business acumen and, as their relationship had gradually become more intimate and personal, she'd stopped questioning his decisions and motivations. However, she'd never seen him as a musical force, someone who could mold her sound in addition to guiding her career. She trusted Paul Stevens for that and wasn't sure if Richie knew his flanger from his elbow.

Oh well, she thought, I've come this far with him and everything's been great.

The mornings were getting a little rough after she had overindulged, though. Cocaine was lots of fun at first, but unlike alcohol or marijuana, which would simply make you sleepy and leave you relatively unaffected the next day, this drug wouldn't leave you alone. She would feel like a marvelously clever conversationalist after about six lines, witty and charming. She'd been acutely shy as a child, insecure despite her exotic beauty, never sure if she was smart enough, or interesting enough, and she'd rediscovered herself, reinvented herself through her contact with Richie Roeper. This was one of the main things that had attracted her to him.

He had introduced her to people that she felt she never could have met, had she remained on the path she was on.

It didn't matter to her if she could see through most of these hangers-on as if they were made of cellophane; there was a certain decadent glamour about them, and it drew her in inexorably.

She remembered, in particular, an intense conversation at 7:00 AM in an obscure after hours club in the meat packing district on the lower west side of Manhattan about the relative merits of cloth versus disposable diapers. Neither she nor her fellow debater, a three hundred pound truck driver named Fred, had ever had any experience with children, but that was beside the point. It was the impassioned quality of the discussion that seemed truly important to her.

What was beginning to worry her was the way time flew by and how she would have to ingest more and more cocaine just to maintain the initial euphoria. She had smoked it a couple of times with Richie, most recently after they'd come back to her apartment after drinks at Electric Willie's, but she didn't like the sensation of smoke in her lungs, although the initial rush wasn't unpleasant. Besides, whoever it was who did publicity for crack wasn't doing much of a job. In Angeline's sensibility, cocaine was affluent and elegant, done demurely with silver utensils. Crack was something that people in projects did. The fact that the two are simply different forms of the same thing didn't register with her.

She took a couple of quick sips from the champagne bottle and passed it back to Roeper, who glanced at his watch.

"Hmm. They should be here by now," he said.

As if on cue, the buzzer sounded on the intercom. Hunter, who had returned to the control room, answered.

"The receptionist says there are twelve strange looking people downstairs who say they know you and want to come in," he told Roeper.

"That must be Beep and his traveling circus. Send in the clowns," Roeper said, laughing and furiously rubbing his hands together.

A few moments later, Beep pushed through the studio doors, trailed by his entourage. Beep, this evening, had selected a pig's snout as the accessory for his lime green tuxedo and was carrying a large, sturdy leather briefcase with him. He waved and bounded up the step to the control room. Roeper, grinning from ear to ear, got up and gave him a big hug. A large black man dressed as a geisha followed him into the control room, reached up and pulled a print of Miles Davis blowing blue heaven out of his trumpet from the wall, and placed it down flat on an equipment rack in back of the room. Beep placed the briefcase on the console in front of Roeper, twisted a couple of numbers on the combination locks, and unfastened the lid.

Richie reached in and pulled out one of four large sandwich bags crammed full of white powder and tossed it on the glass surface of the Miles Davis print. A tiny Asian gentleman wearing white leather chaps and a monocle reached into his mouth, pulled out a sharply pointed platinum tooth, and sliced the bag open roughly, spilling its contents across the glass. He dipped the tooth into a large mound of the powder and put it back into his mouth with an audible click. He whistled, an exotic bird's trill, and smiled broadly, revealing a mining company's entire inventory represented in his palate.

Minerals ranging from slate to zirconium were represented in his dental ware, along with such standards as silver and gold.

"Up to your standards, Che?" laughed Roeper. The little man nodded. "Then it's good enough for me." He reached behind him, picked up a hollow rod section of a spare microphone stand and placed it close to his nose. Turning toward the frame and its contents, he checked out the wide-eyed reactions of the people around him. He guffawed loudly and put the metal tube down, opting instead for the red leather case ever present in his jacket pocket. All in attendance were soon indulging themselves in both drugs and alcohol. Edgardo Rincon, a plastic cup of champagne in hand, stepped back into the control room, now jammed with people lining up in front of the frame. He motioned towards Roeper, getting his attention.

'Oh, yeah," Roeper said, wiping his nose. "Hey everybody, wait up a second. We gotta take care of some business first. You all have to earn your way here." He waved toward Hunter, who had since retreated to the side of the room with a beer. "You ready to record some concussion?"

"O.K."

"Alright, let's get this show on the road. Edgardo, that's your name, right?" Rincon smiled and nodded. "You've got my instructions down? Let's go, then. I want everyone to be quiet as a mouse here. I have to concentrate, make sure it sounds just right. You guys are witnessing history here tonight, the birth of a star." He winked at Angeline and patted her on the knee. A respectful hush fell over the room, most of the occupants not realizing that no matter how much noise they made, none of it could leak through the glass to the studio where the music was being recorded.

Hunter activated the microphone connecting the console to Rincon's headphones.

"Let's get a level, Edgardo. Hit it hard about four inches away from the mic."

Rincon, relieved that not all the inmates who had taken over the asylum were insane, complied. Hunter adjusted three of the knobs and two of the faders on the console and looked over at Roeper, who pointed dramatically at Rincon and shouted "Action!"

Hunter pushed the record button and the sound of subtly echoed piano filled the room, the final chord of the phrase slowing down into a delicious arpeggio. The second time through the phrase, Rincon slowly shook the tambourine, picking up speed through the arpeggio and punctuating the release with a slap on the plastic edge, just as the drums came in. It sounded perfect and a beaming Roeper turned toward the crowd frozen behind him, a sort of cokehead's last supper, surrounding the print, not daring to make a sound. "I told him to put that in, just there. Fucking perfect!"

Rincon made his way through the rest of the song, using his unerring instinct to play perfectly through a song he'd never heard before, though he knew the basic formula for this particular style of music. At a certain level of expertise, a player can simply follow his muse to get the desired effect. There's no substitute for rehearsal and familiarity with the material, but for simpler forms of music, experience in the genre is frequently the best teacher. After the last chorus of the song faded out, Hunter pressed the red "stop" button on the console and the entire group crowded into the control room burst into spontaneous applause. Angeline smiled tentatively, unsure if the applause was genuine, or due to the promise of free drugs. In any case, it felt good.

"O.K. Eduardo, what else do you have on the table that'll spice up the music?" asked Roeper, holding on to the console microphone.

"Uh, Richie, that's Edgardo," said Hunter, behind his hand.

"I'm sorry, you're mixing me up with someone who gives a shit." Roeper was happy with his put-down and looked back to see if his cleverness had been properly appreciated. Unfortunately, the crowd involved in the feeding frenzy going on behind him was oblivious to his wit. "Hey, don't huff all the stuff up! Beep, the record company's not paying for all this shit just for your pals to get high. Gimme one of those big straws!"

It was like when the alpha male lion claims his kill after the pack has brought down an antelope. Beep's posse parted and let him in, and Roeper would've made the Hoover Vacuum company proud. He finally sat back in the producer's chair, tears running down from his red and widened eyes.

"Alright," he said in a strangled voice. He reached down and retrieved a half-full champagne bottle, took a couple of long pulls from it, belched loudly, wiped his eyes and tried to focus on the table full of percussion. "The long thing over at the end, the brown thing. What does that do?"

"It's a tuned rattler from Senegal," replied Rincon.

"Nah. I've got enough snakes in this room already. Don't need to have them taking over the whole place. How about those bongos in the corner. Can you play them?"

"The congas? Sure." He sat down on a metal folding chair and placed the small congas on his lap. He struck them first with his fingertips and then the side of his palm. "Am I close enough to the mic, Hunter?"

Hunter adjusted a fader and looked over at Roeper. Roeper once again shushed the crowd and dramatically signaled for the tape to be rolled. Rincon listened intently, not making a sound until the second verse, where he played a subtle syncopated counter rhythm to the regular drum kit. It added a jazzy latin feel to what was previously a fairly straightforward rock beat. He stopped playing again during the chorus, tapping his foot to keep track of the measures. When the bridge of the song came in, he held back until the very end, where he blazed in with a rapid flurry of his hands, and then returned to what he was playing on the previous verse as the song reached its conclusion. After the music in his headphones had faded out, Rincon looked up and cocked an eyebrow, as if to say, "How was it?"

"He's tremendous!" Angeline said, "Where did Paul find this guy?"

"Maybe the yellow pages. I don't know." He handed her the oversized straw. "Hey, save some for my star, here. Go ahead, Ange, knock yourself out. You've earned it. Beep, chop her a six-pack. Give her your best home cooking."

Beep took out a large razor blade, and, with the precision and speed of a sushi chef, chopped up a large rock of cocaine from his own personal stash, sealed in a smaller bag emblazoned with the emblem of a laughing clown with a red nose. He produced six thick eight-inch lines of white powder in perfect diagonal parallel order on a separate mirror, so that the star didn't have to snort with the mere commoners.

Roeper finished off the balance of the champagne bottle and gave a thumbs-up sign to Rincon.

For the next hour and a half, Roeper would point vaguely at another percussion instrument on the table and have Rincon play it on the next subsequent song. Whether it was some sort of strange synchronicity or just pure luck, the instrument choices fit fairly suitably with the songs they were chosen for.

Roeper, having finished off his fourth bottle of champagne and inhaled a highway full of white lines, was frenetically dancing along, not necessarily with the music that was playing, but to some internal drummer whose beat was getting faster and faster and who would periodically shift from a 4/4 beat to more esoteric rhythms. Angeline, amped up after having also consumed a great deal of both liquor and drugs, tried to persuade Roeper to have her try a few more vocals. He relented and she hurried back into the vocal booth. Hunter, cautiously eyeing the events as if he were locked in a cage with hungry tigers, swiftly adjusted the microphone levels accordingly. Beep plopped down into the chair next to Roeper and gazed longingly through the studio glass.

"Gorgeous. God, what a body. Look at that move!" he whispered.

"Hey, that's my woman you're talking about!" growled Roeper.

"Oh, Richie, you can have her!" Beep replied with a laugh, "I'd lick the sweat off of the back of his thighs in a heartbeat." He pointed and waved at Rincon, who looked up and waved back cheerfully, unaware he was an object of lust. "He'll be mine before the end of the night, I can just tell."

Roeper smiled patronizingly at Beep, and sang, "When you wish upon a star," in a hoarse croak. "You know, Beep?" He looked at the almost empty champagne bottle, "this stuff does absolutely nothing to quench your thirst. My throat feels like the fucking Sahara. Hunter, is there any cold beer in the cooler? Get me one."

Hunter went into the studio and fished around in the ice chest for beer. In the meantime, the hangers-on had formed a conga line. With the leaders carrying a few of the more portable percussion instruments, they did the cha-cha throughout the studio, the large black man in the geisha outfit, named Ajax, leading the way. Hunter returned with a six pack, taking two cans for himself, before handing the balance to Roeper, who yanked the top from one can and guzzled three quarters of the contents. They watched the conga line loop the studio. Edgardo Rincon, realizing his part in the recording process was done with, picked up a pair of maracas and joined the end of the line, a big grin splitting his face. Beep looked over at Roeper, winked and said, "Well, I might as well get a close-up." He jumped up from his chair and quickly joined the conga line, his hands against Rincon's hips.

Roeper observed with bemusement as, after a couple times around the studio, Beep leaned over Edgardo's shoulder and whispered something in his ear. Roeper's eyebrows arched as he saw Rincon smile back at Beep, who was getting more adventurous with his hand placement. Hunter, tapping his toes and starting to get into the swing of things, said, "Angeline's gonna have a tough time keeping a straight face singing with these nuts dancing around the studio."

"Huh? Oh, yeah," replied Roeper distractedly, "where'd she go?"

"I thought she was going to do some more vocals, for what song, though, I'm not too sure." Hunter craned his neck but couldn't see if anyone was in the vocal booth. "Maybe she's in the bathroom."

"Yeah, believe me, that chick takes forever to get ready for anything." He polished off the rest of the beer and immediately opened another one. "Ya know, Hunter, this could be a big step for your career, working on this recording. If this takes off, I'll make sure you get taken care of, not to mention there'll be lots of other projects. Keep up the good work."

"Wow! Thanks," said Hunter, not realizing that he was listening to the cocaine talking.

Down in the studio, Beep had his hands down Rincon's front pockets and was gyrating his pelvis against him. As the procession went around the studio area for the fifth time, Beep suggested they move into the vocal booth for some privacy. Rincon assented and they let the line continue on without them as Beep pulled the door of the booth open. Roeper, observing the developments, nudged Hunter.

"Check this out. Turn the microphone on live in the vocal booth. This should be a hoot," he chortled as Hunter hit the button.

"Oh shit!" suddenly bellowed a voice from the monitor speakers. "Angeline. Oh my God! Is she…?"

"What the fuck?" muttered Roeper.

He hurriedly got up and ran to the vocal booth, where Beep and Rincon were standing at the door with horrified expressions on their faces. He arrived to the sight of Angeline lying crumpled unconscious on the floor, her lower face covered in the blood that had seeped from her nostrils and more blood oozing from a cut on her forehead, where she had hit her head on a music stand on the way toward the floor.

13

"Ow! Goddamn it!" said Pete, after hitting his head on the music stand. He'd been on his hands and knees, rewiring the reverb, echo and compression units into the back of the P.A., and hadn't noticed the music stand lurking next to it until it was already too late and he'd made hard contact with the back of his head. He touched the point of impact on his skull and brought his finger back in front of his eyes, looking for blood. None was to be found, though there was a lot of dust and grime on them from having spent time behind the amplifiers and drum risers in his studios. He'd given Greg the night off to study for exams, and was catching up on some overdue maintenance work. He knew it wasn't going to be too late a night. Only two bands were scheduled to play that evening.

The buzzer sounded and Pete let the deliveryman from the Chinese restaurant in through the door. He'd gotten off the phone with them not fifteen minutes ago, and here was the order already, sliced pork with a spicy garlic sauce, a spring roll and fried rice. He wasn't particularly worried about the quality of his breath tonight. He took a bottle of cream soda from the fridge and started into his repast with a fork.

Despite his drumming experience, which frequently called for him to hold two wooden sticks in his hands, he was clueless as to how to use chopsticks, unless there was a sudden need for him to perform a drum roll on the aluminum dish in which his food had been delivered. He was in the process of doing this when the telephone rang

"Half Moon Bay Studios."

"Hi, could I speak with Mike Hunt?"

"Hey, Styx, what's happening? You recovered from the other night yet?"

"Not a lot, guy. Yeah, for the most part. I've managed to scrape off the major cobwebs." Johnny's voice was still a little hoarse, but he sounded better than in their last phone conversation. "Hey, you got a studio free tonight? I've got a buddy over here who plays some guitar and I was thinking we could jam a little, if you've got the space."

"You're not bringing over the dominatrix that worked you over, are you? Then again, if she looks like Lita Ford, it could get interesting."

"Sorry to ruin your fantasies, but the guitarist is a guy. Come to think of it, that might help your fantasies. So, how about it, is there a room free?"

"Yeah, no problem. The last band finishes up at 9:00 tonight and I've got some time. The only stipulation is I need to get home by midnight. There's a Pink Panther marathon on one of the cable channels."

"Really? Great, I love those movies! What *ruume* will we playing in tonight?" asked Johnny, imitating Peter Sellers' immortal Inspector Clouseau.

"I do not know. I must have speaks with the proprietor. Does your guitarist bite?" responded Pete with a laugh, performing his own imitation.

"Nah, you may be pleasantly surprised."

"Well, no one's in Studio C tonight, so why don't you get here around quarter of nine? This way you guys can get tuned up in advance. At least the other guy can. I know you don't bother with anything as sophisticated as tuning your instrument. I'll let the other bands out and we can kick out the jams for a little."

"Sounds cool, I'll bring a couple of six packs. You sure it's no problem?"

"None at all, and I'm looking forward to it. It'll be nice to show a couple of amateurs like you and your bud how a kick-ass drummer can make a difference," said Pete, puffing his chest out. He frowned as peals of laughter came back to him over the phone line. When Johnny had recovered, he cleared his throat and said,

"O.K., see you soon, bud," and hung up.

An hour and a half later, the buzzer rang and Pete opened the door. Johnny sauntered in with a grizzled looking fellow toting a gig bag guitar case. A cigarette dangled between his lips. Pete's eyes looked like two saucers as his brain tried to reconcile what his pupils were looking at.

"Hi, Pete, how you doing?" said Johnny, a look of amusement crossing his face. "Oh, Keith, this is Pete. This is his place and he's gonna be playing drums tonight. Pete, this is Keith."

"Ow are yer, mate?" said the guitarist in a gruff English accent. Pete, dumbfounded, stuck out his hand.

"Pleased to meet you. Oh Christ!" he turned to Johnny, who was doing his best not to burst out laughing, "You might have mentioned who you were bringing down, Styx. How the hell did this happen?"

They walked into the office just as one of the bands emerged from Studio A to pay Pete. They stood gapemouthed, the drummer dropping his sticks on the floor, as

the English guitarist nodded to them and looked around.
Pete unlocked the door to Studio C and let him in. Johnny
was drinking this all in, enjoying every moment of it with a
face-splitting grin.

"Believe it or not, they've got him involved in the
Speedo commercials, and he stopped by this afternoon to
talk to a couple of the honchos at the agency. We wound up
hanging out at a bar for a couple of hours afterwards and I
asked him if he felt like jamming a little. He said he was
into it, and so here we are. Man, you should have seen the
look on your face. I never have a camera at the right time!"

"Hell, I wish I'd known, I would've cleaned the place
up," said Pete, hoping the office didn't reek of garlic sauce.

"Honest to God, I don't think he cares much. He just
likes playing guitar, and this is a chance for him to do it with
no fanfare. I think he must miss this type of thing."

"It's safe to say I'm pretty pumped to play right now,
I'll tell you that much! Christ, I hope I don't mess up. I never
practice enough." Pete grabbed a pair of drumsticks from a
shelf behind the desk and started furiously loosening up his
wrists.

"Whoa, easy there, Trigger. Relax, man. You're not au-
ditioning for his band. This is just to have a little fun." He
handed Pete a shopping bag. "Hey, these aren't very cold, the
fridge in the deli downstairs wasn't working too well. You
got any colder than these?"

"Sure. I'll stick these in and bring the cold ones out." He
turned to the musicians who had moments ago emerged from
the studio and were now talking excitedly amongst themselves. "Hey guys, will that be cash or plastic? I'll bet you

didn't know Keith's a regular here. Try to keep it under your hats, though, would you? He likes to chill when he's here."

"Yeah, sure, no problem," replied one of the musicians. He handed Pete three twenties and received six dollars in change. Pete ushered them out the door and locked it.

"Watch my bookings triple for the next month," Pete said to Johnny. "I owe you one, bud."

"Well, just don't do your Neil Peart impression to-night and we'll call it even. He likes to play blues and old rock and roll songs."

"You mean, he doesn't know '2112', or 'Tom Sawyer'?" Pete said, referring to a pair of Rush's signature songs. "Hell, where did he learn how to play guitar?"

"I don't know, Pete, maybe he knows the singer's sister. You know, it's not what you know, but who you know, and who you blow, in this business."

"You're probably right, Styx," Pete reached into the depths of his refrigerator and pulled out a 12 pack of beer. "These cold enough for you?"

Johnny touched one of the cans and drew his finger back abruptly.

"Damn, that reminds me of the date I had with Lisa Carter in eleventh grade."

"Lisa Carter? Hell, I'll put 'em back in the freezer then, if you like. That's not nearly cold enough."

"Well, pal, you ready to jam? Is my spare bass still in your closet or did you sell it on Ebay?" Johnny asked.

"I think we tried to use it for firewood when the heater went out last winter, but just like when you play that old thing, it just wouldn't catch fire."

"That's cold, bud. Maybe not Lisa Carter cold, but still…."

They entered Studio C, where Keith was sitting on a Fender twin amp, tuning his guitar. Pete unlocked a closet in the room, reached in and pulled out a battered guitar case and handed it to Johnny, who had just passed two of the beers to Keith. Keith looked on with interest as Johnny took out the bass and attached the strap to it.

"Ere, wot's this, mate? Is that one of those old Fender Jazz teardrop basses?" he asked.

"You got that right," said Johnny. "I found this in a pawn shop on Ninth Avenue in Hell's Kitchen. She's scuffed up, but plays nice. I think it's a '64 model."

"Mate, it looks like a '63 or '62 to me. See the stacked knob pots?" He pointed to the volume and tone knobs. "They only made those before '63. 'Ell, I'll give you two thousand in cash for her when we're done here tonight. If you like, make it twenty-five 'undred."

"I don't know, Keith, she's always been close to my heart, this one," Johnny said, eyeing his bass affectionately.

"Make it four grand, then. 'Ow about that?"

"Honey, I think you've found a new home," Johnny said to his bass and kissed it tenderly on the fifth fret.

"Thanks. I'll throw in some backstage passes for you gents next time we play the States. Any town you like. We'll fly you both in for the gig."

"Hey, that's great!" said Pete. He sat down behind the drum set and adjusted the crash and ride cymbal heights. He then removed a drum key from the large key chain linked to his belt and speedily tuned the snare and tom toms. Meanwhile, Johnny got his sound down on the Gallien Krueger amplifier set on top of a twin stack of sixteen-inch Cerwin Vega speakers.

"I love this rig!" exclaimed Johnny. "Whenever I'm in this room, I feel like the Lord of the Low Frequencies."

"You're not just another pretty bass, that's for sure," replied Pete with a laugh. He finished setting the drums to his liking and went over to the mixing board, setting microphone levels for the three of them.

Every so often, life gets a little perfect, and the next three hours of Johnny and Pete's lives could be described as such. Something about being in the presence of a musical legend inspired rather than intimidated them, bringing them to previously unreached heights, and when they saw Keith's approving smile, they knew something of what heaven must be like. They ran through a series of blues and rock standards, Keith hoarsely shouting out chord changes for the ones they were unsure of.

Johnny had a dream come true when he showed Keith a couple of songs he'd written over the years. They were reborn that evening, flourishing in the vibe connecting the three of them. Keith even mentioned that he might like to record one of them, a swampy number titled "One Man Party", whenever he got around to doing his next solo record. Cloud nine was a few floors down from where Johnny was standing right then.

The beer disappeared as fast as the ashtray on Keith's side filled up. Pete, who normally despised cigarette smoke, couldn't have cared less. His beats alternately drove and followed the other two, laying back off the beat, and his fills were crisp and concise. For the two friends, this was a childhood fantasy long since given up for dead and the joy showed on their faces and in their playing. Keith fed off the atmosphere, too, shaking the neck of his old Telecaster guitar as he wrenched leads out of the instrument. He and Johnny alternately sang lead and even shared a microphone on the choruses of a few songs.

Keith finally wiped the sweat from his brow and glanced at his watch.

"Mates, this really's been a gas. I 'avent 'ad a good blow like this in an age. When you guys come out to see us, I'll bring along a couple of me other mates, and do this again. You could've been pros, 'ad you kept at it. Ah, it's not the life for everyone, though. We still on for that sweet sounding bass of yours, there, droogie?"

Johnny wiped down the neck of his bass with a felt cloth before putting it back in the old case and handing it over, not without a small pang of sorrow, to Keith who extracted forty reasonable facsimiles of Benjamin Franklin from his pocket and handed them to him. Johnny, the pangs having subsided instantly, thanked him and pocketed the wad of cash. Keith picked up a flyer advertising a local band from the floor, took a pen from his tattered denim jacket and scribbled on it, before handing it to Johnny.

"The first's me cell phone, the second me answering service. I bloody hate cell phones, so the second one's a better play to get a hold of me."

They walked out to the office. Keith shook hands with the two of them, thanked them, and loped out the door, another cigarette dangling from his lips.

"O.K., I can die happy now," Pete said, after locking the door. He reached into the refrigerator and retrieved two of the beers that Johnny had originally brought, now at Lisa Carter levels of chill. He handed one to Johnny. They knocked the tops off, clinked bottles, looked at each other for a brief moment, and put their arms around each other in a ferocious hug.

"This was truly one of the greatest things that's ever happened to me," Pete said, his eyes moist. "Thanks, guy, and that's from the bottom of my heart. Do you understand, I mean, do you realize, what just fucking happened here?"

"No. What?" said Johnny innocently, and then burst out laughing.

Pete pulverized his shoulder with a punch and then hugged him again. Johnny winced as Pete squeezed the breath out of him momentarily. He then pulled out the flyer that Keith had handed him and showed it to Pete.

"Can you believe this? I sure can't, not to mention the four G's sitting in my pocket. She was a real nice bass, played sweet, and I'm sorry to see her go and all that, but that makes, uh," he calculated for a moment, "well, about an eight hundred percent return on my investment."

"I hope you know you're buying tonight," replied Pete.

"Hold on a moment, I feel inspired," said Johnny, clearing out the space in front of him with a wave of his arms.

"Today I mourn the loss of my bass,

Though it has gone on to a better place.

And if I was in a better space,

Kyra would be here, sitting on my face."

He lingered dramatically for effect, looking up at the ceiling as if his inspiration was heaven sent. Pete looked up as well, but only noticed that the paint was peeling in a large area of the corner. He was in too good a mood to mention that the peeling hadn't been there before Johnny's poetry recital.

"Very touching," Pete replied, after a respectful moment of silence to let the depth of Johnny's poetry sink in. "Kyra was cool, but I'll tell you, guy, I especially felt a connection with Astrid. She seems like a very special lady to me. She's beautiful, smart, and funny. You know, that's kinda rare, male or female."

"I didn't know beauty meant so much to you in males," answered Johnny, flicking an eyebrow.

"Smart and funny are almost impossible to find, so, like in your case, I've learned to settle for less."

"Then again, you're about as good a judge of character as O.J.'s wife."

Pete choked on his beer at that retort. All of a sudden, he started and looked at his watch.

"Oh, hey, 'A Shot in the Dark' starts in ten minutes. I don't want to miss that one. The scene with the pool table is worth the price of admission all by itself." He hurriedly threw his drumsticks back into a drawer in the desk. "Let's grab a cab back to my place."

"Sure. You got anything to eat in your fridge that's any younger than the Cubs most recent World Series trophy?"

14

After a quick stop at a deli for supplies, they took a cab to Pete's apartment and found themselves in front of the television, watching Herbert Lom doing his hilarious slow boil as Peter Sellers' Inspector Clouseau character infuriated him to the point of insanity and murder. Munching on beef jerky, chips and sliced carrots, they howled with laughter at the misadventures playing out on the screen in front of them.

"Hey, you know something? Britt Eklund looks a little like Astrid, though I think there are a few more curves on the road you're driving," said Johnny, mentioning the beautiful Swedish actress of the movie.

"Great minds think alike, pal. I was just noticing the same thing, especially the profile, the nose. You know, I've got to see her again. There was, like, this instant chemistry, not just physical, but more…, I don't know how to explain it. I sincerely liked being with her, and I got the feeling, though I've been wrong on this subject a couple of hundred times, that she really liked being with me."

"Well, you know, a woman could do a lot worse than you. Granted, you're stupid, cheap and ugly, but your heart is in the right place, and that's the most important thing. Smart women will pick up on this, and Astrid was able to make it that far and see through all your deformities."

"Thanks, Styx, with friends like you, who needs hemorrhoids?" said Pete, throwing a carrot stick at Johnny, who laughed and ducked.

They watched the rest of the movie, whooping and laughing until the credits rolled. The next installment of the series, *The Revenge of the Pink Panther* began and Inspector Clouseau was talking to a blind beggar with a monkey while a bank was in the process of being robbed behind him. The two of them had tears streaming down their faces, they were laughing so hard, and whenever their eyes would meet, they would burst out again uncontrollably.

"I gotta tell you, Styx, this is one of the best nights I've ever had. Good God, we were jamming with one of the great guitarists in rock and roll, a goddamn legend. And you know something? I think he had a good time, too."

"Yeah, I know what you mean. He had a big smile on his face the whole time. I think at first, he thought I was just some idiot working at the office."

"First impressions count for a lot, you know. His instincts are pretty sharp. But seriously, though, I'm not 'minkeying' around here, I appreciate everything you've done for me, not just tonight. You're the closest thing I've got to a brother."

"Wasn't that what Cain said to Abel?" retorted Johnny, though his expression betrayed how much he was moved by Pete's last statement. "Hey, guy, you know we're a team, always have been. We kinda lost touch for a while. I want to hang out with the dude I knew back then. It seems like he's there, right beneath the surface, and I think all it would take to bring him back is some fun, some laughs."

"There haven't been a boatload of those around in the last few years, that's for sure. I'll tell you, I don't miss being a cop anymore. That job can suck the marrow out of your bones, if you're not careful. I miss the guys, though. There are some very solid people on the job, and with what you face every day, everyone becomes family."

"Yeah, still, I never thought you were cut out for a cop's life, not that you weren't good at it. I'm sure you were real good. The thing is, underneath it all, you've got the heart of an artist. You feel way too much to stay uninvolved emotionally."

"You know, that's what I feel got lost in the shuffle. I gave so much of myself to the job I almost died inside. Everything revolved around it. I know I lost touch with you for a while, too. I wasn't supposed to discuss my work with anyone, but it was all I was doing so there wasn't much else for me to talk about."

"It's funny that after a while, Rose hated that you were a cop. She would've been happier if you'd been the drummer for Motley Crue."

"Can you imagine Rose hanging out with those guys?" said Pete with a laugh, picturing his straight-laced former wife presiding over backstage orgies with the legendary hard-partying heavy metal band. "However, this would mean I'd also have married Heather Locklear and Pamela Anderson."

"True. Well, there are pros and cons to every job."

"At least I ended my career with a bang, though there are still a lot of whispers about me, even to this day. Did I tell you about when I went to give Charlie Grimson my statement about the O.D., and some jagoff at the front desk made a snide remark about me?" Johnny shook his head, and Pete added, "I wanted to shove that guy's nightstick right up his ass. Can you imagine that? The moron doesn't even know me."

"One thing about people, Pete: most folks are lazy. If they can dismiss you as a type or fit you into a box with a label on it, they do. It's a rare person who views everyone as individuals. Most won't take the time. You're sure right about going out with a bang. All said, you are one lucky bastard; to be alive and getting out of the whole thing with just a busted shnozz is a miracle."

"Anyhow, it effectively ended my modeling career."

"What went through your mind when those thugs found out you were a cop, if you don't mind me asking?"

"Guy, you can ask me about anything you want tonight, you've certainly earned it. And besides, I feel so good right now, nothing could ruin this evening."

"Ugh, I hate it when people say that," said Johnny, knocking on the side of the scuffed wooden coffee table.

"Very superstitious, wash your face and hands," sang Pete. "You know, even if I love Stevie Ray Vaughan, his version doesn't hold a candle to Stevie Wonder's original. You think it's a Stevie thing? Only people with that name can record this song?"

"I sure as hell wouldn't want to hear Stevie Nicks do it. I think we each need another beer, that's what I think." Johnny lifted himself out of the chair and went to the refrigerator. He came back with a couple of cold ones. "You know, I mean it. If this is something you'd rather not go into, I understand completely. No problem."

"Nah, it's cool. Brothers should be able to talk to each other about anything, right?"

"Hell, if you put it that way." Johnny sat back down and slid a bottle across the coffee table into Pete's waiting hand.

"First thing you notice is the looks on their faces. These are tough, very hard guys, but still you can see a little disappointment in their faces, disappointment not only in you, for turning out to be the enemy, but they're pissed off at themselves for getting taken in by someone they had accepted. That emotion turns to anger fast and I've seen what happens first hand in that situation. I've seen guys beg for their own deaths, and they were criminals. I'd rather put my own gun to my head than go through what they would do to a cop." Pete shuddered at the thought.

"So what did you do when they found out?" asked Johnny.

"Well, it's not like I had fifteen options to choose from. Things were really tense, more than usual. The honcho had brought in some new enforcer, this huge bald guy named El Conejito. He was like one of those guys you get in the advertising business," he pointed the top of his bottle toward Johnny, "like an efficiency expert or someone they get to weed out the office of dead weight, and he started getting rid of guys right and left, guys who weren't up to the level he wanted. He wasn't Colombian like the other guys, he was American, but he had the respect and the ear of the guys in charge, and whatever he said, went. Anyway, he had no problems with the job I was doing, but somehow, and to this day I still don't know how, he found out I was a cop. The crew I was working with, they weren't the best actors in the world, so I knew something bad was up, and I managed to sneak in a couple of grenades that I'd swiped earlier into the meeting I was gonna to have with the bosses. It was in the warehouse where they cooked up the drugs, lots of volatile chemicals there. They took my guns early, but didn't search

my sleeves, where I had the grenades. You remember me telling you about my buddy on the force, Mike Tippins?"

Johnny nodded.

"He had a designed a harness that could hold small
caliber guns in your sleeves and eject them into your hands
if you bent your arms at a certain angle."

Johnny whistled. "Real James Bond stuff, eh?"

"You know it. When they showed surveillance pictures
they had of me talking to the police lieutenant who was my
contact, I folded my arms as if I was confused. In fact, what
I did was to pull the pins out of the grenades, cause if I was
gonna go down, I was going to take the whole bunch of them
with me. Anyway, when I unfolded my arms," Pete motioned
with his arms in a shrugging manner, palms outstretched, as
if to say, "Who me?"

"I let them roll out on the floor. I knew I had eight
seconds to get out. We were in a warehouse and the office
was on the second floor. They all went for the door, except
for the big American, who dove right through the window.
The problem for them was that seven guys going through
one doorframe, all at the same time, you can imagine it's not
the most efficient way to leave a room. Under other circumstances, it would've been kinda comical, like a scene from
some old silent movie with the Keystone Kops. I counted to
three and went for the window too. At least the big guy had
taken most of the glass with him." Pete's eyes were distant as
the recollections refreshed themselves in his mind.

"Wow! That's an unbelievable story, guy," said Johnny
with awe in his voice, "you sound like a completely different
person when you're telling me about it."

"You know how drummers are supposed to have a good sense of time? I was a beat late, and the grenades went off while I was in mid-air. Maybe it was the junk I was on, I don't know. Thank God I wasn't too high at the time and I could still act pretty quickly. If they'd caught me when I was in the bag, it would have been all over. What a fucking noise those things made when they went off in that confined area. It was like being inside of John Bonham's bass drum. Your head feels liked it's getting squeezed." Pete paused, pulled on his beer and looked at Johnny "You know, I've never told anyone but the internal commission this story?"

"All I can say is, guy," Johnny finished his own beer, "I want the movie rights to this one."

Pete looked at him hard for a moment, his eyes damp, and then a raucous laugh erupted from his throat. He almost lost control, his sides aching with the release.

"No one else will have it aside from you, my friend, and that's a promise," he was finally able to sputter out, wiping his eyes. "I can even hear the theme song you'd come up with:

A cop is a cop, of course, of course
Even when he's strung out on horse, on horse."

Pete didn't know whether to laugh or cry, so he did a little bit of both; a ragged sound coming from the bottom of his soul and the back of his throat. Johnny reached over and put his arms around his friend. Pete hugged him back hard.

"Jeez, what a night."

"That night, or tonight?" asked Pete with a laugh.

"Well, both, now that you mention it. Some more suds, good sir?"

"You know where they are," Pete said. Johnny bounced up from the couch and returned with two more open bottles.

"So that's how you busted your nose, when you hit the pavement after your swan dive?" Johnny asked.

"No. I hit hard because the explosion added some acceleration to my takeoff, but I rolled with it and came back up quick. I saw El Conejito running down the street, and I really wanted to nab the big bastard, but before I got a chance to go after him I got hit in the face by a head."

"What?" said Johnny, a puzzled look on his face.

"Yeah. One of the guys still in the room must have had his head blown clear off by one of the grenades, and it flew through the window. I remember seeing something flying at me out of the corner of my eye. I just had a split second to turn and *whap*! I woke up with uniformed cops all around me, getting strapped on a stretcher and loaded into an ambulance. The grenades must've caused a chain reaction when they went off and ignited the chemicals in the warehouse 'cause they were wheeling bodies out of there like it was a Roman chariot race. When I got to the hospital, they tested my blood, found the heroin, put me through detox, and cut me loose with a partial pension."

"You know, there are some seriously bad jokes floating around in my head right now," said Johnny.

"When aren't there? Believe me, I've heard every last one of them already."

"O.K., in deference to our friendship, I'm going to try to hold back the tide, but I can't promise you anything."

"That's big of you," replied Pete. He pointed at the television. "Oh, check this out, this is when Clouseau sucks the parrot into the vacuum cleaner."

They watched the rest of the movie in silence, aside from their guffaws, for a while. As the credits were scrolling on the screen, the telephone rang.

"Who would call me at three thirty in the morning?" Pete asked.

"Maybe it's Astrid."

"Yeah. Hey, that would finish this evening perfectly!"

"I don't know, guy," Johnny said, his lips quivering in an attempt to keep from breaking up, "you don't want to get ahead of yourself."

"You made it a whole forty-five minutes without a bad joke. I'm proud of you." Pete face beamed as he picked up the receiver.

"Oh, hi, Hunter. No, it's cool. I'm watching TV. What's up with you at this hour?"

There was a long silence while Pete listened. He ran his hand through his hair and muttered a few 'uh-huhs' into the phone. Johnny saw the muscles in his jaw start to work.

"I'll be there as soon as I can," Pete said, slamming down the phone. He looked at the beer bottle sitting next to him, picked it up and hurled it against the wall, where it smashed into small fragments.

Johnny stared at him, a questioning expression on his face.

"That stupid, stupid bitch. I can't believe this. Christ, how could she be so dumb?" He turned to Johnny and said, "I knew all this was too good to be true. Who just told me, 'Whenever everything is going your way, it probably means you're on the wrong side of the road'? Goddamn it. You remember Hunter, the guy I was telling you about from the recording studio?" Johnny nodded. "He was in a studio doing a session with Angeline. She overdosed on coke and is in the emergency room at Bellevue hospital. I'm going over there now."

"I'll go with you."

They arrived at the hospital by cab in ten minutes and rushed to the emergency room, where they were directed to the intensive care unit. Hunter was waiting for them in a hallway next to the elevator and grabbed Pete's arm as he hurried by.

"It looks like she's going to be alright, man. I just heard from one of the doctors a couple of minutes ago. He's still over there, if you want to talk to him." Hunter pointed to the nurses' station, where a doctor was conferring with two orderlies and signing papers on a clipboard.

Pete ran over to the doctor and introduced himself, asking about Angeline's condition. The doctor on duty, who introduced himself as Dr. Ralphs, gave him the rundown.

"She's in stable condition now. The young lady had a mild stroke, brought on by an overdose of what we believe, so far, to be an almost pure form of cocaine. Are you aware of what happens when someone suffers a stroke?"

Pete shook his head.

"A blood clot enters the brain and cuts off the flow of oxygen to the necessary areas, causing tissue damage. We've given her Coumadin, which we hope will break up the blood clot. Luckily, she received treatment fairly rapidly, so the chance of permanent brain damage is not great. How she reacts to treatment overnight should give us a good indication."

"Is she conscious? Can I see her?" Pete asked agitatedly.

"She's not conscious at the moment. You can see her through the window of the intensive care ward, though you can't enter the ward itself." Dr. Ralphs motioned for one of the nurses to bring Pete to the window. "We'll know a lot better tomorrow as to how she's going to come out of it. When as we have more information, we can decide what type of recovery therapy should be implemented."

"Thanks, Doc," said Pete. The nurse led him through the doors to the intensive care unit. They walked down a corridor until they reached a long, narrow plate glass window. The nurse pointed to the third bed from the left.

"She's sleeping peacefully now."

Pete saw Angeline lying in the hospital bed, looking very small with the top of her head bandaged and an oxygen mask on her face. He pressed his hand against the glass and noticed all the other smudges made by palms and fingers over the course of the day. He imagined that if this glass was never cleaned, all the marks left there would eventually paint a portrait of hopes dangling precariously by threads. He sent her a mental message, turned, looked back once more, and followed the nurse back to the waiting room where he found Johnny and Hunter. They looked up at him and he shook his head, hands in his jeans.

"The doctor thinks she's gonna be okay, but he doesn't know if there's going to be any permanent damage. This is so freaky."

"Freaky doesn't begin to tell the story, Pete. You have no idea what happened. Sit down for a minute," said Hunter, removing his tinted glasses and rubbing his eyes. Pete sat on a low couch next to Johnny. Hunter described the studio party and the events leading to the discovery of Angeline's unconscious body in the vocal booth.

"Oh Christ. I knew that bastard was trouble from the minute I heard about him from Angeline, but I never dreamed it could get out of hand like this. I tried to warn her." Pete ran his hand through his hair. "She just didn't want to hear about it. It didn't fit in with what she's trying to be."

"I wanted to say or do something about it, Pete, but I pussied out. I feel like such an asshole."

"It's not your fault, Hunter. The only thing that would've happened is you would've gotten fired like Poppa Stevens, and I wouldn't have even found out about this. Do you think for a minute that Roeper would've called me? Speaking of which, where is the bastard? Why isn't he here?"

"After I called for the ambulance, he said he couldn't handle the scene, and him and that weird guy in the tuxedo and the pig snout mask took off somewhere. The rest of the hangers-on dispersed quickly once they saw the party was over and the paramedics and possibly the police were going to show up."

"A guy in a tux and a pig snout?" said Johnny. He and Pete exchanged looks. "Did you get this guy's name, by any chance?"

"I don't know. Not a real name, but Roeper was calling him something like Peep, I'm not real sure. There was a whole lot going at once there, believe me. I thought I was gonna catch a break professionally here, but I can't work with someone I can't respect. I couldn't believe he would just leave her there like that."

"Peep? Was the name Beep, Hunter?" asked Pete, leaning forward.

"Could be, Pete. I honestly don't know. There are so many fruitcakes that come and go. All I care about is getting the sound right. You know, things were sounding great until Roeper and Mr. Personality showed up and brought along his merry men," answered Hunter, waving his hands. "Why, do you know him?"

"Not really, but I think I know where I can find him and that scumbag, Roeper. I'm going to take it to the bank," Pete said, a dangerous look on his face. "I think it's time he and I had a conversation."

"And I want to see Little Bo Beep," said Johnny. "I'm almost out of placebos."

"This is no joke, Styx. I'm going to rearrange that bastard's face. He took something beautiful and crapped all over it."

"You're going schizo on me, guy. First, you can't wait to see if Astrid's called, then you want to go after a worthless dirt bag who's banging what has obviously become your old girl friend. This is something you need to let go of. C'mon, man, let this go," Johnny grabbed Pete by the shoulder.

"Yeah, yeah, I know what you mean. I know." He shook his head and pushed Johnny's hand of his shoulder, not unkindly. "But let it go? That's something I don't think I can do. You know what's going through my head right now? I'm picturing someone I've been very close to, maybe even been in love with, spending the rest of her life as something diminished. I don't even know how bad, all because of a sack of shit who didn't even have the heart to see how she's doing or the balls to face the music. It's even kind of funny: music and Richie Roeper in the same sentence."

Pete frowned. "You know, he doesn't know the first thing about music. I was jamming with her band at the beginning. I have no real illusions about my playing. Look, I'm a decent drummer. There are thousands of guys better than me, but I can hold my own. We sounded fine. What she's doing doesn't require Terry Bozzio, or some other monster drummer. All Roeper wanted to do was to get me out of the picture, anyway he could, and as fast as he could. You know, I've never actually met the guy, been introduced to him. One day he had some guy come in, the flashiest looking and playing drummer you could imagine, twirling drumsticks all over the place, and I looked like one of those wind-up monkeys with the cymbals in his paws next to him. Angie and I had a long talk and she made me understand that the visual is so important in music these days, with videos and all that, and it would be a big plus for her to have this guy in the band. To cut a long story short, I sure wasn't going to stand in the way of her dreams, so I did an exit stage left. You know, I didn't even mind that much at the time. I felt like I was taking one for the team. Two weeks later, I was talking to Ange, and she mentioned that the drummer had left to go on tour with some glam rock outfit and they'd hired someone else."

"That's messed up, man. I didn't know," said Hunter, "they must have auditioned about forty guys for the spot. I asked Richie about bringing you in and he said you couldn't make it."

"There you go. I just feel like I owe him so much, Styx, and I want to give it to him with interest. What better place to deliver it than a bank?" said Pete, cracking his knuckles. "This is not entirely about Angeline. There's more than that."

"Exactly why you shouldn't be doing something stupid," implored Johnny. "It's not your safety I'm concerned about. I'm worried about his and I don't want you to throw away what you've got now just to get even with someone."

"Point taken, Johnny," Pete looked him straight in the eye. "Now get the hell out of my way."

"I'll go with you."

"Alright, but don't try to do your 'voice of reason' bit."

"Guys, I'd go with you on this excursion, but I think someone should stay here to see how the lady's going to pull out of it, if she does," said Hunter.

"I wouldn't want you to jeopardize your career or anything, Hunter. You've done more than enough. Thank God you were here for her, and thanks for getting hold of me."

Pete and Johnny shook hands with Hunter and took the elevator down to the lobby, where taxis were waiting in a line. They jumped into one and headed down to Chinatown. It was a silent ride.

Pete was thinking what he would do to Roeper when they finally met while Johnny was thinking of how to keep the situation from getting out of hand. He'd seen Pete in action a couple of times when they were teenagers and knew that his friend had a bit of the berserker in him. Once he'd had to wrest a chunk of brick away from Pete just as he was going to bring it down on the skull of someone in a brawl. The taxi pulled up in back of a large black stretch limousine idling in front of the club. "Look, I know what you're thinking," Pete said. "I'm not stupid, and I'm not going to do something stupid here. Still, I gotta tell you, I'm glad you're here. For one thing, I have no idea if that Beep guy has any muscle backing him up in this club."

"Christ, I never even thought of that, Pete. Whaddaya want to do if a bunch of thick necked guys come riding to the rescue?"

"We'll cross that bridge when we get there. Hey, wait a minute, what's this?" Pete pointed at three figures leaving the doors of the club. The first two were looking around furtively, as if expecting someone. The third, a tall, goateed man in a ponytail, wearing sunglasses at four o'clock in the morning, had his hand in a jacket pocket and he ushered the first two toward the limo with his free hand.

"That's Beep and Roeper, all right," said Pete, "they don't look too happy, if you ask me."

Pete, about to pay the taxi driver, watched the limousine door open and the three men step in. He put the money back in his pocket.

"I want you to follow that limousine, but stay back," he told the driver. "Give them five seconds after they leave. I'll make it worth your while."

"Oh Christ, Pete. What are you getting us into here?" said Johnny, slapping a hand to his forehead.

15

"Hello, gentlemen. I trust you've been having a good evening," said Frank Bender to a very nervous looking Richie Roeper and Beep as they entered the limousine. They sat in the seats behind the driver, concealed to them by the darkened glass partition. Alice lounged on a side seat, wearing a white pantsuit and grinning wickedly. Ronno climbed in after the two men, sat next to Bender and removed his sunglasses. He pulled out the pistol he'd been holding in his pocket and directed it loosely at Roeper's chest.

"You know, motherfucker, I think you've got an attitude. You dress like some sort of internet dot fairy dot fucking com. I'd like to grind up those faggot granny dyke glasses of yours and feed them to you."

Roeper hastily took off his tinted glasses and put them inside his jacket.

"Is that a challenge, pissant?" growled Ronno, his good eye widening while his other one remained impassive. It was truly a horrible effect. He leveled the gun and Roeper raised his hands in supplication. Ronno pulled the trigger and liquid squirted out of the barrel in Roeper's direction, drenching his clothing. Bender, Alice and Ronno laughed at Roeper's shocked expression, while Beep sat next to him with a grin indicating that he was with them all the way on this prank.

"What the fuck!" exclaimed Roeper.

"You'd better get that suit to a cleaner soon, man. Bleach tends to mess with the color a little and it's gonna make accessorizing a bitch, unless you work some sort of two tone, gradient kind of thing."

"Bleach! You sprayed bleach on me? What the hell is wrong with you?" Roeper rose in fury, "I'm going to….."

Alice sat him down immediately and abruptly with a rapid backhanded forearm shiver, bloodying his nose.

"Does it hurt? I can make you feel better, if you like," she offered.

Roeper sat there, stunned, and shook his head. A drop of blood fell from his nose and landed in a bleached area of his jacket. His evening, which had started so beautifully, was rapidly deteriorating into a nightmare.

"That's the price you pay for consorting with the wrong company," said Ronno, who then withdrew a far larger gun with a silencer attached to it from a shoulder holster and pointed it at Beep, the smile frozen on his face as if it had been cryogenically sealed. "Just in case you're wondering," Ronno continued, cocking the gun. "This ain't a squirt gun, sweetheart."

"Would you like the pleasure of searching these gentlemen for concealed weapons, miss?" Bender asked Alice.

Alice, whose teardrop makeup this evening had altered to a pair of streams crossing over at the bridge of her nose, reached over to pat Roeper down and rifle his pockets while Ronno kept his gun trained on Beep. She made her way down his pants until she discovered a Taiwan Lightning stiletto knife stuffed into Roeper's boot. She flicked it open and waved it in front of Roeper's terrified eyes, as if hypnotizing him with a shiny object. She lowered it so the tip of the knife slipped into his bloodied nostril and turned it as she slowly applied pressure. Roeper closed his eyes.

"Please…. Please don't."

She pulled the stiletto out of his nose. There was about a half-inch of blood on the tip. Roeper opened his eyes and Beep looked on in horror as Alice slid the knife into her mouth and licked the blood from it.

"Type O negative, if I'm not mistaken. Am I right?" she asked Roeper with a wide-eyed innocent expression. He nodded hurriedly.

"Miss, you never cease to amaze me with your unique talents," said Bender, with a shake of his head. "Now please give me his briefcase before you take care of our other guest."

Alice got up to sit next to Beep. She took the briefcase and handed it over to Bender, who rested it on his lap.

"Hey, if you want it, it's yours. There's a few grand worth of stuff in there. Let me get out of this car, and you can have the whole thing. No hard feelings. I'll write it off as a loss," said Beep, trying hard to maintain a cheerful disposition. "The combination to the lock is '2001'."

"That's awfully generous of you. You know, I appreciate a cooperative person. It makes things easy and then there's no need for messy and unpleasant behavior. Now, there are just a couple of things that will get in the way of things being smooth and easy. For one thing, I have a feeling you know who we are," Bender arched his eyebrows. Beep shook his head.

"I have no idea, though judging by the nice wheels, you're a big player. I don't know why you're interested in me.

I'm small time, and about to get smaller once you keep my stash." He motioned toward the briefcase.

"Before we go any further, let's just make sure you're not carrying any surprises." He motioned to Alice, who frisked him. She found a bulge around his calf. She moved close to him and whispered in his ear.

"Is this what I'm hoping it is? I might put up a fight for you."

She then took Roeper's switchblade and deftly slit his pant leg from the crotch down to the ankle.

"Oh, too bad," she pouted, "I was getting my hopes up." She reached down and pulled a small caliber revolver from an ankle holster. "I'm afraid he's not the stud I was expecting him to be. As a matter of fact, he seems to be shriveling up a little." She tapped him in the groin with the handle of the stiletto before handing the gun to Bender, who put it in his jacket pocket.

"But your real problem is that we have found out who you are," said Bender. "In any case, that's not the real problem. It's the man you work for, Sal Cangelosi. I'd like to talk to him and can't seem to find him anywhere. However, I was able to find out about you through some people on the street who, in retrospect, you perhaps shouldn't have trusted. Are you beginning to see where I'm going with this?"

"There must be some sort of mistake here. My friend here," Beep motioned toward Roeper, "is a big record producer and manager. Have you ever heard of Dale Patterson? He's got the number three hit in the country right now. We're in the music business. We were in the studio tonight, finishing up some tracks. Those are just party supplies in the case." He tried his most winning smile. "It's always good to be prepared."

"Like a boy scout? Yeah, it looks like you've scouted enough boys in your time." Ronno turned to Roeper. "So you're Patterson's manager and producer? Hey, I really like his stuff. It's a shame what happened to him."

"Yeah, it sucks to see a talent like that cut down," said Roeper, who was trying desperately to figure some way out of his current situation. He glanced out the window and saw they were driving unhurriedly along the East River on the lower side of Manhattan, an area that would be very deserted until fishermen began arriving with their wares in an hour or so at the Fulton Street fish market. The only other moving object he could see was a taxi a block behind them.

"What's your name, Mr. Big Time Producer?" asked Ronno.

"I'm Richie Roeper." He almost extended his hand to shake Ronno's until he noticed that Ronno was still holding a gun.

"To tell you the truth, I don't think I would've recognized your name anyway. I can't read the credits printed on CD inserts anymore. The lettering is too small. On albums, I used to pore over every last detail, but my eyesight's not so great, as you can see." Ronno pointed to his drooping eye with his free hand, the one not holding the pistol. "But enough about me. If you're a producer, you must know quite a bit about music. I used to play some piano as a kid. My Mom forced me to take lessons before I killed her, though that's not why I did it. Just kidding," he chuckled to himself. "But I always liked music theory, even minored in music in college. So you should have no trouble telling me how many sharps there are in the key of F major."

Beep was thinking they were maybe, just maybe going to pull this off. He discreetly removed the pig snout and put it in his tuxedo pocket. This thought rapidly dissipated when he saw the look on Roeper's face. As far as Roeper was concerned, the only F major he knew about was the fucking major mess he found himself in right now, and he was in this mess thanks to the asshole with the nose masks sitting next to him in the limo.

"F major, you ask? Heh, heh. Haven't done that one in years. Uh, there are four or five, depending on what instrument you're playing."

"Is that your final answer? Or would you like to use a lifeline? You might be needing one soon," said Ronno, beginning to enjoy himself. He could feel mayhem coming shortly, his favorite foreplay, and found it very arousing. He glanced at Alice to see if the prospect of blood was having the same effect on her. After the interrogation of the Jamaican assassin, their eyes had met and she'd led him into a bathroom in Bender's brownstone where she'd urged him to fill her every orifice as hard as he could, in any order he desired. He was looking forward to a return engagement. Ronno met her eyes, which glinted but betrayed nothing.

"Yeah. Guitars have four sharps and Senegalese rattlers have five."

"Senegalese rattlers? I've heard of Thai sticks, but that's a new one on me." Ronno frowned and tilted his head in Roeper's direction. "And sorry to say, there are no sharps in F. There's one flat, kinda like the way you're gonna fall pretty soon."

Bender opened Beep's alligator leather briefcase and perused the contents. "Quite a collection you have here. Nicely arranged, too. Did you have the briefcase custom made?"

Beep nodded nervously as Bender spun the case on his knee to show it to the others. Red velvet partitions held a variety of bags containing brown and white powder. Another partition enclosed a series of glass bottles with different colored pills, each bottle fastened in place by a leather strap.

"Why do some of the bags have the clown logo and the others don't?" asked Ronno.

"That's the high end stuff that Richie keeps for his artists. It's almost pure. There's practically no cut in it. The face is for ironic purposes. It means there's no joking around with anything in one of those bags."

Roeper's face was dripping sweat by now. The combination of all the cocaine and the stress was causing his heart to gallop and he was having trouble catching his breath. He decided to put his cards on the table.

"Look, I don't know what's going on here, and I don't want to know or have any part in this. I'm a fucking producer. I've got contacts in some very high places. If I'm missing, people are going to come looking for me, asking questions. I'll bet publicity is not something you want. If your problem is with Beep here, it's really between you and him."

He turned to an ashen Beep. "Sorry, man, but I gotta cut you loose." He returned his focus to Bender. "You seem like reasonable guys. Beep sells shit and I buy it sometimes. I don't know what or who his connections are. Can't you settle this without me? I can pay you guys to forget about me and

I'll just disremember I ever knew him. Shit, I can score blow thirteen ways to Sunday. I don't need this fag to get high."

"Looks like the ball's in your court, my friend," said Bender to the aghast Beep, his mouth open in a horrified expression, before pointing a finger at Roeper. "However, you don't impress me in the least." He pushed a button in a console of the limousine door, activating the intercom to the front seat. "Bunny, pull over and let that cab pass us. Have Verden get the plastic tarp out of the trunk and bring it in the back here, along with the tool case. I don't want the interior to get stained."

The partition between the driver and passengers lowered to reveal Bunny and another very large man wearing a purple bandanna and a grin displaying fewer teeth than a mouth normally has. The cab containing Pete and Johnny rolled past the stationary limo and turned right at the next corner, where they promptly paid the cabbie and got out of the vehicle.

They peeked back around the corner and saw the man in the purple bandanna fish some indeterminate objects out of the trunk of the limo and bring it around to the side door, which, when opened, created a small pool of light in the surrounding darkness of the side street. The man climbed inside and the door shut behind him. There was no movement from the darkened vehicle for the next thirty minutes.

"Pete, we gotta think about this, or do something else," whispered Johnny after they'd pulled their heads back from around the corner and retreated into the shadows. "We have no idea what the hell is going on here and there's more of them than there are of us."

"Nah. Sooner or later they're going to drop Roeper off somewhere and that's when he and I are going to throw down. They're probably doing some more coke in the car before going to some after hours place. The problem now is: how are we going to keep up with them when they go?"

"Maybe we can ask them for a lift," said Johnny, the sarcasm heavy in his voice.

A small fish van pulled onto the curb across the street from them. The driver stumbled out of the front of the truck, obviously drunk, and went into an alleyway to relieve himself, leaving the motor idling.

"Hold it, I think we just got lucky. Come on."

They sprinted across the street and jumped into the van, quickly driving it back down the road from whence it had come. Its former driver ran unevenly out of the alley, still trying to zip up his fly. Pete gunned the van around the corner. As he slowed down and pulled the van around the third corner, he saw the brake lights of the limo disappear on to the ramp leading to the Williamsburg Bridge, connecting Manhattan with Brooklyn. He accelerated until he was apace with the limo, about six car lengths behind.

"This van is the only thing that smells worse than the situation you're getting us into," said Johnny, wrinkling his nose in disgust at the fishy smell of the van's interior.

Pete ignored Johnny's comment and started singing the chorus to the Beastie Boys' song "No Sleep Til Brooklyn".

16

E ven though it was after four o'clock in the morning, the traffic was relatively heavy on the bridge, due to some roadwork going on in one of the lanes. Pete and Johnny drove slowly past hardhat wearing construction crews in fluorescent orange vests, the limousine now four cars ahead of them. Finally the lane cleared and they picked up some speed. Fifteen minutes later, they were only two cars in back of the limo and cruising through the Bay Ridge section of Brooklyn, an affluent area with many stately pre-war brown-stone houses lining its streets. The limo pulled up in front of one of the brownstones. A large tree, which would cast its cooling shadow throughout the hot summer, stood in the small courtyard in front of the building.

The van was stopped at a red light, enabling Pete to observe, from thirty yards away, four individuals emerge from the back door of the car. First to exit was Roeper, then the goa-teed man who had ushered him and Beep from the bank club, followed by a tall red haired woman wearing a fitted white pants suit. Finally a short man with slicked back black hair wearing an expensive looking sports jacket and black jeans came into view. A hulking figure materialized from the front passenger door, but his face was hidden from Pete's view amid the shadows provided by overhanging tree branches.

The woman took something resembling a key out of her pocket, bent over the lock of the wrought iron gate for a few seconds, and opened it. The group promptly made their way up the walk to the brownstone, where she opened the front door. The limo then pulled out around the next corner. The light turned green. Pete drove the van straight through the intersection and parked halfway up the block.

"Well, so much for that," said Johnny. "They're in some swanky place now, planning to shove half of Peru up their noses. They're going to be there until God knows when."

"Shit. You're probably right," Pete replied. "I was hoping maybe they were going to some after hours place where I could get that rat alone."

"I wonder why Betty Beep didn't get out with the rest of them, though. You'd think with that briefcase of his that Hunter was telling us about, he'd be the life of the party."

"Yeah, you know, that's true. One thing for sure, I can't take another minute of this fishy van. I hate seafood to begin with and this smell is going to make me heave before too long."

"I'm with you," said Johnny. They exited the van and closed the doors behind them. "Any idea if we're close to a subway out here? I know Brooklyn like I know Botswana."

"I think the N or R lines stop somewhere around here, but I'm not sure where. If we go over the river and through the woods, a couple of blocks past Grandma's house, we should be able to find it," Pete replied with a tired look. "Before we try to get back, though, I want to see whose brownstone this is."

"Oh, come on. Don't start playing detective here. We shouldn't have watched those Pink Panther movies tonight. Let's call it a night, for chrissakes," Johnny said, throwing his hands up in the air.

"It'll take two seconds, I promise. I just want to see the address number or see if there's a name next to the mailbox. Maybe this is where the bastard lives."

"What if someone walks out while you're looking?"

"I thought you said they're in there snorting up a storm. Hey, if someone comes along, I can always say we're lost and looking for where we are. You know," Pete chortled, "it wouldn't exactly be a lie."

"We could pretend we're selling Girl Scout cookies."

"O.K., that'll be our backup if Plan A fails."

"Hey, it'd be perfect. Roeper steps out, you pop him one in the kisser, and we leave, short and sweet. By now, he must be wasted enough to really believe we're Girl Scouts."

They walked around the corner and casually made their way toward the brownstone, past the open gate and moved toward the mailbox, set in the wall by the front door. Pete peered at the label in the darkness, but couldn't make anything out.

"I think it's blank, Styx, or some sort of smudge on the label. I don't know. Anyway, at least we've got the address now." He pointed at the numeral '43' embossed on the mailbox.

"O.K., what now? It's not like we're waiting for the cavalry to show up."

"What a weird way to end the evening," said Pete. "Talk about anti-climaxes."

"Not much else to do except try and find the subway, unless we luck out and run across an empty cab out here."

"I'll be damned if I spend two more minutes in that fish truck, so that's out. Maybe we could ask the limo driver to get us back into the city if we found him."

"Good idea. Can't hurt to ask, anyway. After jamming with Keith tonight, it would be the appropriate way to get back home, after all."

They rounded the corner and turned down the block where they had seen the limousine turn.

"Man, this is a quiet neighborhood," said Johnny. "I'm used to seeing people walking around twenty-four seven. Nice brownstones, though. Can't be cheap to live here."

"All you got to do is sell a couple of your jingles and this could all be yours," replied Pete. He craned his neck. "Hey, I think the limo's parked a little further down on the other side of the street."

They crossed the street and approached the driver's door. As they drew within a few feet, the window rolled down a third of the way.

"Hey, how's it going?" called Johnny.

"Can I help you gentlemen?" growled a voice from the darkened driver's seat. All that was visible was the lit tip of a cigarette.

"Yeah, we're hoping you can," answered Pete. "We're kind of stuck out here, haven't seen any taxis. We saw you drop off some people a block away. I'll give you forty bucks to get us back into Manhattan."

"That's tempting, but I've got to wait here. Sorry, guys."

"You sure?" asked Johnny. After receiving no reply, he added. "Do you at least know where the closest subway is?"

"Yeah," a bandanna wrapped head moved closer to the window. "Go back up three blocks, then turn left for two and you'll find a station."

The driver flicked the cigarette butt out. The window rolled soundlessly back up as Pete and Johnny gave their thanks. They turned to go back the way they'd come. As they passed the rear of the vehicle, they heard a thump.

"What was that?" Johnny asked.

Two more thumps.

"Sounds like it's coming from the trunk," said Pete, stepping closer to the limo.

The front door swung open. The hulking driver quickly emerged and headed their way. The purple bandanna was completely incongruous with the formal chauffeur attire.

"Get away from there. Now!" He ordered.

"Yeah, sure. No problem," said Johnny, backing up a couple of steps.

"What the hell is going on here?" asked Pete.

The driver seemed uncertain as to what to do. His eyes darted between Pete, Johnny and the trunk of the car. His decision was made by a more violent thump and the sound of a panicked, muffled voice emitting from the trunk. The driver pulled out a silenced pistol from a holster under his jacket and trained it on the other two.

"Oh, Christ," said Johnny.

"You guys are in the wrong place at the wrong time."

"What does this have to do with Roeper?" asked Pete, trying to sort out what was happening.

The driver's eyes narrowed. "You know Roeper? Don't move a fucking inch."

Still covering Pete and Johnny, the driver removed a cell phone from a belt holder and hit a speed dial button.

"Yeah, it's Verden," he spoke into the phone. "There's a complication here. A couple of guys who know Roeper showed up. I got it covered." After a pause, he continued.

"The clown in the trunk's making a racket." Another pause. "No problem." After disconnecting the call, he gave them his gapped-tooth smile and pulled out the key ring for the limo. "You guys wanted to see what's in the trunk?"

"Nah, that's fine. Probably just a suitcase shifting around," babbled Johnny, waving his hands. "If you don't wedge them in the right way..."

"Shut up." Verden pointed the gun at Johnny.

Pete made his move then and lunged at the chauffeur's arm in an attempt to grab the pistol. Verden blocked Pete with his shoulder and slammed the butt of the gun against Pete's head, knocking him to the street. Pete rose unsteadily to his feet, rubbing the side of his head.

"You want to wind up like him?" Verden said, popping the trunk open with a push of a button on the key ring.

Beep raised his head, eyes imploring, veins straining in his neck, his screams muffled by the duct tape wrapped around his face and his hands manacled behind him. His lime colored suit was slick with blood and he was loosely wrapped up in a plastic tarp.

The chauffeur chortled. "Kind of like a jack in the box. Well, pop goes this weasel."

He fired once. The bullet slammed through the bridge of Beep's nose and exited through the back of his head, flinging him back prone against the spare tire. Pete and Johnny looked on, horrified expressions on their faces, as Verden closed the trunk.

"You guys want to go to a party?"

17

"After you. It should be open." Verden gestured toward the front door of the brownstone. Pete pushed it and the heavy door swung open silently. Next to the door was an elaborate looking alarm system, looking like it came from a military installation. A green light blinked "Disabled" next to a crystal L.E.D. display.

"Boy, they'll let anyone in here," said Johnny.

"It's kind of like one of those cockroach motels," said the deep voice from behind them with something resembling a laugh. He shut the door behind them and locked it. "Go upstairs."

They marched up a narrow, dimly lit staircase with their host following close behind them. He motioned them to a closed door at the end of the carpeted landing. They could hear muffled voices from within the room. As Pete was about to reach for the handle, the big man put a hand on his shoulder and stopped him. He knocked three times rapidly and opened the door a crack.

"Boss, our guests have arrived."

"Please show them in," came a commanding voice from inside the room.

Verden pushed the door open and they entered a long, rectangular bedroom, complete with a couple wearing pajamas in a large four poster bed. There was a crowd of people in the room and the space became totally silent as flashes of recognition registered on the faces of half the inhabitants and bewildered looks, based on these reactions, shone on the others' faces.

Alice was most surprised to find one of her recent conquests standing in front of her a few days after the fact. In the past, some of her unluckier partners hadn't been able to even stand for weeks. She'd enjoyed herself tremendously with Johnny, his stamina had proved to be very stimulating for her and, though he'd been in a state of chemical hypnosis and susceptible to her every suggestion, she still felt a certain fondness for him.

She considered for a moment that Johnny was some sort of double agent sent to spy on her, but quickly dismissed the notion. She'd asked him a few questions over the course of the night and knew who he was and what he did for a living. No amount of memory implants could withstand the effects of the drug he'd been administered. A rush of pleasant memories came flooding back to her. She masked it fairly well, though not well enough for the astute eyes of Frank Bender.

Those dark eyes took in the situation rapidly. His finely tuned senses had always enabled him to maneuver the murky waters of organized crime throughout the years and warned him of undercurrents circulating here of which he should be wary. He noticed the involuntary flush of Alice's cheeks, the widening of her eyes and wondered what the cause was. He couldn't be absolutely sure with her, whether it was blood lust, lust, or just plain blood. People he couldn't control made him nervous, a feeling he never had for very long.

Control wasn't difficult, if you knew what motivated people. If you knew that, it was simply a question of what buttons to push, and the right time to push them. His attention to Alice's reaction, however, was short-lived. The distraction came from the trio of reactions from Bunny, Pete and the man Bender's crew had found asleep on the couch in the living room of the brownstone. All three of them simultaneously exclaimed, "What the hell are you doing here?"

At first, Johnny assumed he'd stepped into a robbery. He saw two men, a Mutt and Jeff combination: the short man with slicked back dark hair and the bald giant with his left arm in a sling. They were standing by the bed at the end of the room, silenced guns drawn, in which the couple still sat, propped up by pillows. An upholstered couch pressed against one wall. In front of it stood, also with guns drawn, the man with a strangely dragging eye, whom he'd seen prodding Beep and Roeper into the limousine, and a woman, her long copper hair done up into an ornate bun with what looked like a Chinese knitting needle. She looked oddly familiar to him, though he couldn't place where he knew her from; it was like he remembered her from some erotic dream, or nightmare, that he'd had one night. No way, he thought, would he forget a woman who wore her makeup the way she did.

Across from these two was a fully stocked walnut stained bar. In front of it stood two men, the desultory looking Richie Roeper, and a man whose eyes widened in shock when he recognized Pete.

"Pete?"

"Mike? What the hell is going on here?" said Pete to Mike Tippins.

"I know the guy on the right, boss," Bunny motioned to Pete. "He's undercover narco. I had his ass pegged a few years back and he slipped me." He trained his gun on the new arrivals and said to the chauffeur, still standing in back of Pete and Johnny. "Verden, keep a real tight lock on these two. Make sure you check they have nothing up their sleeves, and I mean that literally."

Pete felt something hard poking him in the neck and heard Johnny's rapid intake of breath.

"Pretty safe to say that only one of them's a cop." Ronno said with a laugh. "The other dude looks like some sort of surfer or something. You a butthole surfer? You go on sphincter safaris, pal?"

Johnny knew his best bet was to stay quiet and pray he'd only lose his wallet. He felt Verden's free hand pat him down, looking for a weapon.

"Conejito, I never thought I'd see you again," a bewildered Pete said. "I don't know what the hell is going on here, and I don't want to, though it's probably too late for that now. I'm not a cop anymore and my beef is with this piece of shit right here." He pointed at Roeper.

Roeper gave a bitter laugh. "No offense man, but unless you're carrying the bubonic plague, I'd have to rate you as one of my lesser problems right now. And, by the way, who the fuck are you, anyway? I don't know you."

"You bastard. Angeline's in the hospital with a stroke right now because of you." Pete lunged, but Verden's strong arm grabbed him, restraining him effortlessly.

"Don't move a hair if you don't want to get pistol whipped again," Verden hissed in his ear as he frisked Pete.

"Oh, this I don't fucking believe. You're her boyfriend, aren't you? You stupid jackass, oh God!" Roeper laughed. "You came here to try and kick my ass? Welcome to the big leagues, kid. You might try working on your timing a little, especially if you're supposed to be a drummer."

The man in the bed stirred and swung his legs over the side of the mattress. A dark brown beard covered his swarthy face. He was overweight and beads of sweat stood on his forehead. When he spoke, a good-sized slice of Sicily was still in his voice.

"Frank, what's this traveling circus you bring here with you tonight? You and I should be able to discuss business calmly and quietly, like gentlemen. You come into my house like a thief in the night and now I've got some bad soap opera going on in my bedroom."

"Sal, I truly apologize for this intrusion, but I have some, how shall I put this, issues that require immediate resolution," said Bender. "Lately, whenever I go out, whether it be on business or even personal matters, such as a colleague's funeral, I find I've become the subject of target practice by assassins and snipers. You can imagine what this does to my indigestion. I can see from looking at you right now just how stressful it can be to be looking in the little hole of a pistol like this one." He waved the gun. "You look nervous and jumpy, and I don't blame you."

He fired once into Cangelosi's pillow, ten inches from his head. Goose feathers puffed out of the hole. He turned to Bunny and said, "You know, we should really have these triggers better calibrated. I barely pulled on it and look what happened."

"Let me try mine," Bunny replied and pointed his pistol at Cangelosi's head.

"Wait, wait!" bellowed Cangelosi, "Frank, this is no way to settle matters."

"Hang on a second, please, Bunny." He put a finger up. "Sal, we go back a long way, though I'll throw it all away in a second, you know that. This city has more than enough to go around for both of us. This rash behavior of yours surprises me. Perhaps you've let personal matters cloud your decision making processes, hmmm?"

He looked over at the attractive brunette woman in the bed, cringing with the covers pulled up to her quivering chin. "Hello, Trudi. How are you? Please don't get up. We won't be long here. Anyway, Sal, I'd like to know how you can tell where I'll be at certain times. It's not like I advertise my whereabouts in the newspaper or use a publicist."

"First, I'd like to know how you found me here. This is a secluded hideaway, my little love nest, if you will." Cangelosi gestured broadly with his hand to indicate the overly ornate furnishing of the room.

Pete had been so surprised to see Mike Tippins and Bunny that he hadn't noticed his surroundings much. It was a low budget reproduction of the inside of a Venetian palazzo designed by someone who had never left Newark. The ceiling was painted baby blue, with surly looking flute playing cherubs done in relief in each corner. The shag carpeting was burgundy colored. Faux Corinthian columns framed the windows and blue silk ties dangled from the four posts down to the white satin sheets of the bed.

Ronno stepped toward the bed, reached into his pocket and said,

"We found one of your associates, or should I say, former associates. You remember the guy with the tux and nose masks? What was his name, Leap, Creep, something like that? Anyway, in the end he was more than happy to let us know your whereabouts. You could say he fingered you."

With that, he removed his hand from the pocket and casually tossed six severed fingers and a thumb onto the bedspread. Cangelosi paled, his eyes widening in horror. Trudi let out a small yelp and ducked her head under the covers. She kicked the satin sheets violently, and the fingers scattered from the covers in every direction.

"Tic-Tac, anyone?" offered Ronno, pulling a plastic container of mints out and popping one in his mouth. Verden chuckled from behind Pete, the gun still pressed into the back of his neck.

"Ronno, you sure know how to do things in style. That's a good one!" He said.

Bender scowled at Verden, who immediately wiped the smile from his face. He turned back to Cangelosi, lifted his eyebrows slightly and said,

"Sal?"

"Frank, I don't need to know where you are. I can always call you. Your business is your business. My business is mine. This town is big enough for the two of us, no problem," he said very quickly, wiping sweat from his forehead.

"Hey, it looks to me like this is something you guys might want to settle amongst yourselves, and I got nothing to do with any of this, so if you don't mind, I'd like to mosie on out of here," interjected Roeper.

"It's cause of you that me and Johnny are here, guy, so you might as well stick around," replied Pete.

"Eat my shit. You're fucking annoying me. Hey, you," he motioned in Ronno's direction. He reached into his pocket for his money clip. "I've got well over thirty grand in here.

I'll give it to you now if you cap this douche bag and his friend for me right here."

Ronno pursed his lips in thought. "What do you think, boss? I could use the extra money."

"Ronno, don't I pay you enough? I always try to look out for you. After all, you are family," he hesitated before deciding. "O.K., but just this once. Try not to make a habit of outsourcing yourself as an independent contractor."

"You heard the man, fork it over. I'll do the job for you," Ronno said to Roeper.

Roeper sneered at Pete and tossed the clip to Ronno, who caught it.

"There's two less assholes in the world now," said Roeper.

Ronno turned his pistol and aimed it at Pete's head. Pete's eyes locked with Roeper's.

"Nothing personal, cop. A job's a job." Suddenly, a strange look came over his face and he said. "Oh, you know, I don't feel so good."

His hands started shaking, as if palsied. The pistol waved wildly in the air. He pulled the trigger. Roeper screamed and fell to the floor thrashing; a bullet in his shattered kneecap.

"Oh, hey, man, I'm sorry. I think I forgot to take my meds this morning. I get these attacks sometimes," Ronno smirked and chambered another round. "This guy may be a cop, and he'll die tonight, but you're not worth the paper you're printed on." He spit on the money clip and tossed it back near Roeper. "I ain't gonna kill you fast, either. You shoulda protected Dale Patterson better, if you were his manager. You fucking suck, dude. Hey, cop boy, you know this sack of shit better than I do," he motioned to Pete with his pistol. "Is this guy really in the music biz?"

"Sad but true," said Pete.

"This is why I can't hear any good music on the radio anymore? Cause of guys like this? Fuck you, pal. This one's for your clown bags, you vulture."

Ronno shot Roeper in the elbow, drawing fresh screams. Roeper went into shock, twitching on the carpeted floor. Everyone in the room, with the exception of Trudi, who was still cowering under the sheets, observed Roeper's convulsions for a few moments and then Bunny dispassionately put two quick bullets in his head, ending the spectacle.

"Thank you, Bunny. I hope we'll have no further interruptions," said Bender, looking around the room.

Pete's eyes widened. "What's that you said about clown bags? I found a bag of heroin like that on Patterson when he died."

"Looks like he was getting his artists to the top of the charts with a needle instead of a bullet," replied Ronno.

"Does anyone else have an agenda I should be aware of, or can I continue my conversation with Sal here? You were saying, Sal?"

The incident with Roeper had given Cangelosi a few precious moments to think about how to save his skin. While everyone's attention had been focused on Roeper for a few moments, he had discreetly snuck his hand behind his pillow and slid a small revolver under the covers next to him.

"Frank, I think we've been set up. The Jamaicans have moved in on a couple of the smaller guys and they've been getting bolder. They even had the balls to whack one of my guys. You remember Tex Rothstein, Frank? He'd been with me for a while, running some small stuff. Anyway, they got him and you shoulda seen the mess. I don't know what it was, maybe some sort of Rasta religious rite or something, but they found him with his throat cut so bad his head was almost off and this weird face paint all over him, like he was some sort of sacrifice. We live in unfamiliar times now, Frank. I long for simpler days."

"That's too bad, Sal. I remember Tex. Nice man, if a bit squirrelly. It's interesting you mention the Jamaicans. Maybe I've been barking up the wrong tree, because the first attempt on me was made by a fellow with dreadlocks. I don't like to profile, but the odds are good he was Jamaican. The bastard got away in his car. I was lucky to escape with just a scratch."

"Frank, we've got to team up and get those munion bastards. If we show any weakness they'll be on us like a pack of hyenas," said Cangelosi emphatically.

"You think it's that serious a threat, Sal?"

"You gotta let 'em know who's the boss or else you lose control. One of the first rules of running a business, something I don't need to tell you, of all people," Cangelosi replied with a throaty guffaw. "You and me, we've got to get together and send them back to their crappy island in a box."

"Actually, it was an ancient Sumerian rite that I performed," said Alice. All eyes turned to her. "It dates back to when their civilization was at its height and they painted their warriors' faces in such a way that the Gods of their underworld would fear them and allow them passage to heaven."

"What do you mean?" stammered Cangelosi.

"Do you play chess?" she asked, smiling disarmingly.

"I don't think I'm following you. Frank, what's this woman talking about?"

Bender smiled and stroked his chin. Alice, turning on her Southern accent a touch more, continued,

"If you did, you would recognize an end game when you saw one. Here you'd have a knight," she motioned to Mike Tippins, "or perhaps a bishop. Are you Catholic?"

Tippins, his hands stuffed in his pockets, simply stared back at her.

"No matter. As I was saying, a king, a knight and a pawn are no match for this kind of assault, especially when we're armed and you're not."

"Let's make sure this one's not carrying anything either," said Bunny, pointing at Tippins. "I got surprised once by that guy," he waved his pistol at Pete, "and I won't get fooled again by some cop. Check him out, Verden."

Verden removed the gun from Pete's neck, shoved it in his belt and shuffled over to Tippins. "Alright, buddy, get your hands up."

Mike lifted his arms high. Suddenly a massive roar filled the room as an explosion surged from Tippins's chest from the flat, shotgun-like device that blasted buckshot forward, triggered by straps hooked up to Mike's arms.

Verden flew backwards, his face, throat and chest in tatters, knocking Alice back into the couch. As Ronno turned and squeezed the trigger to end Mike Tippins's life, Cangelosi drew his gun from under the covers and shot Ronno in the head, right over his drooping eye. Ronno's slug flew wide, but Bunny's didn't. Tippins slumped to the ground. A bullet had torn away a large chunk of his throat. The bed looked like a massacre in a hen house, feathers flying everywhere, as Bender and Alice, who had drawn Verden's gun from his belt in addition to her own, riddled it with lead. The impact of all the bullets knocked Cangelosi clear off the bed and the quivering lump under the covers that had been Trudi now was still, red stains gradually spreading through the satin sheets.

Bender raced over to where Ronno lay on the floor and cradled his head while Pete stepped over Roeper's body to where Tippins writhed on the carpet. He pulled off his jacket and pressed it to the gaping wound in his throat, trying to staunch the flow of blood. His eyes betrayed his despair as he understood there was no way to extricate Tippins, Johnny and himself out of this situation in time to save Mike's life.

"Jesus, Pete, what've I done?" Mike's voice came out as a hoarse whisper and his hand grasped Pete's sleeve.

Bender let out a cry of anguish. He ran over to where the bullet riddled body of Sal Cangelosi lay slumped against the side of the bed and started savagely kicking it.

"You killed my little brother, you mother fucker! Oh God!" He stifled a sob and buried his face in his hands, before returning to Ronno's prone body. Alice and Bunny exchanged a look. Neither of them had known of the fraternal relationship between Bender and Ronno.

"Take it easy, Mikey, I'll get you out of here. Just hang on," Pete told Tippins.

"I just wanted to make some extra on the side. I'm not a bad cop. You gotta know that."

"I know, Mikey. You're one of the best. Don't talk. Save your strength, man." Pete felt the jacket saturate with

Tippins's blood. "Eileen and the boys need you to be strong here."

"I was trying to set these bastards up against each other and make some cake for my family." Tippins's eyes were glazing over.

"You did a hell of a job here, Mikey. I'll try to finish it for you." Pete's eyes welled with tears. "Come on, man. You want to see Sean and Mikey Jr. play for the Mets? You got to hang in there now."

"Oh Christ, Pete, don't let it go down I'm dirty. Don't let that happen. Promise me." His hand gripped Pete's sleeve tighter, then started loosening.

"Yeah, Mike." Pete hugged him tight.

"Promise me, Pete."

"I promise, Mike. Mike, hang on, for God's sake," Pete whispered desperately into Tippins's ear.

Tippins' hand fell from Pete's sleeve and hit the carpet. After all the gunfire and screams, the room was silent for a long heartbeat. Pete saw the far away stare in Mike's eyes and laid his head down gently on the carpet at the identical moment that Bender did the same for Ronno. They turned towards each other, their gazes met, and for a moment it seemed possible each could let the whole thing go, mourn their losses, and go their separate ways. But then Bender's dark eyes hardened. They both stood up.

"I don't know what part you've played in this, but believe me, I'm going to find out," Bender said.

"What part we've played in this? Are you out of your fucking mind? You people are shooting and killing each other. There are dead bodies all over the place," Johnny gesticulated wildly, "and you want to know what part Pete and

I are playing in this?" His eyes bulged. "We don't have any fucking part in this at all! This is wrong, totally wrong! We wanted to smack Roeper around." He raised his arms in frustration. "Jesus, and I didn't even want to do that, but I was covering Pete's ass. Then we walk into some scene out of *Scarface*. I don't care what you think, pal, but I'm seriously unhappy that my friend and I are in this room right now. Haven't you had enough here? Good God, man, look around you for a minute."

"All I can say is if you think you're unhappy right now, remember this moment well, because it will soon seem like a fond recollection compared to what's coming next," Bender replied in a low voice. He motioned to Bunny. "You got some rope or cuffs so we can keep these two steady?"

Bunny grunted his assent and produced two pairs of handcuffs from within a jacket pocket. Bender covered them with his pistol. Alice pushed the rest of Verden's body from her legs and stood up while Bunny cuffed Pete and Johnny, cross-handed, to each other. Bender wiped his brow and sat wearily on the bed.

"Miss, would you mind mixing me a scotch and soda, straight up, from the bar. I'm sure Sal would have those ingredients readily available," he said to Alice. She strolled over to the bar and removed a tumbler from a small wooden cabinet behind it.

"Can I get you one?" she asked Bunny, who frowned and shook his head, keeping the focus of his concentration on Pete and Johnny. He, like everyone else in the room, wasn't certain what was going on, but he'd underestimated Pete once, and was wary. Bender sauntered to where Pete and Johnny were cuffed together. He stared at them intently for a few seconds, holding eye contact with first one and then the other. He took a deep breath.

"Gentlemen, you are undoubtedly aware by now that I'm not going to dick around here. You, my friend," he reached up and grabbed Johnny by the chin, "are either an innocent bystander in this unfortunate scene or an Oscar caliber actor. In the end, it makes no difference. Now you're a witness. I can see from the way Bunny is checking out your friend that he considers him to be the more dangerous of the two of you. He also has demonstrated compassion for a fallen comrade. We're now going to see how far and how fast he'll go to save another friend. Bunny, do you still have the clippers?"

Johnny watched in horror as Bunny produced a small, sturdy pair of wire clippers, already encrusted with what Johnny assumed was the blood of the late, lamented Beep, who would regrettably never play the piano again.

"Pete? That's your name, right?" Bender asked Pete, who glared at him sourly. "Are you going to tell me what I want to know before I get started with your friend here?"

"What the hell do you want to know? I don't see what I could possibly tell you. We came here looking for Roeper. Someone I care about is lying in intensive care in a hospital because of that bastard. We went to the club where he was hanging out. We saw him get into your limo and followed it. I have no idea what business he has, or had with you, and I don't care. I'll tell you right now I'll say anything you want to hear to avoid Johnny getting hurt, but I can't make up things that don't exist. I have no idea what that guy," Pete motioned with his head toward the slumped, bullet-riddled body of Cangelosi, which was leaking heavily onto the rug, "was doing to you and your business, except it looks like he just stopped doing it. I'm not a cop anymore, haven't been one for five years. What else do you want to know?"

"Not the kind of enlightenment I was looking for, Pete. I'm afraid your friend here is in for a very long night," Bender replied with a shrug.

Alice came over with an amber tinted glass tumbler containing Bender's scotch. He swallowed half the glass in one gulp, sighed, and turned to her.

"Ah, that hits the spot." He squinted and looked more closely at her. "Miss, I think you're missing one of your, uh…." Bender motioned vaguely towards her face.

Her usually immaculately created teardrop makeup effect was missing the tear running parallel to the nostril on the left side of her face. Puzzled, he glanced down momentarily into his glass. On the bottom was the last little piece, and it dissolved in the second he glimpsed it. He looked up at Alice, recognition dawning in his eyes. Bender opened his mouth to say something, but all that came out was a funny sound; it almost sounded like a birdcall. Whatever species of fowl he was trying to attract, no one will ever know. Perhaps it was the Delaware sparrow. His bladder had discharged its contents into his bloodstream and his skin turned a pale yellow.

In the time it took for Bunny to turn toward Bender's falling body and realize what was happening, Alice had, in a lightning fast movement, taken the steel Chinese knitting needle holding her hair together in a bun and buried it into Bunny's jugular vein so hard that the point of the needle came out on the other side of his neck. Blood gushed out from both wounds. Bunny, a shocked expression on his face, tried to level his pistol to take a shot at Alice, but fell heavily to the floor before he had a chance to pull the trigger. The gun went off as the giant hit the ground, the bullet going into the foot of the hapless Cangelosi, who'd already absorbed enough lead to start a pencil factory. Bunny's legs kicked on the carpet for a few seconds and then he lay still, face down. Alice shook her copper hair loose with a toss of her head and smiled.

"You two look like Siamese twins that way," she said.

"I'd be eternally grateful if you would unlock these handcuffs," said Pete, surveying the carnage in the bedroom.

"Maybe later," she replied.

"There's something that's been bothering me from the minute I walked in here. Well, more than one thing, but it seems to be the only thing left," said Johnny. "It might be stupid of me to mention this, but I get the strangest feeling we've met, or went to grade school together, or something, I don't know. Do I know you from somewhere?"

"You could say that, Johnny dear. We've been intimately acquainted. You don't remember?" Alice responded with a taunting laugh and a mock glower, "I am so disappointed."

Johnny knew he was skating on very thin ice and his response could either doom him and Pete or set them free.

"I'm sure I could never forget someone like you, and I'm not just saying that to be charming."

"Oh, but that is so very charming. I could tell you were a charmer, the first time I looked in your eyes." She reached down to where Bunny's body lay, put her shoe on his head and, with a grunt, yanked out the needle. They eyed her nervously as she advanced a step in their direction. She looked casually at the needle and then ran it crosswise across her lips, deftly cleaning the blood from it with her tongue. She quickly wrapped her hair with her free hand and then stuck the needle back into the bun.

"There, that's much better." She looked at herself in the mirror hanging on the wall in back of the bar. Frowning, she noticed the bloodstains, courtesy of Verden's dead body, spattered on the front of the jacket of her pants suit. "I'll never get these out. This outfit is ruined," she sighed.

"Is there any club soda in the bar?" asked Johnny, who was starting to think there might be a way out of this, after all. "That usually works well on stains."

"Maybe food, or grease or wine; once you get blood rubbed in, it's pretty much over. It's no big deal. I'll find something in one of the closets in this place. I doubt that woman was the only visitor to this brownstone." She motioned towards the bloody lump, which lay unmoving under the covers of the bed. "But the real question is: what am I going to do about you two?"

"I have absolutely no idea who you are and would be very happy to forget about this whole thing and go home," said Pete.

"That's a recurring theme tonight. I was thinking something along the same lines, perhaps not quite in the way you envision it, though," she replied, tilting her head thoughtfully.

"What do you mean?" asked Johnny.

"It means we might have to trust each other some. You, I guess, a bit more than me," she paused. "I have a good lie detector built into my head. I believe you're in this place and situation by accident and you are who you say you are.

I know that Johnny here, in addition to being quite a stud, also has nothing to do with the business you two have witnessed here tonight. The reason those two," she waved a hand in the direction of Bender's and Bunny's bodies, "are dead and you're alive is, frankly, I've seen too many innocent people pay for the sins of others; that and the fact that I knew they were going to try to kill me when this was over." She showed them a small electronic device she had withdrawn from her pocket.

"What's that, some sort of listening device, a bug?" asked Pete.

She nodded.

"Being careful means being alive, in my business," She reached behind the bar. "Would you like a beer?"

"After seeing this, I'm going to need a few," said Johnny.

"One should be enough for both of you. Alcohol doesn't mix well with drugs," Alice replied, as she opened a small refrigerator under the bar and removed a bottle of Peroni beer.

"We don't do drugs," said Pete.

"That's where the trust part comes in," she said and poured the beer into three glasses. "You see, I can make sure you two don't remember a thing about what you saw here tonight. That's my insurance. I'll be out of the country after I tie up a few loose ends, but you'll want to go back to your normal lives." She peeled the two closest tears to the corner of each eye and dropped one into two of the three glasses. The tears dissolved instantly.

"How do we know we're not going to turn yellow and die like Captain Friendly on the floor there?" asked Pete.

"You don't. But, as you can see, dear Johnny survived my first encounter with him."

"That's what happened? You drugged me?" asked an incredulous Johnny. "Why?"

"I like a certain amount of compliance in my men sometimes, depending on my mood. I'd like to tell you what you did with me the other night, but you might have some trouble handling it. Take my word for it."

The way she smiled right then was chilling enough to prevent him from asking.

"This is an interesting drug," she swirled the glasses. "It's my own concoction, and, if I may say so myself, works beautifully. It combines complete obedience in the subject with the ability to make post-hypnotic suggestions and wipe out memories."

"So, what you're saying is, we'll wake up tomorrow with no idea what happened here?" asked Pete.

"Almost certainly not tomorrow. The day after is a safer bet. And you might feel a bit under the weather. So how about it, gentlemen, shall we drink a toast?" She brought over the two glasses containing the dissolved tears.

"How are we supposed to drink with our hands cuffed like this?" Pete inquired.

"I'll take them off as soon as you finish your glass, I promise."

"What do you think, Pete?" asked Johnny.

"I honestly don't know, Styx. But the thing is, if she wanted us dead, I don't think we'd be having this discussion right now."

"Yeah, Pete, but what if she wants to set us up to take the fall for all of this."

Pete looked at Alice inquiringly.

"Set you up?" she said, "What would be the point? It's a gangland shootout. No one knows that any of us are here. Tell you what, I'll even stage it so your dead cop friend comes out looking like a hero who died in the line of duty." Her face hardened. "Don't test my patience or goodwill anymore, guys. Drink up. Who's first?"

"Normally we do the rock, paper, scissors thing to make these kinds of decisions. I guess we can rule that out," said Johnny, looking over his shoulder at the manacles around their wrists, "but since these are unusual circumstances, I'll volunteer, since apparently I've done this before. And guy," he glanced back at Pete, "If I croak here, don't drink the other glass."

Alice came over to Johnny and held the glass up to his lips.

"To all the girls I've ever loved," he toasted and drank down the contents as she slowly tilted the glass back. Five seconds after she took the glass back from his lips, Pete felt Johnny's body go rigid behind him.

"Styx? Are you alright?" he shouted. "Talk to me, Johnny!"

"Your friend is fine. Don't worry," Alice said as she came around to face Pete with the other glass of beer.

"Hey, can you do us one favor, please?"

"What, you want a blindfold and a cigarette?" she asked with a smile.

"No. But you can selectively remove memory, you said, right?"

"Actually, I can be quite precise with what you can and can't remember. Science has come a long way in this field."

"The reason I'm asking is because, up to the moment we started chasing after Roeper, this had been one of the best nights of my life in a long, long time. I'm not going to bore you with the details, but if you can leave everything in up to the point of following your limo, I'd appreciate it."

"I'll see what I can do. If you've lied to me about anything, I'll find out pretty fast, you know. And then you will both die, and not pleasantly."

"Do I look like I've got something to lose here?"

"No, and you don't look stupid, either. But you never know."

"Alright, then let's get this over with."

She brought the glass up to his lips.

"Any last words?" She asked.

"How about: 'Throw off those chains of reason and your prison disappears.'"

"Oh, I like that! Good choice."

He opened his mouth and drank down the contents of the glass. Moments later, Pete's body, like Johnny's had a minute earlier, stiffened, and his eyes stared forward unblinkingly.

Alice ambled back to the bar, where the third glass of beer was waiting.

"What a night," she said to everyone in the room, all of whom were paying no attention to her whatsoever. She reached down into the bar and found a bottle of Jack Daniels, unscrewed the cap, took a large swig and chased it down, in one swallow, with the beer.

Alice took Verden's gun and fired a round into Bender's head and another in his chest. His skin had already lost most of its yellow pallor. She was fairly sure that no coroner would look for an exotic boutique poison in a room full of bullet-riddled individuals. She fished around in Bunny's trouser pockets and found the keys to the handcuffs. With a smile playing on her lips, she strolled back and forth in front of Pete and Johnny, unbuttoning the jacket of her suit.

She then removed it, slowly, sensuously, like the stripper she'd been, a long, long time ago. All she wore underneath it was a lacy white brassiere that concealed only some of the scars she'd inflicted on herself over the years with an assortment of sharp, and sometimes, very hot, objects. She reached between the two men and undid the cuffs. Most people, at that moment, would rub their wrists to try and get their circulation going again, but Pete and Johnny didn't move an inch.

"You know, it would be such a waste to have two nice, handsome specimens like yourselves here and not have just a little bit of fun. Maybe even get the two of them to do each other while I watch. And the smell of fresh blood is sooooo exciting."

18

Pete was running through the low-ceilinged stone walled corridors of a cathedral, chased by something hideous and unimaginable. Running was difficult for him because one of his legs was dragging, so he was forced to hop along as fast as he could. He rounded a corner and glimpsed a large mirror on the wall to his left. Glancing at his reflection, he saw the reason his leg was dragging was due to his deformed back, a large hump near the right shoulder blade. With great difficulty, he climbed a rickety wooden ladder at the end of the corridor and made his way into the bell tower of the cathedral. There were large open-air portals around the perimeter. He lumbered towards one and looked out. The streets of Manhattan seemed tiny and insignificant below him and he realized the cathedral had been built precariously on top of the Empire State Building. He raised his head and screamed into the night sky.

"Sanctuary!"

He then made his way to the massive brass bell hanging in the center of the chamber. There was a long braided rope attached to it. He leapt and dangled from the rope, swinging himself wildly to and fro. Pete wanted the entire city to hear his call to arms. The booming peal of the bell he had expected to hear was a disappointment, though. It had a digital ringing sound, significantly quieter than what he thought a bell that size should produce. He frowned and let go of the rope.

Still half asleep, he reached over his pillow to answer the phone and stop the ringing. His head was throbbing badly and he mumbled into the phone, "Hello?"

"How would you like a free subscription to *Bachelor Chef*?" announced a cheery male voice.

"What?"

"We picked your name from our database of single men to receive *Bachelor Chef* magazine. Every month you'll get delicious recipes that can be prepared using only a toaster and a hot plate. And we'll send you this entertaining magazine absolutely free, sir, if you choose our no-fault auto insurance, which, I assure you, has very low premiums. Would you like me to describe what it covers?"

"I don't own a car."

"Oh. Well, the insurance is still very inexpensive and you would receive *Bachelor Chef* magazine free for a year. In this month's issue, the cover recipe is the Toaster Tomato Surprise, a mouthwatering dish which..."

Pete hung up the phone and moaned. In addition to his headache, his stomach felt like a mud-wrestling match was going on inside of it. He got up slowly and made his way to the bathroom. His reflection stared back at him in the mirror with bloodshot eyes. At least he had lost the hump jutting from his shoulder in the dream, but he discovered cuts, bumps, bruises and chafe marks all over his body and a lump on the side of his head. When he urinated he found that his genitals were also sore. He looked at the clock radio on one of the shelves in the bathroom and it read 11:30.

"What a night," his reflection said to him. He wasn't due at the rehearsal studio until 5:00 that evening and so figured he still had some recovery time. He decided to shower after he got some coffee and a bagel into his system. The thought of the alternating hot and cold blasts of water seemed like a cruel punishment to him at this moment and he gave his unpredictable shower a look as if it were a medieval instrument of torture.

After throwing on some jeans, sneakers and a sweater, he went downstairs to purchase a large coffee, an onion bagel with chive cream cheese, some apple juice and a newspaper. He retrieved the mail from the mailbox in the lobby of his building without looking at it, got back into his apartment, and devoured the food, realizing that he was ravenous. He was munching on broken potato chip pieces left in the bottom of the bag on the coffee table by the couch, when he saw there was a message on his answering machine. He pushed the play button.

"Hey, man, where are you, dude?" Greg asked. "It's seven o'clock. I just got here to find two pissed off bands waiting outside the door. Call me at the studio."

Pete was puzzled. He glanced at the microwave and it read 11:55, so he knew the clock in his bathroom was correct. He glanced down at the back of his newspaper and saw the date read Tuesday, October 22nd. His eyes widened in shock. The last thing he remembered was leaving the hospital early Sunday morning.

"Oh my God, Angeline!" he exclaimed and quickly found the number of the hospital. He was transferred by the hospital operator to the correct ward and was told by a nurse that Angeline had regained consciousness Sunday afternoon and was coherent. No signs of permanent brain damage were evident, though they would be keeping her there a few more days for observation and tests. One thing the nurse had said at the end of their conversation struck him as odd.

"We haven't told her the bad news about her boyfriend yet."

Pete wanted to ask the nurse what she meant by that, but an emergency had arisen at the hospital and she had immediately hung up the phone.

He sat down on his couch, thoroughly confused. He had been so fuzzy headed that he hadn't even glanced at the newspaper when he had bought it. If he had, he would have noticed the back page, containing the sports headlines, was all about the Jets and the Giants, New York's two football teams, who had played on Sunday. He was still trying to figure things out when he flipped the paper over to the front page, where the headline "HIT RECORD MAKER, HERO COP KILLED IN DRUG GANG WARFARE" blared, adorned by photos of Richie Roeper and Mike Tippins.

"What the hell...." Pete's words trailed off as he commenced reading the story. According to the newspaper, early Sunday morning there had been a shootout in the Bay Ridge section of Brooklyn. Drug kingpins Sal "Mustang Sally" Cangelosi, nicknamed for the quantity of his sexual conquests, and Frank Bender had been found slain. Bender's brother Ron, chauffeur Allen Verden, exotic dancer Trudi Wilde and an unidentified man had also been found dead in the bedroom of a posh brownstone building owned by Cangelosi, along with decorated officer Mike Tippins and music manager Richie Roeper.

All had died of bullet wounds, with the exception of the unidentified man, who had died of blood loss from a neck wound caused by an unidentified pointed weapon. The police were still searching for the weapon.

Officer Tippins was said to have been working undercover on a case involving the two gangs and had bravely died in the line of duty. Roeper's involvement was unclear, though rumors of rampant drug use and shady connections had surfaced. The article mentioned the recent tragedy of Dale Patterson and hinted that many of Roeper's previous clients had also suffered from drug problems. A few of them had entered clinics, suffering from what was termed "exhaustion".

A search of the neighborhood had turned up another body, shot once in the head at close range and stuffed into the trunk of a limousine parked around the corner from the crime scene. Although the corpse was missing all the fingers of his right hand, fingerprints of his left hand identified the body as Brian Peterson, a low-level dealer in the Cangelosi gang. Also found in the trunk was a briefcase containing large amounts of cocaine, heroin, ecstasy, and other exotic designer drugs. A police spokesperson was not saying if other suspects had survived the massacre or if all the participants were accounted for. There were no witnesses and no current leads.

"This is way too weird. What the hell is going on here?" he said.

He picked up the phone again and dialed Johnny's number.

"Hello." Johnny sounded as bleary as Pete felt.

"Hey, guy, I'm not looking for Dick Hertz anymore. He's here."

"Oh, hi, Pete. I was just going to call you. Man, I think there's really something wrong with me. I had another blackout. I woke up about a half hour ago, all thrashed again, and have no idea what happened since we hung out last night."

"Then you haven't read the newspaper yet?" inquired Pete.

"Nah, I haven't looked at anything yet. It's usually in front of my door with the mail. I'm mainlining some espresso here, trying to get my act together. Why, what happened?"

"Get it and call me back after you've read the front page."

"You're sure being mysterious. What's up?"

"I'm serious, Styx. I don't know what the hell is going on. Just check it out and get back to me ASAP."

"Sure. I'll call you back in a few minutes." He hung up the phone.

Five minutes later, Pete's phone rang. He picked it up on the first ring.

"Holy shit! What's up with this?" Johnny's voice leapt through the receiver.

"Damned if I know, Johnny. I don't remember a damn thing after trying to find Roeper at the club. We must have missed him by minutes."

"Well, looks like that was the best thing that could've happened to us. If we'd found him at the same time as the guys who did, our pictures would be on the cover of the paper too."

"Scary thought. But what's really weird is I don't remember what happened after we got to the club either, and I feel banged up as hell."

"You too? This is bizarre," said Johnny. "This is like it was a few nights ago. I'm beat up and have no idea what happened."

"Yeah, but if this happened to me too, there must be something weird going at that bank club. It sounds funny, but it's not; someone must've slipped us some sort of date rape drug or something. It looks like this has happened to you the last two times you were there."

"It's a good thing we didn't wake up each missing a kidney. I've read about stuff like this happening to people. It'll be a cold day in hell before I ever go back to that club again, that's for sure," Johnny said with a shudder. "Hey, and wasn't the cop who got killed an old buddy of yours? I've heard you mention his name."

"Yeah, it's a damn shame. I can't believe it. I was just at his place a couple of days ago for a barbeque. He's got a wife and a couple of small kids. I'll call the precinct to find out when the service is going to be. Poor Eileen; she must be in shock."

"That's horrible," he commiserated.

"At least there's some decent news. I called the hospital and it looks like Angeline's doing O.K. I'll probably stop by and visit her today."

While talking to Johnny, Pete sifted through the mail lying on his coffee table. He hadn't noticed the thick airmail envelope with a return address from Sweden. He hurriedly ripped it open. It contained a note and an open-ended round trip first class airplane ticket to Stockholm.

"Hey, guy," Pete said, his spirits soaring, "I just checked my mail and Astrid sent me an airplane ticket!"

"Check the destination. It's probably to South Dakota or somewhere, so she doesn't have to see you next time she comes to New York," came the sardonic reply.

"Very funny. No, it's to Stockholm and the note says, among other things I can't repeat to you, that she's dying to see me and can't get me off her mind."

"Good for you. Let me check my mail to see if Kyra did the same for me."

Pete could hear Johnny ruffling through some papers.

"Nope, nothing but credit card come-ons and my electric bill and...What's this?"

"What's what?" asked Pete.

"I got this small package addressed to me. No postage and no return address. Just a drawing of what looks like a drop of water in the upper left hand corner." Pete heard the sounds of Johnny opening the package and exclaiming, "Oh my God!"

"What is it?" Pete noticed a similar package scattered among the bills and junk mail and reached for it.

"There's a bunch of cash in it; a whole lot of cash!"

Pete put down the phone and excitedly opened his package. He dumped the contents on the coffee table. A three-inch wad of hundred dollar bills wrapped in a rubber band landed with a thump and a single piece of paper floated down on top of it. Pete picked up the paper and read it. All that was written on it, in a feminine handwriting, was:

"Throw off those chains of reason and your prison disappears".

Pete picked up the wad of cash from the table, riffed through it, and whistled softly. He lifted the phone and said,

"I got one, too! Johnny, what the hell is going on here?"

"I don't know, Pete. I'm clueless here. Is there a note in yours?"

"Yeah, it's a quote from 'Hemispheres', one of Rush's records. You got one too?"

"Yours is a quote from Rush? That's strange. Mine says, 'From all the girls you've ever loved'."

"You sure you're not missing a kidney or a bladder or something?" Pete checked the myriad scratch marks on his body for a deeper cut or incision. "Maybe this is a cut of what they were able to sell it for on the black market."

"No. I'm a little the worse for wear, but in one piece," said Johnny. "There must be over ten grand in cash here, guy. What on earth did we get ourselves into?"

"I have no idea, Styx, but the money sure comes in handy. I'm not exactly making a fortune with the studio."

"It always does. But where does it come from? Do you think this has something to do with Roeper? You know, Hunter was telling us about all the cash this guy carries around with him, or used to."

"Hmmm, not a bad point," Pete considered Johnny's idea for a moment. "But then what's with the notes? That doesn't sound like Roeper's style, does it?"

"No, and it definitely looks like a woman's writing on both the note and the envelope. Do you have some funny looking shape in the area where you'd normally have the return address too, Pete?"

"Yeah. It looks like a drop of water. Did we pass a sign-post that reads 'The Twilight Zone' lately?"

"Sure seems that way. So, what are you gonna do?"

"I think I'm gonna see if Greg will take a thousand bucks in cash to cover for me at the studio for a week or two while I jet over to Europe. That's for starters."

"Ah, to be young and in love," said Johnny.

"Hey, I think I've earned it."

"Sure, sure. It couldn't happen to a nicer guy. Wait!" Johnny paused for effect, "I think I feel my muse coming on again."

"I can hardly wait," Pete replied wryly.

"It seems my talent is lost on the likes of you."

"It seems your talent is simply lost."

"This is a good one, guy," Johnny cleared his throat, "here goes:

There once was a man named Pete,

On whom a Swedish lady was sweet.

When she paid for his fare,

It was clear she didn't care

About the smell that came from his feet."

"You're a piece of work, Styx," Pete laughed, "and my feet definitely smell a hell of a lot better than your poetry."

Made in the USA
Charleston, SC
12 April 2012